BY JOSH MALERMAN

Bird Box
A House at the Bottom of a Lake
Black Mad Wheel
Unbury Carol
Inspection
Goblin
Pearl (previously titled *On This, the Day of the Pig*)
Carpenter's Farm
Malorie
Ghoul n' the Cape
Daphne
Spin a Black Yarn
Incidents Around the House

Incidents Around the House

Incidents
Around
the House

A Novel

Josh Malerman

NEW YORK

Published in the United States by Del Rey, an imprint of Random House, a division of Penguin Random House LLC, New York.

DEL REY and the CIRCLE colophon are registered trademarks of Penguin Random House LLC.

Hardback ISBN 978-0-593-72312-8
Ebook ISBN 978-0-593-72313-5

Printed in the United States of America on acid-free paper

randomhousebooks.com

1 2 3 4 5 6 7 8 9

First Edition

Book design by Diane Hobbing

Image on title page by AdobeStock/Pb

For Finnegan and Elliott
For, when children, seeing things

Author's Note

The unique format of this book is intentional: left-justified for narration/action, indentation for dialogue, with spaces between. All in the name of perspective: This story is told by a child.

—JM

Incidents Around the House

1

Good night, Daddo!
Good night, Mommy!

Mommy and Daddo leave my room.
I pull the covers up to my chin.
Other Mommy comes out of the closet.

Hi, I say.
I'm so excited to see you again.

2

Bela, Mommy says to me. Eat.

I'm not hungry, I say.

But still. Eat.

I'm not—

I've got minutes, only minutes. Then work. Remember? That's the place I go to make all the little money so we can buy things like food. So, you? Eat the food. Help me out here.

Little money? I ask.

Sometimes it feels that way, hon. Like the money I make is physically smaller than what other people get.

I eat. Mommy always gives me oatmeal. Daddo never gives me breakfast because one time he gave me eggs and sausage and I ate till I threw up and Mommy got mad at him and so now only Mommy gives me breakfast. But Daddo does the dishes.

I love you, Mommy says. Bela?

My mouth is full of oatmeal.

Say I love you too, Mommy says. Don't make me ask you to say that, 'kay?

'Kay.

I love you, Bela.

Love you too.

What's on your mind? she asks.

Nuthin'.

But there is something on my mind. I'm looking at the recycle bin.

Bela, Mommy says. *Eat.*

Where does it go? I ask.

Where does what—

But she looks to where I'm looking.

Are you seriously asking me about recycling right now?

I nod. She looks impatient.

I don't know where it goes, she says.

Is it a better place?

Better place than what?

Than where we are?

Mommy looks at me the way she does when I say something that surprises her.

I don't know what that means, Mommy says. The whole point is that it comes back, as . . . something else, I guess.

Something else.

I think of carnations.

Bela—

But she doesn't need to tell me again. I eat. Then she's up from the table.

Be good for your daddo, Mommy says.
When will you be home? I ask.
I don't know yet. Might be late. I don't know.

She looks frazzled. That's the word Daddo uses when Mommy looks like this. She's wearing her brown leather coat. Her black pants. I don't have to go anywhere because it's still summer. Daddo works all the time. Mommy's schedule is all over the place. That's how she says it.

Bye, Bela, Mommy says.
Bye.

She leaves the kitchen. Daddo is in the den working already, and I don't hear her say goodbye to him before she leaves out the front door. I go quietly upstairs to my room. I wait for a second by the table with the flowers in the hall.
Other Mommy is already standing outside my closet doors.
I don't want her to make the face I think she's about to make.
She gets impatient like Mommy does.
I know she wants to talk about carnations.
I go into my bedroom.
And I wave at her.
And I sit on the end of my bed, where I know she likes to talk.
She's been coming out of the closet a lot more lately.
She walks over to me now. Sometimes it's like she floats.
She sits on the bed too. Slowly. Next to me.
And she asks:

Can I go into your heart?

3

The first time I told Mommy and Daddo about Other Mommy they laughed. It was good-night time and I told Mommy good night and then I said it again and Mommy said,

Why did you say that twice, Bela?

And I said,

I was saying good night to Other Mommy.

They both smiled and their eyes got wide and Daddo made a funny sound like from a spooky movie. Then Mommy's smile went away and she asked,

Who's Other Mommy, Bela?

But I was embarrassed. So I said,

I'm tired!

Daddo laughed again and shut the light and they left my room, but I saw Mommy look back once through the crack in the door.

Her eyes looked right at mine. Then she and Daddo went to their own bedroom.

Then Other Mommy made the grunting sound she makes when she stands up on the other side of my bed, in the space between my bed and the wall, when she's been crouched down there on the carpet waiting for them to leave.

4

Mommy only left for work ten minutes ago, but Daddo already calls to me.

> Bela, you up there?
> Yeah.
> Bela?
> Yeah!
> Come on down. You don't have to play alone.
> I'm not alone.
> What?
> You're in the house too.
> Come on down. We'll find something for you to do.
> I'm doing stuff.

Daddo comes up the stairs. Other Mommy steps into my bathroom.
The kids at school say I'm lucky I have a bathroom connected to my bedroom.

> What are you doing in here? Daddo asks.
> Stuff.

You're just standing in the middle of your room.
No, I'm not.
Bela.
I was thinking what to do next.

Daddo sniffs the air like he smells something bad. I don't want him to see Other Mommy in the bathroom. I don't want her to talk to him. I don't want her to ask him what she always asks me.

What's that smell? Daddo asks.
I don't smell it.
Are you serious? It's totally disgusting.

He sniffs again. He goes toward the bathroom.

I'm ready to go downstairs, I say.
Hang on.
Now, Daddo!
No. Hang on.

I hang on as Daddo goes into the bathroom. He goes in far enough so I don't see him. I wonder if Other Mommy is making that face at him.
Then I hear the toilet flush and Daddo steps out again.
He taps my belly.

You okay? he asks. Smells like a gas-station bathroom in there.
What does that mean? I ask.

He looks once back to the bathroom. The noise of the toilet stops. It's done flushing.

Come on, Daddo says. Let's hang out downstairs. You can play a game in the den while I work. We got that amazing Michigan puzzle.

It is a great puzzle. All the roads and cities and the state bird (the robin) and the state flower (the apple blossom) and the state flag, my favorite flag of any flag in the world.

Okay, I say.

He smiles, but he looks at me the way Mommy looked at me that one night through the open bedroom door. Like he thinks there's more to what I'm saying than what I'm saying.
Behind him, Other Mommy is peeking out of the bathroom.

Let's go, I say.
You get as restless as your mom, Daddo says. I guess energy needs somewhere to go.

I think of energy going someplace else. I think of carnations.

Am I wrong in saying you used to play outside more often? Daddo asks.
I don't know.
I'm not trying to make you feel weird, he says. I just have many memories of you through the den window, seeing you on the front lawn, running around.
I don't know.
What's Deb doing today?
I don't know.
What about some other friends?

We both just kinda look at each other because we both know I don't have any other friends. There's Mommy and Daddo and Deb. And Kelvin too.
Other Mommy has been my friend as long as I can remember. But lately she won't stop asking me the same question. It used to be she'd wait till night to come out of the closet, but now she's out before I even get out of the bed in the morning.

Whatever, Daddo says. I just wanna make sure you're doing as much as you used to do. Exercise. That kind of stuff.

He's right. I used to do more. I used to play outside. But then I'd see Other Mommy watching from the windows upstairs. And what if she came downstairs to talk to Daddo in the den while I was outside?
Daddo rubs the top of my head.

No worries, he says. We all go through phases. I mean, when's the last time I exercised at all?

He smiles and I try to smile too.

The puzzle, he says. Think of it as . . . *mind* exercise. I say that counts.

I follow him out of my bedroom. We head downstairs and I don't look back because I know she's still peeking.
It feels like she's always peeking these days. Night or day.

5

Daddo works at his desk and I sit on the couch and work on putting the puzzle together. There's no door for the den and across the foyer is the entrance to the dining room. I try not to keep looking up, but every time I hear a creak I do.

Well, I wasn't aware of that at all, Daddo says into his phone. Probably woulda helped me to know that.

The puzzle is hard. I like that Daddo believes I can do it. I like the books in his office too. I like adult books. I can't read all the words but I like looking at them anyway. Pages in any book are pretty, I think. I told Daddo that once and he picked up a book and opened it and looked at a page for a while and then said, *I don't know if I see it, but I like that you do.*

This damn Himalaya account, Daddo says.

He's off the phone now.

What's wrong with it? I ask.
It's just a lot of work.

Work is fun, I say.
Yeah, well . . .
It beats doing nothing.

Daddo laughs a little.

Did I teach you that? he asks.

I shrug.

Well, that's a good philosophy, he says. Still, some projects take more out of you than others.
Yeah. Like when Mr. Brown has us give our speeches in class.
You don't like giving speeches?
I get scared.
O, don't be that way.
I can't help it.
But trust me, Daddo says. You wanna get over that right now. You don't wanna have stage fright your whole life. If there's one thing I could teach my younger self . . .
It would be to not have stage fright?
Totally.
Why?
Because it comes up a lot in life. Think about it: I've been on the phone for an hour this morning. It's like I'm giving speeches. You know? Right now Mommy is probably giving a speech, kind of. Hell, even when you call the insurance company you give a little speech.
I don't call the insurance company.
No literal jokes.
But they're funny.
Maybe. A little. But really . . . next time Mr. Brown asks you to give a speech? Give a wild one. Get up on your desk and shout it. Whatever you gotta do to get over that stage fright now, do it.

I think about that. Mommy would tell me *not* to get up on my desk. But I know what Daddo means. I'm jealous of the kids who aren't afraid. Who don't have a reason to be afraid.

I won't be afraid of speeches anymore, I say.

Daddo holds up a hand because someone is calling his phone. The ceiling creaks. I pretend to put the puzzle together, but I'm not paying attention anymore.
The ceiling is creaking.

Not right now, I say.

I shouldn't have said that out loud. I don't want Daddo asking me about Other Mommy.
But Daddo's talking on the phone and didn't hear me anyway.
I look up.
She used to come only at night. Then sometimes during the day.
The first time I saw her in the daylight I hid.
I think she's getting closer. Even though she's already in the house. Even though she sits next to me on my bed.
Closer. That's the word I think of.
She used to just stand in the closet and stare at me. Then she came out. Then she started talking.
Then she started asking.

Not now, I say again.

I see an eye up there, like there's a hole in the ceiling shaped just like an eye.
Maybe it's a whole face.
Daddo gets off the phone.

What's up? he asks.
Nothing.

He looks to the ceiling.

    You look freaked out, he says. Was it because of all that stage-fright talk?

I nod.

    Yeah, well, sorry, he says. That's the problem with stuff like that. The more you talk about it, the more it freaks you out. But don't let it.

Daddo makes a funny sound as he breathes out just as the ceiling creaks and he didn't hear it and I don't look up.

    Wanna watch a movie when I'm done? Daddo asks.
    Should we wait for Mommy to come home?
    O, I don't know when that will be.

Mommy used to be home all the time. We used to watch movies and eat together all three of us all the time.

    What movie? I ask.
    Well, that's up to you. Hey, what are you and me?

I smile.

    We're best friends, I say.
    Totally, he says.

He snaps his fingers like I got the answer right. Then his phone rings again and he holds up his hand for quiet.
I look up.
Other Mommy is looking back down at me.
I get up and hurry out of the den while Daddo talks. I don't want him seeing her.

I take the stairs and I hear creaking up there and I know Other Mommy has gotten up off the floor, bringing her face up from the carpet.

I hurry. I'm gonna tell her to leave Daddo alone.

She used to just stay in the closet. Now she sometimes leaves my room.

I hear the mattress creak before I get there. I see her before I enter. She's sitting on the edge of my bed. She's facing the other way.

I don't like to see her like this. Because I can see the backs of her arms and there is dark hair on the backs of her arms.

I hurry in, but I don't say what I wanted to say.

I'm too afraid to say it. I don't tell her not to show herself to Daddo. I don't tell her not to ask him what she always asks me. But I don't have time to ask anyway.

Because she asks me first,

> Bela, can I go into your heart?
> No, I say.
> Please? she says. Let me in?
> No, I say.

She looks upset. In school we were told not to let people other than our parents touch us. Is going inside my heart the same as touching?

> Friends give and take, she says.

I don't know what Other Mommy will do if I say yes.

> No! I say.

She makes that face and I run from my bedroom. I don't look back. I run down the stairs and back into the den and Daddo is standing up at his desk, setting down his phone, and he says,

You pick a movie yet?

Yeah! I say.

Which one? And why are you breathing so hard? You just change an alternator?

I'll show you, I say. Hurry up! I wanna watch a movie right now!

I run out of the den and up the hall toward the living room.

Okay, okay! he shouts. I've never met someone so eager before. Don't ever lose that!

6

Me and Daddo are on our third movie. The sun is down and it's darker in the house, but I watched when he made dinner because our house has an "open floor plan," that's what Mommy calls it, and you can see everything in the kitchen from the living room. We're just up the hall from the den and sometimes Daddo gets up and goes and grabs something from there because he's still doing work even if he's just watching movies and every time he does I want him to hurry back from the front of the house because the stairs are up there at the front and I don't want him hearing any creaking.

We've been watching "easy movies." That's what Daddo calls movies with a lot of jokes and people falling in love. Sometimes, when I'm in my bedroom, I hear Mommy and Daddo watching movies that aren't easy. Loud, scary music and people screaming and sounds of violence. It used to be Other Mommy would stand at the end of my bed and cover both my ears with her hands so I didn't have to hear the not-easy movies. But I was littler then. Daddo rolls his eyes at a joke in the movie, but I can tell he likes it. Mommy makes fun of him for liking bad jokes but Daddo doesn't mind. I think he likes when Mommy makes fun of him. Maybe they fell in love watching movies like these.

I wish Mommy was here to fall even more in love with Daddo.

You hear that? Daddo asks. I think she's home.

I listen for Mommy.

She's not home yet, I say.

Daddo looks at the clock. He frowns.

Thought I heard someone, he says.

He gets up and I get up too.

Urs? Daddo calls.

Ursula. That's Mommy's really cool name. Daddo's name is Russ and that's okay too.

Urs, you home?

I follow Daddo out of the living room and up the hall to the foot of the stairs.

Urs?

He turns to look out the glass-brick windows that frame the front door and I peek into the dining room.
Is she sitting at the dining-room table in the dark? Is that her?

What is it? Daddo asks. Why'd you just gasp?

He looks into the dining room too but he doesn't see her.
Maybe it's not her.
Other Mommy has never come downstairs before.

Daddo steps into the den and looks out the windows and I take a step into the dark dining room and I hear breathing.

Are you downstairs? I ask.

The front door opens so suddenly, I scream.
Mommy is home like Daddo thought she was.

You two! Mommy says.

She sounds a little loud.

You two look like you saw a ghost.

Mommy turns on the foyer light and I look into the dining room and nobody is sitting at the table. Nobody is breathing there in the dark.

We've been watching romantic comedies, Daddo says.

Mommy smiles.

Scary stuff, Mommy says. Then, to me: Have you been good?
She's been weird all day, Daddo says.
Have not, I say.

Mommy struggles to take her purse off her shoulder. She sets it on the bench in the foyer, but she sets it too close to the edge and it falls off.

Whoops, Mommy says. What a *night*.

She picks it up and when she's standing again Daddo tries to kiss her. I think it's because of the movies we watched.

But Mommy just steps past him and into the hall toward the living room and she says,

What would you two do without me. Russ, you want a drink?

Daddo says,

The answer to *that*—

And then at the same time they both say,

Is *always yes.*
All right, Bela, Mommy says. Just because your daddo doesn't believe in bedtime doesn't mean it doesn't exist.

Daddo looks at me.

Do you think it's real? he asks.

I think of what I saw at the dining-room table. The shape in there.

Is what real? I ask.

Daddo smiles.

Bedtime, he says. Is it real or . . .

He wiggles his fingers.

. . . is it fantasy?

Mommy brings Daddo a drink and sips from one she made for herself.

It's real, Mommy says. Real as the hair on your head.

She touches my hair.
I think of the backs of Other Mommy's arms.

Up, Mommy says.

She nods to the foot of the stairs.

Go get ready, hon, she says. I'll meet you up there.

I head up. I hear Daddo whispering behind me. When I turn around they're kissing.
I think of carnations as I climb the rest of the way. I think of how friends are supposed to give and take.
When I look back down, Mommy is walking out of view and Daddo is watching her walk away.
They don't even think there might be someone other than us in the house.
That's really good.
I don't want her talking to Mommy or Daddo about carnations and friends. I don't want her asking them what she always asks me because they might say yes or they might say no and I don't know which is the right answer.
Mommy calls out to Daddo in a loud voice and I imagine them falling in love all over again. I want them to always feel good. I want Mommy and Daddo to hold hands all the time like they used to when we'd walk around the zoo and even the time I saw them holding hands when we were swimming in a lake in Chowder.
That's all I want.
For them to be like that all the time.

Bela.

Other Mommy is sitting on my bed, facing me.

Hi, I say.

I used to be so excited to see her. I used to wait for the closet doors to open. But she scares me now. With all her talk and her question.

Can I go into your heart?

Mommy calls out from downstairs before I have time to answer.

Bela! I don't hear you getting ready!
Make more noise! Daddo says.

They laugh down there.
But Other Mommy isn't smiling.
She's waiting for an answer.

No, I say.

And I run to my bathroom and close the door and grab my toothbrush.
And I make enough noise to block out the question.

7

Mommy sits on the side of my bed. She's wearing what she worked late wearing. She still has her leather jacket on. Her eyes look a little wet.

You smell different, Mommy, I say.

She smells her hands. Smells her shirt.

What do I smell like?

She looks to the door. Like she doesn't want Daddo to hear. I sit up and smell her up close.

You smell like another person.

Mommy looks upset.

Don't say that, Bela.
Why not?
Because it's not nice to tell someone they smell like someone else.

I'm sorry.

She doesn't tell me not to be sorry. She just smells herself again. She takes off her jacket. Her back is to the closet.

Shit, Mommy says.

I fluff my pillow and lie down. In a minute she'll think I'm falling asleep. Sometimes Mommy and Daddo tell me things when they think I'm asleep.
I stay quiet a couple minutes.

I deserve this, Mommy says. I deserve to have my kid say I smell like someone else.

I know she thinks I'm asleep now. I breathe like I am. She's facing my bedroom door. She doesn't see my eyes open a little in the dark.

What the hell am I doing? Mommy says. I have a family. Why would I risk this?

She hiccups. I wanna laugh because a hiccup is a funny sound, but I don't want her to know I'm awake. I don't want Mommy to know I hear what she's saying.

Jesus, Mommy says. *Jesus Christ.*

She closes her eyes and she breathes in really deep and she smiles like she's sad.
Other Mommy steps out of the open closet.
She slides along the wall to where the two walls meet. Her head is up in the corner of the ceiling.
I want to tell her to leave. I want to tell Mommy to leave.

Your father is a good man, Mommy says.

She's crying a little. I know what Mommy and Daddo sound like when they cry because they both cried a lot when Pester died. Pester was our orange cat.

He works hard for you and me just like I work hard for you and him. But sometimes . . .

Other Mommy blends into the dark corner. Mostly.

Bela? Mommy asks. Are you awake?

I don't answer. I'm afraid to speak. If I do, will Other Mommy ask to go into my heart?

There's no rationalizing this, Mommy says. What am I doing . . .

She only talks like this when Mommy and Daddo drink. Mommy must have been drinking while she worked late.
She stands up and picks up her jacket and turns around suddenly and Other Mommy sinks deeper into the corner where the walls meet the ceiling.
Mommy makes a little gasp sound.
She isn't facing me, so I can open my eyes wider and she won't see. I watch her take a step closer to the corner where the wall meets the ceiling.
She says,

Is something up there?

She walks to the dresser by the closet and puts her hand on the lamp like she's gonna turn it on. But she doesn't. Probably she doesn't wanna wake me.
She steps closer to where the walls meet the ceiling.

What did I just see?

When Daddo speaks from the doorway, Mommy jumps.

> What's up? Daddo says.
> *Man,* Mommy whispers. You *scared* me, Russ.

Daddo looks to where she was looking. I close my eyes before he looks at me.

> Ready for bed? he asks her.

Mommy doesn't answer at first. I peek again and see she's still looking where the walls meet the ceiling.
She turns on the flashlight on her phone and points it up to the corner.

> What is it? Daddo asks.
> I don't know. I just . . . I'm hungry, she says. I may eat something before bed.
> There are chicken wings in the fridge, Daddo says.
> That sounds good. Yes. How was Bela tonight?
> Great. Always.

I peek. I see Mommy looking up at the corner still.

> She worked on that puzzle, Daddo says. I think she likes the challenge. What are you looking at? A spider?
> No, I . . . I don't know.

She lowers the light.

> I guess I felt like I was being watched.
> By a spider.
> No.
> By me.

Now they're looking at each other. I'm not sure but I think Other Mommy is in the closet again. I used to think that's where she lives. But one time when I asked her what would happen to me if I let her into my heart, she told me I would go where she comes from. We'd switch places, she said. I told her I didn't want to be in the closet. She told me that's not where she comes from.

     I love you, Urs, Daddo says.
     I know you do, Russ.

I almost said yes to her once before. Daddo told me that people should say yes in life more often than they say no. He said that's how adventures begin. The first time Other Mommy asked to go into my heart I really almost said yes. I didn't wanna make her feel bad. I'd already seen her mad face.
I worry that one day I'm going to say yes. Just because.
One time I heard Daddo's friend Mark at a party downstairs say that if you ask enough times for a favor, people "eventually say yes."
And Mommy said that you can only "tempt" someone for so long before they give in.
Other Mommy is asking me for a favor. She says that's what friends do.
They give and take.
They help each other carnation.
But I don't know what that means.

     I love this family, Mommy says.

She has tears in her voice.
Then Mommy and Daddo are leaving my bedroom together and I'm alone in the dark, and I'm looking at where the ceiling meets the walls.

Hi, Other Mommy says.

Her voice is right next to me.
She's almost too big for the space between my bed and the wall
and she feels too close.
I cry out.
Mommy and Daddo come running back and they're both in the
doorway and I say,

I almost rolled off my bed.

They wait a second and then Daddo laughs.

That's not funny, Mommy says. Bela, be careful.
O, come on, Daddo says. At some point in everyone's life,
they roll off the bed. It's a rite of passage.
Go back to sleep, Mommy says. You won't roll off.

She looks to where the ceiling meets the walls again, but Other
Mommy is crouched on the other side of my bed now.

You good? Daddo says.
Yeah, I say.

Daddo sniffs the air.

What? Mommy asks him.

Daddo thinks about it.

I don't know. Nothing. I keep getting a whiff of something.
Like . . . a toilet pipe.
A toilet pipe? What the hell?
It's gone, Daddo says. But whatever. If something's wrong,
we'll fix it.

He smiles at me.
I can hear Other Mommy breathing on the other side of my bed.

> Good night, Bela, Mommy says. And do me a favor?
> What?
> Sleep in the middle of the bed.

Then they leave. And I think about how Other Mommy used to feel more like a friend. When I first met her, she *was* a friend. And I didn't need any others! We laughed in my bedroom at nothing. She combed my hair. She covered my ears. She held me. Then she'd go back into the closet. And she'd stare at me for a long time from in there. She told me she was making sure I had good dreams. But I didn't always have good dreams.
Sometimes she didn't talk. But I could hear her breathing. And sometimes I'd hear it again, while I was sleeping, her breathing, in the dreams I did have. And sometimes I woke up and saw her hurrying back into the closet.
We were friends then.
Are we still?
Does she still want me to have good dreams?

> Ha! Daddo yells from up the hall.

Something fell in their room.
Daddo is laughing.
Then Mommy is too.

> I told you it's a rite of passage! Daddo says.

I try to feel good about them laughing. I *want* them to laugh all the time.
But I can hear Other Mommy breathing beside my bed.
And I know she wants an answer.
And if we used to be friends . . . what are we now?

I sit up.

I think about calling out to Mommy and Daddo again.

Then I hear her sliding across the carpet.

The closet doors slowly close and I don't call out for Mommy or Daddo.

Let them laugh, I say.

Please, let them laugh, all the time, like this.

Forever.

8

Deb and me are on the swings in Chaps Park. We come here a lot. It's one of my favorite places because the jungle gym is huge and made of wood with bridges and ropes and slides. Daddo always laughs about one time when I was littler and I went too fast down the slide and landed on my face in the sand and looked at him like I was gonna cry but then I started laughing and got up and went back to the ladder because I wanted to do it again. I like the days best when Mommy and Daddo take me here together.

Why isn't your dad here? Deb asks.
He's home working, I say. Mommy's schedule is all over the place.

Deb asks a lot of questions. Mommy says so does her mommy. Her mommy's name is Carly, and Carly and Mommy are talking on the bench by the big trees and the bathrooms.
They use their hands a lot when they talk.
I wonder if Mommy still smells like another person today. I wonder if Carly notices that too.

My mom says the school is gonna make us be checked for weapons, Deb says.

I heard the same thing. Mommy and Daddo got real mad about this. Daddo slapped his palm on the kitchen counter and said the world is "crap." Mommy started to tell him not to say that in front of me, but then she stopped because I think she agreed with him.

It's gonna be really weird, Deb says. We gotta make sure we don't have secrets in our backpacks.

I think of carnations. A backpack full of them.
We swing as we talk. Mommy once told me everybody lives in fear of "something." She said everyone has "that one thing they're afraid of." She told me she doesn't want to live in fear and that if she ever catches me living in fear it would "break her heart."

Would you ever hurt anybody? Deb asks me.
I don't think so, I say.
Like if somebody was hurting me? Deb asks. Would you hurt them for me?
O, then yes.

I swing higher than Deb does, but then she swings even higher and we talk as we pass each other.

Good, she says. Because I would do the same for you.
What would you do? I ask. How would you save me?

Mommy looks to me from the bench. She's wearing big, dark sunglasses. A white scarf around her neck. It's still summer but some days are a little bit colder than others now. She looks like she's in disguise. But I can tell she's looking at me. I think about her on the edge of my bed last night. She said she was "risking" everything.

Well, Deb says, swinging slower now. I guess that depends on what's happening.

I slow down until we're both not swinging anymore.

Let's say I was in my bedroom, I say. And a woman lived in my closet.

Deb giggles.

I like scary stories, she says.
But really, I say. How would you save me from a woman who lives in my closet?

Deb's face gets smushy while she thinks about it. She taps the dirt with the tip of her shoe.

Maybe it's not bad if she lives in there? she says.
But what if it was bad? I ask.
Then I would tell your parents.

I look to Mommy. She's really using her hands while she talks and she's sitting on the edge of the bench.
I think of Daddo snapping his fingers, saying yeah we're best friends.
Are Mommy and Daddo best friends too?

I wouldn't want them to get hurt too, I say.
That's true, Deb says. Well, how would she hurt you?
She could scare me, I guess.

I wouldn't want that.
But she says we're friends. Because we used to be.
Friends? Deb asks.
Yeah, I say. We used to play quietly in my bedroom.
What did you play?

Her question makes me feel weird. I don't know the names of the games we played.

Like staring contests and stuff, I say.
That's weird.
What if she watched me from the bathroom when I was lying in bed? I ask.
Then I would *stab* her! Deb says.

She said it loud and I look to our mommies but they didn't hear her.

Stab her?
Yes, she says. I would say, *Leave Bela alone!* And stab her with a sword.

I think of a mean face.

But what if there are no swords? I ask. What if I woke up and she was lying in my bed next to me?
I don't wanna play this game anymore, Deb says.
What if I woke up and her face was next to mine? What if her eyes were on the bottom of her face?

Deb gets off her swing.

Stop it, Bela.
Would you save me then? I ask.

Stop it. I don't want to hear any more of your scary story.

How would you save me from the woman who lives in my closet?

I don't wanna talk anymore!

I get off the swing and follow her to the jungle gym.

Would you still tell her no? I ask.

Deb runs the rest of the way to the jungle gym. She knows not to run to our mommies because they're talking about something serious and now Carly is doing more talking than Mommy, who is holding her head in her hands like people do when they don't feel so good inside.

Would you kill her? I ask.
Bela, stop.

I'm right behind Deb now. She climbs the metal ladder to the wood bridge.

Would you pour water on her like in the movies? I ask.
Stop it, Bela. Talk about something else!
Would you push her out the window?
Bela . . .
Would you—

But Deb runs across the bridge and into one of the square wooden rooms.
I'm standing down in the sand beneath the jungle gym.

Would you really tell your mommy? I ask. Even if your mommy might get hurt?

Deb comes out and walks to the top of the yellow slide.

Yes! She says. Yes! I would tell Mommy that a mean woman lived in my closet and that she laid with me in bed!

Daddo says some things are a "matter of time." It's "only a matter of time" before something happens that you think might happen.

Are you alone in there, Deb?

She's hiding from me in the little wood room.

Of course I'm alone, Bela!
Are you sure?
Of course I'm alone!
Are you sure?
Stop it!

Mommy and Daddo talk to me when they think I'm asleep. Daddo talks a lot about "the importance of being nice." One time he said:

The older I get, the more I think the barometer for intelligence is how kind you are. Because it's not an easy thing to do, staying mindful, after all you go through in life. It scares me, thinking of you going through all the things your mom and I already have. Everybody who has ever lived has gone through some pretty terrible times and it scares me to think you will too. I don't talk about these things when you're awake because I don't want to scare you. What kind of a father tells his kid they're going to go through hell and back? Well, I guess one day you'll need to know it. And it's not just about crushed dreams and failed relationships. It's much deeper than that. You know, I can still remember the time I realized people are mean. Most people. I was just out of high school, I was living here in Chaps already. I was working this terrible data-entry job and my job was to type in how many hours these home healthcare nurses worked. Would you believe I got paid more to type in their hours than they got to work them? Yeah. Even then I was able to see there was something wrong with that. But here's the thing: there was this guy at work named Oren. And for whatever reason, Oren just did not like these home healthcare nurses. They were mostly women and definitely poor and here this guy who worked in the office with me just flat-out hated them. Well, we would hand out the paychecks weekly. The nurses would line up in the office after helping people in their homes, their apartments, and Oren and I would hand out the checks and the nurses would make sure we had the hours right before leaving. Justifiably so. And more than once, we didn't have it right. And I couldn't figure out why. They turned in their hours, I typed them in, Oren ran the checks. And if a nurse said we got it wrong? I'd tell them not to worry, I'd figure it out. But Oren would push back. He'd tell them they were wrong. They were uneducated and "couldn't add." And there was this glee on his face when he did this and it made me so mad. It still makes me mad now, years later, sitting here with you. But it wasn't just that I realized Oren was somehow docking their pay, out of spite. It was that Oren would often look to me during one of these beratements, and in his face I'd see he expected I felt the same way he did. That I got off somehow on watching these poor nurses suffer and argue too. And no matter what face I made back at him, no matter how disgusted with him I looked, he still assumed I felt the same. You see, Bela? That's real cruelty. That's world cruelty. Where it's not just the idea that one person is cruel, it's that they believe, and have reason to believe, the whole world feels the same.

Deb, you still up there? I ask.

She doesn't answer. She's mad at me.
I'm being mean, I know.

I climb up the slide. It's not easy, but I get to the top. The wood room Deb is in is just the little bridge away.

    Deb? I ask. Are you mad at me?

I cross the wood bridge.

    Deb. I'm sorry.

I hear her in the dark. She's crying.

    Really, Deb. I'm sorry. We can talk about something else.
    Get away.
    I'm sorry, Deb. Don't tell our mommies. Come out.
    No.
    Let's play in the sand, I say. I'm sorry!

I can see a little of her face in there.
She says,

    Bela?
    Yeah?
    Can I?
    Can you what, Deb?
    Can I go into your heart?

I look over the safety railing, down at the playground sand. I see Deb running back to our mommies down there.

    Can I, Bela?

It's Deb's voice from the dark.
Fingers curl around the edges of the entrance to the wood room.
Fingers with hair.

MOMMY! I yell.

I back up too fast across the bridge and my feet hit the top of the slide and I fall backward, down the slide and hit the sand at the bottom, hard, too hard.

I feel dizzy.

Mommy and Carly are coming for me. I don't feel so good, my head hurts.

I think of Daddo on the edge of my bed.

So the goal, I think, is to stay kind for as long as you can, no matter what happens to you. No matter what you go through, no matter how many breaks you get and how many you don't. And I think you always have to remember that if someone is mean to you, they are like that with everybody else too. You see, Bela? Meanness doesn't have to spread. It can stop with the mean person, stop at the threshold of the kind person. I guess I'd put it this way: don't let them in. Don't invite them in. If there's one thing I could convey to you, one thing that would take root in you just like the need to eat and sleep, it would be this: try to stay kind as long as you can. For all of your life. Always be mindful of what others are enduring. And whatever you do, most of all, don't allow someone else's meanness, someone else's cruelty, to get inside of you.

Everybody's standing over me. The sun is up behind them all. I squint. I see myself in Mommy's dark glasses. She's asking if I'm okay. She sounds so worried. She smells like herself again. I look scared in her glasses. I look small.

Deb looks scared too. And Carly holds her like she's worried the same thing could happen to her. Like Deb could suddenly fall down the slide right now.

Bela, Mommy says. What happened? Why did you fall?

I don't have the air in my chest to answer. I cough. She helps me sit up and she pats my back and I see past her and past Deb and Carly.

I look up to the entrance of the wood room on the jungle gym.

> Bela? Mommy says. Are you okay?
> I'm scared, I say. I'm really scared, Mommy.

For the first time ever, Other Mommy is outside the house.

9

She fell on her head, Mommy says. On her freakin' head!
Scared me to *death*. Scared Carly and Deb. It looked so bad.
Jesus, Russ, Deb was white. Blanched.

Daddo looks at me. We're all sitting around the kitchen table.
They're talking about doctors.

> How you doing? Daddo asks me.
> I'm okay, I say.

But I don't feel okay when Daddo asks a question like that. I feel
a bunch of things at once.
So I cry.
Daddo comes over and scoops me up so I can sit on his lap.

> It's okay, he says. You had a playground accident. Happens
all the time.
> She fell hard, Mommy says.

She hasn't stopped sounding worried since I fell.
Daddo looks me in the eyes and says:

One time I was walking the parallel bars and your uncle Klay pushed my feet out from under me. I landed on my ribs. Broke one. Could barely breathe. Your grandma was so scared. Just like Mommy was today. But I was fine. And you look good. You'll be fine too.

   We don't *know* that, Mommy says.

   Then let's take her to the doctor, Daddo says.

He looks to me.

   Wanna go see Dr. Smith, Bela?

I hear creaking upstairs. As Mommy and Daddo get me ready to leave. As they take my hands and walk me to the front door.
I look up.
And I think,
What if I say yes?
Will she stop?
Will she?
If I say yes?
Will she stop getting closer?

   Come on, Bela, Daddo says. Let's go listen to your head and your heart.

10

My doctor looks like Abraham Lincoln. I see him once a year except when something happens. Like when I get sick or like the time I broke my pinkie when Daddo threw me a football too hard. He felt bad about that.

Dr. Smith is tall. He wears a white coat. He has a beard that goes just around the bottom of his face.

The wallpaper is all a bunch of ducks and geese chasing one another. It smells like medicine in here. There's a little sink and a jar with green lollipops and I sit on the gray cushion with the white paper on it. This is where I always sit.

Dr. Smith has a stethoscope in his coat pocket and one time Mommy and Daddo couldn't stop laughing about that on the drive home. They said he looked like a "living cartoon." A drawing of a doctor.

But he looks serious now.

Bela, he says.

Dr. Smith is good at talking.

Tell me what happened, he says.

She fell, Mommy says. Backward down the slide.
I'd like Bela to tell me, Dr. Smith says.

Mommy makes a little face, but Dr. Smith doesn't notice. He's looking at me and wants me to answer.

I stepped back too far and fell down the slide, I say.
Uh-huh. And why were you walking backward?
I was backing up.
Uh-huh. Did you experience any disorientation before then?

I look to Mommy and Daddo.

Were you dizzy? Dr. Smith says. Did you feel strange? Did you think you saw something strange?

I think of hairy fingers in the doorway to that little wood room.
I think of Daddo's phrase, "It's only a matter of time."
I want to tell them because maybe I need to warn them. But if I tell them, will she ask them instead?
I say to Dr. Smith,

No.
Okay, he says. Nothing at all?
What are you getting at? Mommy says.
O, I don't know, Dr. Smith says.
Well, I was watching her the whole time of course, Mommy says.

I think of Mommy and Carly talking on the bench. I think of Mommy with her head in her hands. I guess we both kinda lie to Dr. Smith.

I'm only wondering how Bela felt prior to falling, Dr. Smith says.

That's fine, Mommy says. But I said I was watching her.

Urs, Daddo says. He wants to know if Bela had a dizzy spell. I mean . . . she fell.

That's it, Dr. Smith says. That's it exactly.

Fine, Mommy says.

Mommy is like this when she worries. She talks a lot and fast.

Bela, Dr. Smith says. Any dizziness before you fell?

No.

Okay. And no . . . shock or scare?

I think about it, and Mommy nods for me to answer.

Yeah, I was a little scared.

Ah, Dr. Smith says. And what scared you, Bela?

The geese are chasing the ducks on the walls. The geese look so mean and the ducks look so scared.

Other Mommy, I say.

It's a pattern, they're all the same, but when you look at one goose and one duck, you think the other geese are catching up to the other ducks. You think some of the ducks have already been caught. Are bleeding.

Dr. Smith is looking at Mommy and Daddo.

Really? Mommy says.

Bela, Daddo says, you haven't used that name in . . .

He looks to Mommy.

She said that name maybe a couple years ago, Mommy says.

And who is Other Mommy? Dr. Smith says.

He's asking them. Not me.

We don't . . .
We don't know, Mommy finishes Daddo's sentence.

I like when they do that. People in the romantic movies finish each other's sentences too.

It's a kid thing, Mommy says. Then, to Daddo: We should cancel the party tonight.

Dr. Smith looks at me.

You thought you saw an imaginary friend at the top of the slide? he says.
It wasn't like that, Mommy says. It's a whole jungle gym.
Bela? Dr. Smith says.
I don't know, I say.

I don't want to be talking about this.

How did you know to ask if she'd seen something? Daddo asks Dr. Smith.
Well, because Bela here is as coordinated a child as they come. She's strong. Sure of foot. She bounds right up onto the examination bed and she skips her way out of the office. She loves to dance. For the little I know of your Bela, she's not the type to fall down a slide without reason.
Accidents happen, Mommy says.
They do, Dr. Smith says. They sure do.

But he's still looking like maybe he thinks there's more to what I saw.

Well, let's check on your head, he says. Though I don't see any signs of a concussion in your eyes and your speech isn't slurred and nothing is broken.

He pulls the stethoscope from his pocket and says,

Just watch the geese and the ducks, if you like, Bela. They're more interesting than they let on. Sometimes I think I see a goose catch a duck . . . out of the corner of my eye.

11

Mommy and Daddo are throwing a party tonight. They throw lots of parties. Their friends talk loud and laugh loud and the music gets so loud you can't help but dance. And everybody drinks adult drinks, I know. They get a babysitter for me when they have parties, even though I'm not home alone and I'm not a baby.

His name is Kelvin. Kelvin goes to the high school in Chaps. He's probably the nicest person I've ever met. Daddo met him first. In a sports league Daddo plays in. Soccer. Or softball, maybe. I don't know. But Kelvin is really fun to be around. He's a friend.

There's already music playing downstairs.

And know what? I don't just dance, I'm actually good at it.

Dr. Smith wasn't kidding when he said I'm coordinated. Mommy and Daddo used to laugh when I danced because they said they didn't expect me to be so good. Now they don't laugh. Now they ask me to dance for friends at their parties. Kelvin also knows I'm a good dancer because when Mommy and Daddo go out, I put on the music I like and I dance for Kelvin. Sometimes he dances too.

He's always on the phone when he's here. But he still watches me. Makes sure I don't do anything like turn the stove on and all the other things parents worry about.

I know Mommy wanted to cancel tonight because I fell down the slide. But Daddo said it would be okay. He said Dr. Smith said there was nothing wrong with me. And there isn't. So what better reason for a party than a "clean bill of health"?

Daddo is fun like that. I love him so much.

I hear people downstairs already in the kitchen with Mommy and Daddo. It's Amanda and Dan. They always come early and they always leave early and I wonder if it's because they don't like it when people start talking loud. They have a little baby at home. They talk about wanting more. Mommy and Daddo make jokes about me being "a handful" all by myself, but then they always say I'm the best thing that's ever happened to them. Right now, downstairs, Amanda laughs at something Daddo says. He makes Amanda and Dan crack up whenever they come over. I like the sound of them laughing. If there was a sound that was the opposite of Other Mommy's voice, it would be laughter. The music isn't so loud that I can't hear them talking down there.

So, Bela took a fall? Dan asks. Amanda told me this happened.

It was no big deal, Daddo says. She's fine.

Actually, Mommy says, I was there and it was scary as shit.

I bet, Amanda says. Poor kid.

Doctor said she's fine, Daddo says.

I am fine.

Did she hit her head? Dan asks.

We don't think so, Mommy says. But it looked like it. And it made the worst sound. Or she did. As she fell. It was like she grunted or . . .

Or what? Amanda asks.

Well, it sounded like an old man grunting. Not like a little kid.

I'm sure she was scared, Daddo says. I'd hope no tape recorders are nearby when I make my scared sounds.

Amanda and Dan laugh. But Mommy means it.

It could've been a car's muffler near the park, Mommy says. Or even her shoe on the slide, I don't know. But when I play the sound back in my memory . . . it was like an animal grunting when it doesn't get what it wants.

The doorbell rings. I leave my bedroom. I'm at the top of the steps, looking down at people arriving.

Mark, Daddo says. Well, well, *welcome*.

Mark is one of Daddo's best friends. They have parties just by themselves a lot of nights. They listen to music and drink a lot. They get loud but never mad.

How's Bela? Mark asks. You mentioned the doctor.

But I'm fine. And adults are dramatic. Daddo said that once.

She's fine, Daddo says. Just gave Urs a scare is all.
I bet.
This is why you've never had kids.
This and ten other reasons. Not finding a woman to have one with is near the top.

Daddo starts to shut the door but another couple is here and so the party has already started. I go back to my bedroom. I want to change into my party clothes.
But those clothes are in the closet.

And I don't wanna go in there right now.

Instead, I go to the dresser and try to find something else to wear.

The doorbell rings.

The music gets a little louder downstairs.

I don't like the clothes in my dresser. I look to the closet. It's closed.

I think of carnations.

Did I close the closet doors? Do I ever open or close the closet anymore?

Hey! I hear Kelvin downstairs!

Kelvin is here! I'm so excited, I could scream!

      Kelvin! I yell out.

I hurry to the top of the stairs and see him at the bottom, already talking to people.

      Kelvin! I yell again.
      Bela!
      Come help me get my clothes from the closet!
      Give me a second, he says. Then I'm all yours!

Mommy meets him at the door and shakes his hand. She looks up the stairs and sees me and says,

      He'll be right up, Bela. Come into the kitchen for a minute, Kelvin.

Okay. So now I wait. While Mommy tells him I got scared and fell. But meanwhile, I'm fine.

I head back to my bedroom and more people come to the front door and I can hear Laver and Marsha and Amanda and Dan and Billy and Anita and voices I don't recognize too.

I look to the closet.

It's closed.

I look to the bathroom.
I listen.

    Other Mommy? I say.
    Bela.

But it's real Mommy's voice, behind me at my bedroom door.
She scared me!

    Hey, Bela, Kelvin says.

Mommy and Kelvin enter my bedroom.

    Kelvin is gonna watch you, Mommy says. Like usual. Then,
to Kelvin: But feel free to hang out downstairs too. You know the
drill. Bela is not only welcome, she's wanted. The reason we hire
you is so we can get drunk enough without freaking out where
our child is.

Kelvin laughs.

    Yep. I know the drill.
    And you, Mommy says. You should dance for everyone. If
you're up for it.
    I want to!

Mommy smiles. But she's still worried about me. I can tell.

    So, Kelvin says to me. Clothes are in the closet?

He steps to the closet.
Mommy makes a face like she saw something in the bath-
room.
She goes into the bathroom.
Kelvin puts his hands on the closet doorknobs. He turns to me.

What's up? Are the clothes not in here? You look like you're about to say something.

I'm watching the bathroom. Why is it quiet in there? What did Mommy see?

Bela? Kelvin asks.

I step toward the bathroom.
Mommy steps out again.
She's holding a towel.

Not on the floor, Bela.

I look to the closet. Just as Kelvin opens the doors.

No! I shout.

But it's just my clothes hanging on the hangers.

Bela? Mommy says.

I know she's thinking of me falling at the park.

Those, I say.

I point to the clothes I want to wear downstairs. The clothes I want to dance in. They're purple and blue and they look just like something a dancer would wear on TV.

I thought so, Kelvin says.
You got this, Kelvin? I'm heading back down, Mommy says.

There are so many voices down there. And the music is even louder again.

Thank you, Mommy says to him. Bela, be good for Kelvin.

Kelvin takes the purple and blue clothes from the closet and sets them on the bed.

Get changed in the bathroom, he says. And hurry. They love you down there.

I look to the bathroom.

What is it? he asks.

Then he's up and looking in the bathroom himself.

Worried it's too messy in here? Don't be. Watch.

I carry the clothes to the bathroom door and watch as he quickly arranges my toothbrush and soap so the bathroom looks cleaner.

There. Now you have a nice place to change. You know, Bela, little things can make a big difference. I don't expect someone your age to get that. I didn't get it back then. But it's true. A clean changing room can make you feel like you're changing into a clean person.
I am a clean person!
Ha. Yes. I didn't mean that.

He leaves the bathroom and I bring my clothes inside.
I shut the door behind me.
I wanna get changed really fast, but all I can do is stare at the tub. Other Mommy was in there when Daddo was in here last. And if she's not in there now, and if she's not in the closet . . . where is she?
I imagine her downstairs. Dancing for the people there.

I'm at Bela's place, yeah, Kelvin says out in my bedroom.

He's on the phone. Always on the phone. I think he has a crush
on someone.
I hurry up and change into my party clothes.

Yeah, a lot of people here, Kelvin says into the phone.

I look in the mirror. I look to the tub.

Hang on, Kelvin says. I think I just heard something on the
roof.

He laughs.

Bela? he calls. Do you have squirrels on the roof here?

I leave the bathroom fast. Kelvin is standing in front of the closet
like he's about to slide my clothes apart so he can look inside
better.

No! I shout.

He laughs.
The voice on the phone asks why the kid just screamed.

Wow, Bela, Kelvin says. You're piqued, huh? Thought I
heard something is all. Come on.

I don't close the closet doors. Kelvin and I leave my bedroom.

I'll call you later, Kelvin says.

He hangs up.

I look back to the closet. To where my party clothes aren't hanging anymore. It's like a gap there. A hole in the house.

It's real lit downstairs, Kelvin says. I'm sure we'll become someone's confession booth tonight.

What does that mean?

Ha. It means someone is going to drink too much and decide to tell the young people a secret. You good? What's on your mind?

Carnations, I say.

Like . . . the flowers?

I know what carnations are because I looked them up after Other Mommy told me about them.

Yeah, I say.

What about them?

We're halfway down the steps.

They bring you back to life, I say.

Kelvin laughs hard.

What do you mean?

I'm getting a little hot. Am I embarrassed?

Carnations, I say again. Friends use them to bring each other back to life.

Wow, he says. You are amazing, Bela. Sure, maybe carnations bring people back to life. I've heard of worse things!

We get to the bottom together. It's like slipping into a pool of people. The adults all drink from cups and glasses and some are in the living room and some are in the kitchen and some are on the back deck and the back door is open.

There's a lot of smoke. The kind that makes Daddo and Mark laugh.

> Bela! a lady says.
> Bela! a man says.
> Bela! Are you gonna dance for us?
> Bela! How are you?
> Bela! Hello!
> Bela! Are you going to dance for us?
> Bela? When are you going to dance?

Daddo. There he is. He leaves a group of people and comes to me.

> Hey, you. Hey, Kelvin. You two good?
> Hey, Kelvin says. Yes, we're great. Bela has her dance pants on. And carnations bring people back to life.

Daddo looks at me with a funny smile.

> This is like a stand-up bit, right? Daddo says. You mean *rein*-carnation?
> Yeah, I say.

That's it. That's what Other Mommy told me about when she was on her knees at the end of my bed.

> That's a good one, Daddo says. Then, to Kelvin: Make yourself at home. Eat whatever you want, of course. And Bela, come here, I want you to meet someone.

Daddo leads me to the fireplace in the living room. A woman is sitting on the stones there. She's got red hair and big glasses and she's looking right at me.

Bela, this is Lois Anthony. She works with people all over the world.

Hello, Bela.

She holds out her hand for me to shake it like I'm an adult.
She smiles and it looks like she means it. The word Daddo uses is "genuine" when someone smiles like she does. I think of Daddo saying how people need to be kind. How that's how you know how smart someone is, by how kind they are.

Your father tells me you may be a Sensitive.

I look to Daddo.
He looks away for a second and I know he's uncomfortable.

What does that mean? I ask.

Lois Anthony nods like she was expecting me to ask that.

Some people are able to sense more in this world than others, she says. It's a real talent. Something to be extremely proud of.

I look to Daddo.

Well, we'll get deeper into this later, he says. But just know . . . Lois is definitely someone to talk to about anything you want to talk about. I just wanted you to meet her is all.

Lois doesn't take her eyes off me.

Can I do one thing? she asks.
Sure, I say.

Lois reaches out and puts her hand on my shoulder. She closes her eyes.
She holds her hand there for a little while.
I think she's disappointed.
She opens her eyes.

Didn't sense any magic? Daddo jokes.

Lois smiles.

O, what do I know. Just an old hippie, in the end.

But she's still studying me. Like she was expecting to learn something when she touched me but didn't.

Bela!

Mommy and Daddo's friend Marsha is calling to me from the entrance to the living room. She has a glass in each hand. Her face is already red.

How are you, sweetheart?

Marsha always talks to me when she drinks. She's funny like that.

It's so cute that you hang out with the adults! she says. My kids would *never* do that. They hate me.

Her kids are older than me.
Mommy is there now next to Marsha. She frowns but she doesn't mean it.

Bela, stop judging us, Mommy says.

Marsha laughs and Kelvin appears beside Mommy.

> Bela! Are you partying?
> Yeah, I say.

Mommy looks to Lois Anthony. Then Mommy and Marsha and Kelvin start talking about clothes.

> Bela, Lois Anthony says.

I barely hear her over the music. Daddo and some other people are really excited about this song. They're playing the instruments without any instruments in their hands.

> Come here for a second? Lois says.

Daddo isn't standing near her anymore, but I go to her anyway.

> Do you mind if I touch your shoulder again? she asks.
> Why?

The party is getting louder. Even Kelvin is practically shouting to Marsha by the hall.

> Well, I'll be honest with you. I really thought you might be a Sensitive when I met you, but when I touched your shoulder, I got zero indication I was right about that.
> Okay.
> Yes, that is okay. Except . . . also it's not. I'm usually right about this sort of thing. Can we try again?
> Okay.
> Okay. Here.

She puts her hand on my shoulder. She breathes in deep. She closes her eyes.

I like her face. It's wrinkled in a good way. Smooth skin but wrinkled. She's older but feels young.

Tell me, she says. Are you seeing ghosts?

But this question scares me.

No, I say.
No? Your dad said you might be.

Did he? Did Daddo say that? Ghosts?

No, I say. I don't see ghosts.
How about one ghost?

She opens her eyes.
The ceiling creaks. I hear it over all the music.

No, I say.

Lois smiles like maybe she thinks I'm not telling the truth.

Well, okay, she says. I didn't feel anything this time either.

But she still stares at me like she's trying to figure something out.

Thank you, Bela, Lois says. And I want you to know . . . anything you do see is natural. Even if it feels like it's not.

I start walking away from her and I bump into Kelvin.

Hey, he says. What do you feel like doing? Ready to dance?

So many voices. So much music.

> Yes, I say. But wait, I need my shoes!
> Where are they?
> By the front door.
> Awesome. Let's do it.

Kelvin walks me past the open kitchen. Everybody's talking
and drinking and there are more people than I've ever seen in
our house before. We go up the hall and I see Mommy is in the
dining room, at the table, laughing at a story a man is telling,
and Daddo is on the front porch, smoke like white hair around
him and his friends Mark and Laver. They're laughing, too,
and I wanna see why, so I head that way but Kelvin takes my
hand and says something about "giving them a minute." He
hands me my shoes and I sit on the foyer bench and put them
on. Then Kelvin leads me up the hall again back to the living room, where it's even more crowded than it was a minute
ago.
Mommy won't allow the TV on at parties and Daddo says it
ruins everything unless it's a "nature doc" because "animals are
good to see all the time no matter what."

> This is a real party, Kelvin says.
> It's about to be, I say.

I start dancing.
I'm never self-conscious when I dance, but I feel weird tonight.
Adults smile at me but mostly they just talk and it's like I'm
not a little baby anymore so maybe it's not as fun that I'm
dancing. But Kelvin dances with me and it's a fun song and
even more people are coming into the room one by one and
some women dance with me, and now Daddo and his friends
are in the room and Daddo sees me and waves with a funny

little smile on his face and I think I hear creaking on the stairs and I dance to the creaking just as much as I dance to the music.

Someone is telling a story.

I can tell right away it's a ghost story. Anybody can tell something like that. Ghost stories might not all use the same words, but they all sound like the same words because it's the ghost we think about, not the words.

The man says,

The basement was the one place none of us wanted to go, right? But sometimes Mom made us do it and it was the worst thing ever, every time. Piles of magazines and this old sewing machine that was covered in a blanket, so it looked just enough like a person.

Scary! someone says.

People laugh. More people in the room now. I keep dancing.

The man says,

And one day Mom tells me to go get this box of pictures from the basement. As if worrying about spiders in a box of pictures isn't enough, the fuckin' box is in this dark area down there, about as far from the stairs as you can get.

So you gotta run as fast as you can, someone says.

Yes, the man says. But . . . there's the furnace down there too.

I look between the people and see all the way down the hall. Mommy is standing close to a man in the foyer. He's holding her hand.

Daddo is talking with his friends near me in the living room.

The man and Mommy bring their faces closer together, but then people step in the way and I can't see them anymore.

Did Daddo see that? Does this man smell like someone else?
The man with the ghost story says,

And so I take the stairs down to the basement like I always
do. One at a time, gearing up to grab the box and get the hell out
of there.
What happened? someone says.
I'm telling the story right now, Rachel! the man says.

Everybody laughs.
Everybody except . . .
Lois Anthony is still in the room. Still sitting on the stone ledge
at the fireplace.
Still looking at me.
The man telling the story says,

And so I get to the bottom of the steps and I *bolt,* and I get
to the boxes and it feels like bugs are everywhere and I look up
and see my dead aunt peeking out from behind the furnace.

Everybody says whoa.
The man says,

And Aunt Nettie lifts a finger to her lips and goes, *Shhh-
hhh.*

Everybody in the room kinda breathes in together.
And a woman screams.
And it's the loudest sound I've ever heard.
I look to Lois Anthony, but it wasn't her who screamed.
It was Mommy's friend Marsha.
And now suddenly there is no music and Mommy is beside Mar-
sha and so is the man who had his hand on Mommy's hand and
everybody is telling Marsha it was just a story.

But she isn't scared of the story.
She's pointing to the far side of the living room and she yells,

There was a monster! A *huge . . . thing! Right there!*

Daddo's friend Laver laughs like he's nervous. But otherwise it's
quiet and nobody knows what to say.

My God, Marsha keeps saying. *My God . . .*
Marsha, someone says. Are you stoned?

But Marsha is shaking and she's still pointing and she says,

It was tall . . . dark blue . . . hair . . .

People make room for where she's pointing and we all see there's
just an empty wall and everyone's talking about drinking too
much and being too stoned and some are looking at one another
like whoa, Marsha is upset.
But I look across the room and see Lois Anthony is looking right
at me still.
I step forward and I say,

That wasn't a monster, Marsha.

And Mommy looks at me the way she does when she wants me
to keep quiet. She even looks at Kelvin like maybe he could help
with that.

That wasn't a monster, I say again.

Because she was once a friend. And maybe she still is. Even if she
scares me as much as she excites me.
A friend.

Who was it, Bela? Lois Anthony says.

I think of hair on the back of arms. A face on the side of a head. A voice like a friend who keeps asking for the same thing, over and over, until I give in.
Give and take.
I say,

That was Other Mommy.

12

Daddo thinks I'm sleeping.

He sits on the end of my bed and he's talking to me but really he's talking to himself.

It's late. Everybody's left the party.

I don't know where Mommy is.

And I don't want Daddo to leave my room.

Marsha saw Other Mommy.

What does that mean? Can anybody see her?

First she was just in my closet. Then she crawled to my bed. Then she sat beside me.

Then she was outside the house.

And now someone else saw her too.

I saw Lois Anthony talking to Marsha in the driveway when everyone was leaving. Marsha was sitting in her car with the window down. The person driving the car looked like he really wanted to go and then they finally left.

Lois Anthony looked back at our house and to my bedroom window and I ducked and Kelvin said,

You spying over there?

He was making a joke but I could tell he was scared about what happened downstairs. I didn't know if it was Marsha screaming or me or maybe Kelvin saw Other Mommy too.
He didn't go near the closet as he helped me to bed.
But Kelvin is gone now too.

Maybe I should sleep in here tonight, Daddo says. Yeah, why not. You must be a little shaken up. I guess I am too.

I can tell when he's looking at me and when he's not. My eyes are closed. But I can tell.
He's looking at me.

You know, Daddo says, a lot of people have stories like yours. Like the . . . mommy thing you've talked about a couple times.

He doesn't say *Other Mommy*.
Is he upset?
I don't like that idea. I don't like it at all.

I've got something too, he says. But I'm not talking about that right now because who needs it? God, I'm so stoned.

He definitely thinks I'm sleeping. Where's Mommy? Downstairs?

Ah, Bela. It's all so different, you know? How you think things are gonna be and how they end up being. I know that sounds like something a stoner would say, but I'm not claiming to be much more than that. Am I happy? Yes. Yeah. Sure I am. But I'm also sad. Does that make sense? Sometimes I feel like it's my life's mission to make sure you don't get the second half of that, only the first. I'm sure your grandparents wanted me to grow up to be happy, full stop, no sadness. But it's not quite like that. Adulthood. It's not that it's bad, or dark, or terrible. Jesus, no. In fact it's incredible. Sometimes I think of this one kid, Quinn Dole, from high school. Poor guy wrapped his car around a tree late at night when we were all seventeen and he died and every time I experience something new, I think how he missed out on that. Even on the day you were born. I swear. In the hospital. Your mom was in so much pain and you come popping out and everyone's relieved and the doctor says you look great and Mommy is gonna be great and who do I think of? Quinn Dole. I think of his huge Adam's apple and his spiky black hair and the way his teeth lit up his face when he smiled and I remembered him running, of all things, up the hall one day, when he was late for class, and how his arms and legs looked all disconnected like nothing was working together in concert. How's that for a word there, huh? *Concert.* Yeah, I'm stoned. You asleep? Yeah, you're asleep.

Daddo stands up, walks to my dresser, grabs his drink, sits back down on the bed.
He sits down kinda hard and I have to try hard to keep my eyes shut.

But it's not so much the big events Quinn is missing out on. It's not graduation and first love, real love, and college, and shitty jobs, and dumb decisions. It's not marriage and a kid and buying your first house, though he was present in my head for all those things, too, right? Still . . . it's the *feeling* of life. The experience of aging and living. *That's* what Quinn Dole is missing right now. It's not the kid, it's your *reaction* to the kid. It's me not sleeping for the first year you were alive, Bela. It's the constant worrying about you and what that does to a parent. You know what I mean? It's growth and change, by way of experience, and that's what Quinn Dole is missing right now. It's not love . . . it's *falling* in love and how it literally changes who you are. Hey, Bela, you know my friend Mark?

Daddo drinks. The ice makes a clinky sound.

So get this. Mark takes a photo of himself every day. Did you know that? He's done it for a really long time now. Years. We're talking pre-cellphone stuff here, but also with his cellphone now too. Mark has thousands of pics of himself. I guess everybody does that nowadays, but I think you know what I mean. And in case you don't: Mark is documenting the changes in himself. And that's cool. And we talk about it. But at the same time, I don't know. I'm less interested in the changes on the outside, you know? I lose or gain some weight? I grow my hair out or lose it all? Who cares, right? What I wish I had documented was the *inner* change. That's the stuff Quinn Dole is missing right now. How amazing would it be to check back ten years ago, five, even just one. I guess artists would understand. Hey, Bela? You asleep? Did Marsha really see what you said you saw?

Daddo drinks. He's quiet now. I listen for creaking. Noises other than him or me. Where's Mommy? Did she leave? Is she with that man from the hall? Did she drive him home?

Jesus Christ, Daddo says. That scream of Marsha's.

He stands up. I peek.
I thought he'd be standing above my bed, looking back down at me. I was ready to say I'm awake again. To keep him talking. To keep him here.
But his back is to me and he's facing the closet.

If there is anything in this house, Daddo says, get out. Now.

I open my eyes wider. I look to the closet.

Go somewhere else, Daddo says with his back to me still. If there are such things as ghosts, go somewhere else and be one there. This house doesn't want you. We're happy here.

I don't want Daddo talking to the closet like this.

I mean it, he says. Leave. Leave right now.

He holds up his drink like he's toasting the closet. He makes a
click sound like he's touching his glass to someone else's.
The closet doors creak open.

Hey . . .

I sit up. I can't pretend to be asleep anymore.
Daddo steps closer to the closet. It's so dark in the room I can
barely see him now. What do I do? Yell for him to stop?

Kelvin? Ursula?

He reaches out and closes the closet doors.
He stands quiet for a long time and my eyes get used to the dark
and I think Daddo is looking back at me from the closet and has
been since he shut the door.

You still asleep, kiddo? he says.

I don't answer because my heart is beating too hard. I'm so
scared, I can't move.
He looks to the closet again. He pulls out his phone and uses the
flashlight.

Ah, Daddo says. A hinge is loose.

He laughs.

I'll fix you in the morning.

But still . . . he doesn't walk away. He just stands there.

Is he looking at the hinge? Is he looking at me?

Know what? he says. Screw it. I'm gonna fix this right now.

He leaves my bedroom and goes out into the hall. There's a nightlight there because of me.
I stare at the closet.
She's gonna come out.
I feel like I know she's gonna come out.

Don't, I say.

It's hard to tell where the closet doors end and the walls begin.
Daddo steps into the room with a screwdriver in his hand.

Okay, naughty closet hinge, Daddo says. Let's fix you up so you don't scare Bela anymore.

I watch him as he fixes it. I think of him locking her in the closet and I like the thought of that.

All right, Daddo says. That should be good.

He steps back but still doesn't leave.
He keeps quiet for a time. Just facing the closet.
I think of carnations. Flowers. And how I must've misheard Other Mommy.
Daddo says,

You know, Bela, fear is a super interesting thing. If you think about it, every time you've ever been scared in your life so far, you've also survived whatever you were scared of. Right? You've literally gotten through everything you thought you might not. Everything you thought you weren't strong enough to get through . . . you got through it. Or else you wouldn't be here to know you got through it. Right? And I'm telling you, Bela, *that's* the stuff Quinn Dole is missing out on right now. That's the feeling of being alive.

Daddo, I say.

I scared him, I think.

Bela. What?
Is reincarnation bad?

He carries his drink back to the bed. I'm glad he's farther from the closet now.

Bad? he says. No. Reincarnation is . . . one of the most beautiful things we've ever come up with, I think.

I think of Other Mommy telling me about it. About how it brings friends back to life.
Can I go into your heart?

Maybe Quinn Dole had reincarnation, I say.

Daddo sips his drink.

So you *were* awake. You do that often? Sit and listen to Mommy and me when we think you're asleep?

I don't answer.

Don't worry if you do, Daddo says. I woulda done the same as a kid. How else are you gonna hear about the real world?

He breathes in deep like he's thinking.

But who needs the real world, right? he says. And I like that
idea.
What idea?
That Quinn Dole was reincarnated.
But where would the other person's body go? I ask.
What do you mean?

I don't know what I mean.

If Quinn came back in someone else's body . . . where
would that person go?
I . . . well . . . I . . . I don't think it works that way.
But maybe it does?

Daddo laughs. But he's eyeing me closely.

Is this about . . . you know, he says.
Maybe, I say.
Wanna tell me more? Daddo says.

The closet doors creak open.
Daddo stands up fast and goes right to the closet and closes it
again. Then he takes the chair from my desk and puts it against
the doors and he says,

No more out of you!

He's breathing hard and the ice in his glass clinks as he takes
another drink.
Then he sets his glass on my desk and walks over to my bed.

Slide over, kid, Bela, daughter of mine.

I slide over.

Is Mommy home?

Let's talk more about reincarnation and your mother to-morrow, he says.

He sits down hard on my bed and falls back onto one of my pillows.

Quinn Dole will never know what it feels like to drink too much and pass out in your kid's bed, he says.

Then he's asleep. And snoring so loud I can't tell if anything in the house creaks.

But I'm still thinking about reincarnation. And where one person goes if another person takes their body.

Other Mommy told me she wants inside my body. She told me I would go where she comes from. We would trade places.

Like friends.

Trading.

Sharing.

I'd be helping her.

Like friends do.

Weren't we friends before? I think we used to laugh together. But now I don't know if I'm remembering that right. Maybe it was just me who used to laugh.

And Other Mommy just watched.

Please don't come out, I say.

I watch the closet doors in the dark. Daddo snores next to me.

Don't get any closer, I say. Please. No closer.

But I feel wrong. Bad. Like I'm telling Pester not to want to go outside.

But Pester was just a cat.

Bela . . .

Did I just hear my name?
Is she talking to me from inside the closet?
I slide closer to Daddo.
I close my eyes.
I pretend I'm sleeping.
Maybe if I pretend to sleep, it'll actually come true.

No closer, I say again.

And I keep saying it. Like how people count sheep.
Eyes closed. Next to Daddo.
No closer, no closer, please, no close—

13

Eat, Mommy says.

It's morning. I'm at the kitchen table. Mommy just walked into the house a minute ago. She's still wearing her jacket from the party last night and she looks tired.

Did you sleep over at a friend's? I ask.

She looks at me quick, serious.

Eat.

Daddo is asleep upstairs. In their room now. I saw him facedown and still wearing his clothes on their bed on my way down to the kitchen.
I put my own breakfast together. Mommy doesn't know this yet. She's at the fridge now. She takes out orange juice and then some aspirin from a bottle. She swallows the aspirin with the orange juice.

Man, she says. Not every party has to turn into a séance.

What's a séance?

Nothing. I just mean . . . when are people gonna learn it's okay to have fun without bringing up dark stuff?

Who did that?

That ghost story. Remember?

She looks at me like she hopes I remember.

Yeah, I say. It wasn't scary.

Ha. Well, you're a little scare expert these days.

What do you mean?

Nothing. Eat.

I'm eating.

Well, eat more. Eat till you're round.

I eat more.

Where's Daddo? she asks.

Asleep.

Still?

Yep.

He was up late, she says.

So were you.

Excuse me?

So were you.

Bela.

So was I.

Kelvin didn't put you to bed?

He did but then I was up for a while.

Mommy looks to the ceiling.

Did Daddo tuck you in too?

Yeah. He fixed the closet hinge too. And slept in my bed.

What was wrong with the closet?

He said it was loose.

Mommy looks to the ceiling again.
I left the chair in front of the closet this morning.

Well, good.

She drinks more juice.

Bela?
Yeah.
Who is Other Mommy?

The way she asks it, so sudden, it surprises me.

Bela?
Yeah.
Please, tell me more about her.
Why . . .

Mommy comes and sits with me at the table. She smells like the party still.

Because Marsha Dickman got really scared and friends have been texting me about it all morning. She actually stayed at her brother's house. I'd like to know more about Other Mommy and I'd like to know right now.

I don't answer at first.

Bela?
Her face is weird.
Weird? How?
I don't know.
Well . . . you do though. Right?

Yeah.

Okay. So how?

Um . . .

Bela . . .

Her eyes are sometimes on the side of her head and sometimes on the bottom of her face.

What?

Yeah.

Okay.

Mommy breathes deep.

What else about her can you tell me? Is she small?

No, she's big.

O? Bigger than me?

Bigger than Daddo.

I see.

I think she has to duck when she walks around my bedroom.

Jesus, Bela.

It's weird because the sun is bright. And I feel like we're talking like people do at night.

But she's not always like that, I say.

Not always big?

Yeah.

Okay. So sometimes she's small?

I don't know. Yeah.

What do you mean?

I don't know.

Try?

Sometimes she slides across my bedroom floor on her belly.

This is all very creative.
Creative?

Mommy gets up and looks up and leans back against the counter and crosses her arms and says,

Bela, has she ever talked to you?

A door slams upstairs and feet are moving fast down the hall up there. Then down the stairs.
Daddo hurries into the kitchen.

Bela? he says.

He sees me and I know he was scared I was alone down here.
Daddo looks to Mommy.

Hey.
Hey.
Did you just get in? I thought maybe you passed out in the den.
I went to Marsha's. To make sure she was okay.
Well, she obviously had a little too much last night, Daddo says. I know I did.
Yeah, Mommy says. We gotta stop that.
Yeah. We gotta dry out.

They're both looking right at me and they both go quiet and I eat. Mommy turns on the little radio in the kitchen and Daddo drinks some water.

Are we still going to the zoo today? I ask.

Mommy and Daddo forgot.

O, shit, Mommy says.
That's right, Daddo says.

They go quiet again. Then they laugh.
They laugh hard.

It's not great when our kid remembers this stuff and we
don't, Daddo says.
No, it's not.

They look at each other for a while. But when Mommy goes to
hug Daddo he walks away to the sink and gets more water.

I could sleep the entire day, Daddo says. But I'm gonna go
get ready for the zoo.
Can we get a stuffed vulture? I ask them.

They look surprised.

A vulture? Mommy asks. Bela, of all the animals in the
world, why would you want a vulture?

There are vultures at the zoo. I heard vultures are great because
they don't kill. What they eat is already dead.

I think they're cool, I say.
A vulture you shall receive, Daddo says. If they have one.

He pats my head and I finish eating and I see Mommy is looking
at the ceiling still and she has her arms crossed still and is holding her elbows.
Like she's cold.
Then she looks at me like she hasn't forgot the question she
asked me.

But she doesn't ask it again.
Even as Daddo walks out of the kitchen to get ready Mommy
doesn't ask again,

Bela, has she ever talked to you?

14

My teacher last year, Mr. Jeffery, says some places aren't just those places to people. He says some places mean other things. He said:

The grocery store might be someone's safe place. So maybe they go there to buy just one or two items. Because it feels good just to be there. And the park could be someone's place to think. Every time they go to the park, they work their problems out. A location can be a beacon to someone else, even if they're only dots on a map to you.

I think the zoo is that for Mommy and Daddo. They have long talks whenever we go to the zoo. They usually tell me to go on ahead, to go into the reptile house on my own while they follow behind, talking.
I think Mr. Jeffery would say the zoo is not just the zoo for Mommy and Daddo.

You still hungry? Daddo asks me.

We're in the reptile house now. I'm looking into the cage of a really green snake. Bright-green eyes. It looks like he was painted.

She just ate, Mommy says.

Yeah, Daddo says, but what's wrong with a second breakfast?

He winks and I laugh.

I'm glad we're at the zoo. It's more than just a place to us.

There's the big guy, Daddo says.

He points to the alligator behind glass but the alligator isn't so big. There are snakes in here that are a lot taller than I am.

But I go to the glass and look the alligator in the eye and I think he's looking at me but it's hard to tell. I can see Mommy and Daddo reflected in the glass. They're talking close to each other's ears like they don't want anybody else to hear.

They're looking at me when they talk and I know they're worried about things.

Do they know she's getting closer?

I wanna see the butterflies, I say.

But they don't hear me. They're arguing. Mommy points at me and Daddo is telling her not to get "so worked up" in the reptile house. That only makes Mommy madder.

I look the alligator in the eye. I wonder what he sees. At night. In here.

Do things come out of the closets at night in the reptile house? Things that climb over the glass and crouch next to him? Things he thinks are friends but then he isn't so sure?

Maybe the alligator doesn't know the answer to the questions he's asked at night either.

I wanna see the butterflies, I say again.

But they still don't hear me. Mommy is talking about me being "creative" I think. Daddo is saying don't worry. But I don't think

Daddo could pull the worry from Mommy's eyes even if he had that screwdriver.

He's asking about last night. Asking about Marsha and Marsha's house.

Mommy starts to walk away from him. From me too.

I wanna see the butterflies! I say really loud this time.

Mommy stops walking away and comes toward me.

We know, she says.

But they're at the end, Daddo says. Penguins and lions first. And did you know, Bela, the order of the animals at the zoo is the same as the food chain in nature?

Really? I ask.

Yep, Daddo says. The butterflies are king of the jungle. They eat all the lions.

Not true! I say.

Mommy and Daddo look at each other but neither laugh.

I'm thinking of how Mommy told Daddo she slept at Marsha's house but she told me Marsha slept at her brother's.

Naw, you're right, Daddo says. But I bet butterflies are the king of *something*.

The alligator isn't where he was anymore. I don't see him at all and I wonder if he's hiding in the shadows under the branches and leaves. I wonder if he's scared of the closet doors at night. We leave the reptile house and pass the little monkey fountains and follow the elephant footprints to the new place where the penguins live. Mommy and Daddo call it a "habitat." I didn't know the word before today. I ask Daddo to carry me even though I'm too big to be carried. He gives me a piggyback ride

the rest of the way. It feels good when he carries me through the doors of the new penguin house. Like how things used to be.
Before my closet doors started opening at night.
But then I worry:
Am I able to remember a time before the closet doors opened at night?

Look, Bela. You can really see them. They're all out today.

He sets me down and I hurry to the glass. The penguins are on the ice in a little pack.
Some dive into the water while some come back out. Some waddle and some don't move at all.
I look back and see Mommy and Daddo talking by the entrance. Daddo is using his hands like he does when he's trying to be patient with something. Mommy looks like she doesn't want to talk anymore.
I bite my lip. They're fighting again.
I look back to the penguins.
A big one slides into the water and I watch him get deeper until I can't see him anymore.

Hey, Bela, Daddo says. Did you know they have to thaw the penguins out of ice cubes?

They're next to me again. I love when Daddo jokes. But his jokes don't feel real right now.
I know they're fighting.

Not true, I say.
I don't lie, Daddo says.

And I think to myself: this is true.
Daddo doesn't lie.

We leave the penguins and follow the path to the lions. The air is chilly. Colder now. Mommy says the animals come out when it's colder.

We walk. I think about Mr. Jeffery and how places mean different things for different people. Is our habitat, our house, a safe place for Mommy and Daddo?

Hey there Russ, Ursula, Bela. Fancy meeting you three here.

I recognize the voice even before I see who it is.
Lois Anthony is at the zoo today too.

Hey! Daddo says. Wasn't expecting anybody else from the party to be out this early.

Lois laughs.

Yes, well, a bit of a headache. But I have a firm rule: no hangover of mine is going to stop me from doing what I planned to do. If hangovers broke my plans, I'd become a hermit.

Daddo laughs. But Mommy doesn't.

And you, Lois says to me. How are you doing? I wonder if hangovers are contagious. Maybe you feel a little tired like your parents do? Or maybe you're the one tiring them out?
I feel good, I say.
That's good.

Lois Anthony really looks at you when she looks at you.

Hey, she says to Daddo, I wanted to let you know that my group meets on Fridays at—
What group? Mommy asks.
Well, I was talking to your husband about it at the party.

What group?

I wanna see the butterflies, I say

That's fine, Mommy says. Let's do that.

You wanna see some butterflies? Daddo asks Lois Anthony.
King of the food chain?

Mommy looks impatient.

No, but thank you, Lois says.

Who did you come here with? Mommy asks.

I'm alone. But I have a routine, so to speak. I clear my head
at the Chaps Zoo.

Mr. Jeffery is a smart man.

Then we'll see you soon, Mommy says.

She takes my hand.

Great to see you three, Lois says. And remember: Fridays at
Sneakers. We like to have a few drinks when discussing the unknown.

That's great, Mommy says. The unknown.

And we walk away.

What group? Mommy asks Daddo as we walk.

I don't know, Daddo says. But did you really need to be that
way with her? She said a bunch of people meet up to talk about
occult stuff. Sounds cool.

Seriously?

Yeah. Why is that weird?

Seriously?

She's interesting, Daddo says.

How so? Mommy says.

All that crystal and cosmic stuff. It's interesting to me.

O, come on.

Why?

Because it's baloney.

Is it any more baloney than anything else?

We're at the doors of the butterfly house.

Yes, Mommy says. Some things are absolutely more baloney than others.

Well, I don't know, Daddo says. I think things can just be fun, in and of themselves. Like a magic show. Is a magic show baloney?

These people base their lives on this stuff, Mommy says.

I don't know that. You don't know that.

The woman who works at the zoo reminds us to close the first door before opening the second.

It gives you mayonnaise brain, Mommy says.

Daddo laughs.

Mayonnaise brain, really?

It makes you mushy. It makes you believe in shit. I'm not saying there's nothing to believe in. But the kinds of things that woman is into . . . it's mayonnaise.

Do you believe in ghosts? I ask Mommy.

Mommy and Daddo look down at me together.

Come on, Daddo says.

Why, Bela? Mommy asks.

Lois Anthony believes in ghosts.

We wait for the first door to close behind us before opening the second one.

Sounds like you guys know Lois very well, Mommy says.
No, I say.

We go through the second door. We're in the butterfly house now.

A night of drinking with some far-out people sounds fun, Daddo says.
Bela? Mommy says. Why don't you walk ahead a little bit? Find something great for us to look at.

I walk ahead.
I can feel them arguing behind me.

Hey, butterflies, I say. I see you.

There are so many plants in here. And it's hot. Daddo calls it "humid." And there are so many butterflies, I can't see them all. Blue ones and green ones and black ones and yellow ones and ones with spots and ones with stripes and ones so big they could cover your hand.
Look there! A red one!
I hurry through the big leaves. I've never seen a red one before.

Wait! I call.

The big leaves touch my hair and I try to keep up with the red one.
And it lands! It lands right next to a blue one. On a huge green leaf.

Why, hello there, I say. I'm Bela. And my parents have been arguing all day. Who are you?

The red butterfly flaps its wings and I think he can see me. I think he's looking back at me.

I came all the way from my habitat to see you, I say. And my parents use the zoo to fight.

The red butterfly flaps its wings and the blue one moves too.
It blinks.
Like an eye blinks.
I smile because I don't know what else to do.
I feel hot. Hotter.
It looks like an eye between the leaves.
I take a step back because I don't know what else to do.
A blue eye. Buried in the green leaves.
I think of something crouched beside the alligator. I think of the doors of the butterfly house opening like closet doors.

O, no, I say.

I turn around, but Mommy and Daddo are still back there, around the bend, arguing.
I think of Other Mommy on the playground.
I think of Marsha's scream.
I look to the blue, deep under the green leaves and I run so fast the leaves hurt my face and the butterflies are flying everywhere crazy and I run into the woman who works at the zoo.

Slow down, honey! she says. You don't wanna scare the butterflies!

DADDO! I yell. MOMMY!

And I see them, turning, hurrying toward me.

> Bela!
> *She could be anywhere!* I yell.

Then I run through the leaves and out the door and I don't wait for the door to shut before I open the second and I hope some of them escape.
I hope the butterflies make it out of their habitat and fly far away.
I hope—

> *Bela,* what are you *doing*?

Mommy and Daddo have caught up to me outside.
Mommy is grabbing my arm hard.

> Bela?
> Urs, Daddo says. Can't you see she's scared?

And he looks scared when he says it too.
They both do.

> Everyone's lost their minds, Mommy says.

She walks away from us.

> It's all right, Daddo says to me.
> She could be anywhere, I say.
> Who? Daddo asks. Are you talking about . . .

But he knows who I'm talking about.
Mommy turns around and comes back to us.

It's because of people like Lois Anthony that *this* is happening. People like Lois fucking Anthony!

Urs.

No, no, no, Mommy says. I don't care how loud I am, Russ.
Whatever this is? This stops now. This stops *now*.

15

Mommy's mad.
She emptying out my closet.
The pile of clothes is big.
She's moving so fast.
Daddo is saying they believe me. Actually, he says,

It's not that we don't believe you, Bela . . .
I don't want any talk about believing or not believing,
Mommy says. We're emptying this closet and that is all. This
whole house needs to be cleaned. Needs to start over.

She throws more clothes on the pile.

It's almost empty now, Bela, Mommy says. See? Nothing.
No nest. And nothing will go back *in* here until whatever phase
you're in ends.
Where do I—
You are not to use this closet anymore. Understand?

Daddo's phone rings. He says it's his work. He steps out into the
hall.

All my stuff is in a pile on the floor. Now Mommy's taking stuff out of the bathroom. She keeps saying,

See? Nowhere for anything to hide. See?

I look into the empty closet. It looks small to me. How come it felt like there was no end to it before?
Mommy comes to me. She gets on her knees on the floor. She pulls old toys out from under my bed.

See? Nowhere for anything to hide. See? And you're sleeping with your door open until I say otherwise.
Why?
Because.
Because why?
Because I said so, Bela.

I look to the closet. It's just a small, empty space now.
I look to Daddo in the hall on the phone.
Mommy stands up beside the bed.

You need to nap now, she says.
Why?
Because you're all worked up. And because you need rest, water, and . . .

She goes to the window and opens it.

. . . Air.

Then she's at the door and she turns off the light and leaves my bedroom and Daddo and her disappear up the hall.
But I can still hear them.
And I see the pile of clothes on the floor outside the closet.
And I hear the wind outside.

And I wonder if the pile of clothes is big enough to hide some-one.

A T-shirt moves a little bit. From the wind coming in the win-dow. And I'm alone in my bedroom and Mommy is mad and the wind almost sounds like a voice, a voice that keeps asking,

Can I go inside your heart?

But Mommy's right. I am "worked up." And I'm tired.
And I lie down and hear the wind blowing into my bedroom.
And the closet is just a small empty space.
I close my eyes and I don't care about the question right now.
Mommy's mad.
And maybe that's good.
Maybe I'm not alone anymore with this if Mommy's mad.
But the wind keeps blowing. Even as I fall asleep. Like a whisper coming into my bedroom. And Mommy and Daddo creak up and down the hall. And they whisper, too, about me, about my bedroom, about the closet.
I almost get up and look at it again. Because it looked so differ-ent without anything in it.
Without anyone standing between my hanging clothes.
Watching me.
All the time.
Watching me . . .
. . . sleep . . .
I'm tired.
Really tired.
And so . . .
. . . I sleep . . .

16

It's later now. Dark out. I slept. But I'm awake again.
The window is still open.
Mommy thinks I'm sleeping.
I can tell.
She's sitting on the edge of my bed and she's talking to me like
she does when she thinks I'm sleeping.
She says,

I never thought I was the kind of person to do this, Bela.
Seriously. In my whole life, I never imagined I would cheat.
There . . . I said it. Because it *is* cheating and that's all it is. I can
twist it all up and say it's natural, I can say it's only a matter of
time before two people drift apart, no matter how much they
love each other. But this is flat-out cheating. Your dad doesn't
know. He should know. It's as clear as July. But . . . he doesn't.
And that's exactly *why* I'm doing what I'm doing and I know
that's why. Because your dad is simply . . . too easy. Too warm.
God, I sound like one of those idiot college girls who only fall
for bad guys, women who wouldn't give a nice guy the time of
day. But I married one, dammit. I'm *married* to one. I'm sorry,
Bela. Not because I'm doing what I'm doing, but because I'm

not sure anything could stop me from doing it now. Christ, you think he's the only one I've been with? God. I've been cheating since before we got married. That's the truth. Since before you were born. It's who I am. It's what I am. I lust.

I don't know how long she's been talking. I don't know what time it is.
I look to the closet.
It's all dark there. An open, dark space in the dark.

Still . . . *still* . . . it stings. Because no matter how right you think you are, no matter how much sense a thing makes as you're doing it . . . you're still doing something you never imagined *you* would do. I'm sure you have dreams, Bela. Things you want to accomplish, the kind of person you want to be. And while it might be hard to accept, your parents were once your age and they had ideas and dreams too. And I think maybe your dad is living his. Yes. I think maybe he is.

I think Mommy is crying.

I have no doubt he always imagined himself being a kind father, a good man, raising a child right, being loyal to his wife. I know he was already thinking that way in college because he told me he was, in so many words. But me? Christ. In college I was looking to hook up with every boy I met. And I did. For the most part. And some of this your dad knows and some of it he doesn't and it's never made me feel like I do right now. Not until all this stuff started with you.

Yes, she's crying.

There we were, the three of us living our lives, and you suddenly start seeing things and talking about something else living in the house and falling at the park and screaming at the zoo and so now I have to be focused on my family at the exact moment I only want to focus on myself. Is that selfish, Bela? It might be. *Forgive me.* But for what? Let's say we never had you, Bela. Would that have been selfish? Of course not. If there's no child, there's no child to do right or wrong by. But we *did* decide to have you. And so . . . is there no respite from that? Is there no way to live your own life without it being called selfish by someone less independent than you? I can only imagine what the other parents in town would say if they knew what I've been doing. Maybe some of them do. But I would tell them what I'm telling you now: parenthood should not be a prison sentence. And if you want to be with one of your husband's friends? You should do it.

I close my eyes all the way.
I think Mommy was drinking while I was sleeping.
And I hear Daddo. And it scares me.
I hear him up the hall. He's making the house creak.
Does Mommy know he's coming?
Should I tell her to keep quiet?

And the worst of it, Bela, the *worst* of it is that I believe, in my heart, no, I *know* that if your dad were to find out? He'd be okay with it. Yes. He'd tell me he understands. Because he understands *everything.* He'd tell me we're just people and that people have nuance and that relationships come in waves, in seasons, and if I felt so lost in the cold winter of this one, he'd knit a blanket to keep me warm. And while that may sound to someone else like the best partner a person could have . . . maybe I don't want the best partner a person could have. Maybe I want some grit, some spit, some mud, some blood. Is that so hard to forgive? Who is good and who is bad? What is right and what is wrong? You ever think, Bela, how people say that light shows what things really look like, but they also say that light and dark are equal and need each other and you can't have one without the other and so . . . is it so crazy to say that maybe what we see in the dark is the truth too?

The creaking in the hall.
Daddo is getting closer.

I wanna *feel*, Bela. I wanna eat good food and drink good drink and sleep good sleep . . .

I wanna say something. I wanna warn Daddo not to come in right now.

. . . but the world tells you you can't. Not once you've had a kid. Nope. Then it's all prison gruel and curfew and institution-issued rations. Hell, even all our clothes are supposed to match, us parents. Have you ever seen us all gathered at a barbecue? A party? We're fashionless, passionless prisoners, Bela. Prisoners to our children.

I don't like this at all.
Daddo's just outside my bedroom door now.

You know what I've been thinking about lately, Bela? I've been thinking a lot about reincarnation.

What?

I wonder what I'd come back as. A better person? A better mom? Would starting over change things? It might. It might make everybody happy. That's the beauty of reincarnation. A second chance. If someone would just let me in. You know? It's what friends do. They let each other in. Would you let me in? I bet you would. It would be awfully nice of you. You would re-incarnate me, wouldn't you? Give me *life*?

There's a figure in the doorway.

Bela?

But it's not Daddo.
It's Mommy.

Who are you talking to in there, Bela?

I slide out of bed and run for the door and I see Other Mommy
is facing me on the end of the bed.
And her face is crazy.

MOMMY!
Bela?

Mommy turns on the light and she screams and I know she sees
Other Mommy. Then I'm in Mommy's arms and she's running
up the hall and she's repeating Daddo isn't home Daddo isn't
home. The hall creaks behind us and I look over Mommy's
shoulder and see Other Mommy peeking out my bedroom door.
And her face is big and crazy.

Outside! Mommy yells. *We need to get outside!*

She's carrying me down the stairs and my feet bang against the
banister and in my head I keep seeing Other Mommy peeking
like that out my door, and then Mommy is opening the front
door, all so fast, yelling we have to hurry, holding me so tight,
yelling for help, and then she's dragging me by my wrist down
the front porch steps, outside and it's night but the porch light
and the moon make it feel safer than my bedroom and when
we're out on the front lawn we both turn to look at the house
and Mommy is shaking and looking up to my bedroom window

and she moves me behind her legs and she's breathing so hard,
and she says,

>   Bela?
>   Yes . . .

She's breathing so hard.

>   Other Mommy?

And her voice sounds like it's made of fear. And I say,

>   Yes. Other Mommy.

Mommy is shaking, staring up at the house.

>   Okay, she says.

She reaches behind her to hold me there.
But she still faces the house.
And she still shakes. And it feels like she will forever.

>   Okay.

17

We're at Amanda and Dan's house now.

They have a little baby.

Mommy is on the phone outside in the driveway and Amanda is outside with her.

We can hear Mommy talking from in the kitchen. Their house is kinda like ours. No wall between the kitchen and the living room. Daddo says people like open spaces in our neighborhood. Their hallway to the front door is shorter than ours. And they don't have a dining room. Mommy one time said all houses are the same, but I don't think she meant the layout.

Dan is reading a magazine at the kitchen table, but he's not really reading. He keeps asking me questions, like if I'm okay.

He keeps looking to the front door. And he shakes his head at what he overhears Mommy saying.

Then he looks at me again.

Like I might tell him it's all phony.

But I don't.

Late night, Dan says.

He's nice. So is Amanda. But I can tell he's not happy about this. About us being over.
The baby is in a little carriage in the kitchen.

I called your dad, he says. He'll be here soon.

Dan has said that a couple times. That Daddo is on his way. That he was going to stop home first.
I don't want him to stop home first.

Can you tell him not to go home? I ask.

Dan looks at me like I'm a baby. That's because he only has a baby. Not a little kid.

He just needs to grab some things, Dan says.

Then he says loud,

Ursula? I think Bela is about to cry.

I'm not about to cry but then I feel like I might. I think of Daddo going into our house. I think of Daddo seeing Other Mommy on the bed.
Her face big and crazy.

I'm not about to cry, I say.

But maybe I already am. Dan is a nice man. Daddo says being nice is also being smart.

Bela?

It's Mommy. Back inside. She's next to me. She's hugging me. She's so worried. I've never seen her like this before.

Amanda is here, too, now and Dan and her look at each other like this is all crazy.
Like this is all bad and they want nothing to do with it.

We're just gonna spend the night here, Mommy says. We'll figure out what comes next tomorrow.

She can't stop moving. She paces their kitchen. Her eyes moving all over the room.
She saw Other Mommy tonight. She sure did.

Where's Daddo? I ask, even though Dan just told me.
He's almost here, Mommy says.

Amanda is staring at me like I'm bad. Bad for her and her baby.

How big was she? Amanda asks Mommy, and Mommy says loudly:
It wasn't a woman.

I look to Mommy and then look away fast because I don't want to know what she means.

How close is Russ? Dan asks.

Mommy and Daddo say Amanda and Dan are so nice, but they don't seem so nice right now. They seem upset that we're at their house.

It's pretty late, Dan says. You guys can use the extra bedroom.
Extra bedroom, Amanda says. There's not even a bed in there. It's more like an extra closet.

Mommy looks at me and I look at her and she doesn't look away and I know she's thinking of emptying the closet in my bedroom and it almost feels like she let Other Mommy out.

> We're gonna stay awake for a while, Mommy says.
> Ursula, Dan says. What you're describing . . .

He looks at me and I blink but don't look away.
I wanna tell Mommy we should leave. We're scaring them and they don't know we're scaring them and so they're just mad.

> Did you hear that? Mommy asks.

Amanda and Dan look up to the ceiling and they look sick. Mommy says,

> No, in the driveway. I think I heard a car.
> He's here, Dan says.

Mommy goes to the front door and steps outside and I'm alone with Amanda and Dan and I imagine Other Mommy sitting on the edge of their bed, telling them what they don't know about each other.

> Thank God he's here, Amanda says.

Mommy and Daddo come down the hall and Mommy says,

> . . . Wasn't a woman.

Daddo looks at me and tries to smile like he usually does, but his face isn't working and I run to him and we hug in the hall.
He smells like the outside world.

Hey, Bela. You're okay. You're okay. It's going to be okay. Truly. It is.

We're staying here tonight, Mommy tells Daddo.

I think about our house at home. I think about Other Mommy sitting in there alone without us.

Daddo looks at Mommy to make sure she means it. Then he breathes out heavy and says,

I get it. Yeah. I was just there.

I don't like this.

I searched the place, he says.
Maybe not in front of Bela? Dan asks.

Daddo looks at him like he hadn't thought of that.

Come on, Daddo says to Mommy.

They walk up the hall. I can still hear them though. Even when Dan tries to talk over them.

Are you hungry, Bela? Dan asks me.
There was nothing there, Daddo says to Mommy. Nothing like what you described on the phone.
No, I tell Dan.
It was horrible, Mommy says to Daddo. The worst thing . . .
How about some juice? Dan asks me.
No, I say.

Mommy sounds like she's going to cry again and then I remember Mommy wasn't actually crying.

What did Other Mommy say when she was pretending to be Mommy? Was she telling the truth?

  We'll figure this out, Daddo says. Then: What you described . . . Ursula . . .
  A movie then, Amanda says. I'll put on a movie.
  I don't want to think about it, Mommy says. Please.
  What movie do you want to see, Bela? Amanda asks me. *Tangled?*
  It was using my voice, Mommy says. *I heard my voice.*
  She was! I say loudly.

But at the same exact time Amanda turns on the TV, and Mommy and Daddo don't hear me.
I can't hear them now either.
Just certain words:

  Voice . . .
  Taller . . .
  Hands . . .
  Hair . . .
  I think I'm going . . .

Amanda and Dan are blocking my view of Mommy and Daddo.
They lead me to the couch.
But I don't wanna watch *Tangled.*
I wanna listen to Mommy and Daddo.

  Sometimes it's okay to give it a minute, Dan says.

Like we're talking about a game. Or like someone just got a little angry is all.

  Yes, Amanda says. It's okay to process things.

She looks to their baby and Dan smiles but it's more like he wants this night to end.

This movie, Amanda says, is one of Disney's best.

She turns it on and Dan sits on the couch and Amanda walks up the hall to Mommy and Daddo and I hear it when Amanda says,

What would anyone want with Bela?

I don't like this question.
Who said anybody wants anything with me?

What I saw is impossible, Mommy says.

Her voice is shaking.
But then the movie starts and I can't listen anymore.
Dan gets up and gets the magazine from the kitchen and comes back to sit on the couch with me.
I get up and run to the hall.

Mommy. Daddo. Maybe we shouldn't stay here.

They all look at me, worried about me saying this. Amanda has her hand to her mouth how people do when they're sad or surprised that they're sad.
Dan is behind me now.

Sorry, guys, Dan says.
It's okay, Daddo says. Bela, come here. Maybe we all need to talk about this.

Mommy looks up the hall like she's scared of what she might see.
Daddo gets on his knees in front of me.

Bela, is there someone, an adult, at school who has hurt you or said he or she might hurt you? Anything like that?

Mommy hides her face in her hands.

> No, I say.
> No teacher or janitor or recess aide or a coach or anything?
> No.
> Not even another parent? Someone else's mom or dad?
> No.

Amanda sucks in her breath. I see Mommy is still shaking.

> Okay, Daddo says. Then who is she?
> I don't know.
> Well, when was the first time you saw her? This is important.

Mommy's shaking like it's cold.

> When's the first time? Daddo says again.

I think about it.

> I don't remember.

But maybe I do. But if I tell them, they might get mad at me for not telling before.

> Bela, this is important, Daddo says.

I start crying. I don't like this. I don't like this house and I don't like how Amanda and Dan are looking at me and I don't like how scared Mommy and Daddo are.

I wanna go home, I say.

No way, Mommy says. *No way.*

Settle down, Urs, Daddo says. Everybody just . . . take a deep breath.

Daddo stands up and looks at Dan and says,

What am I supposed to do here?

Dan looks stunned.

I have no idea, he says.

You need to go to the police, Amanda says.

Mommy looks like she already said no to this. But like she might say yes now.

I don't know, she says. They'll ask for a description. I don't think I can . . . there's nothing to—

Okay, Daddo says. Okay. I'll call them. All right, Ursula? I'm gonna call them. Let them know someone was in our house.

Daddo leaves the hall and Dan and Amanda follow him. Mommy looks at me. She takes a while before she asks,

That thing . . . was in your closet, Bela?

Yeah.

Always?

No. Sometimes in the walls. Sometimes in my bathroom too.

And you saw it at the park?

Yeah.

Yeah. Okay. Then: It's following you then. My God, it's following you.

She looks up the hall again and now Daddo's voice sounds too far away and what Mommy said scared me and I don't want to be standing in the open anymore and I grab Mommy's hand and I run into the kitchen where Daddo is on his phone and I say,

Daddo! Don't go back home alone anymore!

He shushes me and tells the person he's talking to our address and I know Daddo is going to meet them there and I don't want him going back there alone.

Do you have an alarm system? Mommy asks Amanda and Dan.
Yeah, Dan says. A good one too.
Put it on.
What?
Put it on.

Dan looks to their sleeping baby, breathes heavy, and says,

I've been planning to do that the second I know we're all here to stay for the night. You three have us scared out of our minds.

18

Mommy is sleeping on the couch. She's still wearing all her clothes and her jacket and her head is leaning back and her mouth is open and she looks so tired.

Dan is asleep in a chair in the living room. He has a blanket over him.

Amanda is asleep on a second couch near the chair. The baby's crib is near her.

Daddo isn't back yet.

He called Mommy and Mommy sounded real upset and kept asking if the police did this or that and why didn't they find anything and you better come back here, Russ. But Daddo told Mommy he was going to the police station for something and he might be late.

He's late. It's late.

The world is dark outside and everyone is sleeping except me.

I keep hearing a sound that worries me. It's the sound someone makes before they talk.

The breath they take in, I think.

It's probably Amanda or Dan or Mommy or the baby sleeping but I went up to each of them and put my ear by their mouths and they made different sounds than the one I keep hearing.

There it is again.

Like someone is about to say something. Like someone is in the room and is about to say something.

I took Mommy's phone in case Daddo called, but he hasn't called so maybe I should call him.

The police didn't find anything bad at our house. But what does that mean?

There's that sound again.

It's not a little breath. It's like someone is about to say something. I keep expecting someone to say something.

Is someone here? I whisper.

I wish I didn't ask it and I go under the blanket Dan gave me and I hide because I don't want someone to answer me.

I want Daddo to come back and tell us everything is okay, the police got rid of Other Mommy. The firemen got rid of Other Mommy. The mailman took Other Mommy away.

O! There's that sound again!

I lower the blanket and I wish I didn't.

But I just see Dan sleeping. And Amanda on the couch.

And the baby.

Mommy looks so pale.

I wonder if being scared makes you tired.

But I'm not tired.

I call Daddo on Mommy's phone.

It rings.

And rings.

And he sends Mommy a text message because he thinks it's Mommy calling.

All good, he writes. Just filing a report. How is Bela?

I put the phone down and I listen.

Amanda snores.

Dan snores.
Mommy is looking at me.
I almost scream.

     Did you use my phone? she asks.
     Yeah.

She takes it. She reads what Daddo wrote.
She nods.

     Good. Thank you.

She pulls me in tight to her. She's trying to keep her eyes open.
But they close again.
Daddo isn't on his way yet and—
O! There it is again.
That sound.
That breath.
I look to Mommy because maybe she heard it but her eyes are
still closed.
But I heard it.
From the entrance to the living room.
I heard it there.
Like someone taking a breath before they say something.

     Don't, I whisper.

I stare at the entrance to the living room and I can't stop staring.

     Hello? I ask.

I pull the blanket over my face. I can't look anymore.
I just want Daddo to come home.

O! I say.

Because I heard something move. Something crossed the room.
I lower the blanket and I see Dan is sitting up. He's looking over
his shoulder to the entrance to the living room.
He says,

Who's there?

I pull the blanket back over my eyes because I don't wanna see
this, I don't wanna hear this, I don't wanna be here at all.

Who's there? Dan asks again.

Mommy is sleeping beside me.
But Amanda wakes and says,

Who are you talking to?

Her voice is sleepy.

I don't know. Is Russ back?
I didn't let him in. Did you?
No.

I lower the blanket.
Amanda and Dan are staring at the entrance to the living room.
Dan raises his finger.

You hear that?
No. Amanda says.
No, that wasn't it.
What did you hear?
It was like . . . breathing or something.

They're quiet for a little while. Staring.

I snore, Amanda says.

They're quiet again.

You do, Dan says.

Mommy's phone lights up next to me and Mommy wakes up and we both read the text from Daddo:

I'm back. I'm outside.

Mommy tells Amanda and Dan that Daddo is back and Dan gets up but he pauses at the entrance to the living room and he reaches to the wall and he turns on the light.
Nobody's there.
He looks to Amanda and he says,

I've never been so glad you snore. I might've gone insane if I didn't have an explanation.
For what? Mommy asks.
Just thought I heard something, Dan says. I don't mean to scare you, Ursula.
What? What did you hear?
He heard me snoring, Amanda says.
We're all on edge, Dan Says. We're all—

But Daddo knocks on the door and we all jump at the sound.

19

How you doing, Bela?

Daddo sits next to me on the couch. Dan and Amanda are upstairs in their bedroom now. Mommy is outside. On her phone I
think.

    I don't know, I tell him.
    Are you scared?
    Yeah.
    Yeah. I get it. When I was your age, if the TV was on late at
night and nobody was in the room, I got scared. I can't imagine
how you're feeling. That said . . .

I know he's going to try to make me feel better. I hope he does.

    . . . you have nothing to be afraid of. I understand this all
sounds truly crazy. But you know what? It's the year 2024 and
there isn't any proof of ghosts yet. You see what I mean?
    Ghosts?

Daddo looks at me like I should get what he means.

Can I ask you a question? Daddo says.
Yeah.
What do you think . . . it is?

I don't like this question.

A mean person, I say.
Why mean? Why do you say that?
Because she tricks me.
How so?
I don't know. Maybe I'm wrong.
About?
You don't trick me.
No, I don't. Mommy doesn't either.
You don't trick me ever.
No. Never would. How does she trick you?
She pretends to be my friend, I think.
How does she do that?
She was funny with me. Made me laugh.

Daddo looks even more worried.

What did she say?
Now she only says I should carnation her.
You mean reincarnation again?
Yeah, that.
What does that mean? In this case, what does that mean?

He's really asking himself.

Are you saying she's asking you to . . . reincarnate her?
I don't know.

He breathes deep like he does when he's thinking seriously.

You think she's a ghost? I ask.

I probably shouldn't have said the word. I imagine your mom would tell me I shouldn't say stuff like that right now.

Why not?

Well, because it's scary. And you're young. And the last thing I should do is scare you any more than you already are.

Okay.

Are you scared?

Yeah. Are you, Daddo?

Daddo looks to the living room entrance. He's thinking.

No, he says. Just a little shook up. There's a difference. Actually . . .

He leans back into the couch.

. . . there's a lot of differences with emotions, so many emotions, but we sometimes mistakenly call them all by the same name. Check it out: *scared* is for the . . . unknown. Like you aren't sure how things will work out, so you feel scared about it. But *panicked* kinda implies you know how it could end and you're in a hurry to change that. *Startled* is temporary. It fades pretty fast. So is *shook*. Only it lasts a little longer than startled. Yet, we use the same word . . . scared . . . for all these things. You are *scared* to take the math test. You are *scared* to sleep with the lights off. You are *scared* to board that train. But you see what I mean? Those are all very different scenarios that ask for very different emotions. I think sometimes we think we're scared of something just because we said we are. When really . . . we're something else . . . something a little different than scared . . . and we just don't have the words handy to name it.

So maybe I'm not scared? I ask him.

Maybe. And maybe I'm not. And maybe Mommy's not either. And maybe nobody's truly scared of anything in the whole world. Here, check this out.

Daddo sits up a little bit.

You remember when that teacher Mr. Jeffery gave you a bad grade for that book report you did?
Yeah.
Did that make you feel mad?
Yeah.
And what else makes you feel mad?
When people are unhappy.
I wasn't expecting that answer. That's a good one. So okay, what else?
I don't know.
Give me one more.
I get mad when other kids treat other kids bad.
Perfect. So, if you really think about it . . . the feeling you had when you got that bad grade . . . and it was silly and I agreed with you then and I agree with you now . . . but that feeling, was it the same feeling you get when you see a kid treat another kid bad?
No.
Right. But a second ago both made you "mad." You see? They don't actually make you feel the same thing. And there are so many emotions and you're so young. Believe me, it's not easy sorting this stuff out at any age.

Daddo puts his arm around me and snuggles me closer to him on the couch. We're facing the TV. It's off now.

But I don't know, Daddo says. Maybe you have it easier. In a way. Because feelings must be like solid colors to you. Whereas, eventually, they can all turn kinda this sludgy singular color that rolls around like in a washing machine.

He looks down at me.

I have no idea what I'm talking about. Did you know that?

I smile.

Did you hear that? he says.

Daddo stands up right when the light goes on in the other room. Dan is there.

Hey guys, he says. Where's Ursula?
Out front, Daddo says. On the phone.

Daddo meets Dan at the entrance to the living room.

What's the matter? Daddo says.
I don't know, Dan says.
Why are you looking for Ursula?
Because, man.

Dan looks to me. He whispers to Daddo but I hear him:

Because I thought I saw Ursula in our bedroom.

I look to the ceiling.
I look to the entrance of the living room.
Then I'm off the couch and following them because I don't want to sit here alone.

Urs? Daddo calls when Dan opens the front door.

I hear Mommy outside.
I look up the stairs behind me.

Urs, who are you talking to? Daddo says.

I see someone at the top of the stairs.

I didn't mean to interrupt her, Dan says.
No, it's fine, Daddo says.

The light goes on up there and it's Amanda in her pajamas.

Bela? Is Dan down there?
Never mind, Dan says to Daddo by the door.
Dan? Amanda says.

She's coming down the stairs now.

It was Marsha on the phone, Mommy says.

Mommy is by the door.
I see her in the porch light.
Amanda is down the stairs.

What's going on? Amanda asks.
Nothing, Dan says. I just got . . . I thought . . .

They look at each other like they're upset. Mommy and Daddo
don't see it, but I do.

You can keep talking, Daddo says to Mommy. Dan was just
checking on you.

Dan breathes deep and says,

Hey, you two.

Mommy and Daddo wait for him to say more. They stand in the porch light.

We're just, Dan says, we're kinda . . . listen . . . we're a little freaked out, okay? The baby and all.

I'm sorry, Daddo says.

I know. I know. But still . . .

We think you should maybe stay somewhere else, Amanda says.

O, come *on,* Mommy says. Don't make us find somewhere else right now. Don't make us do that.

Amanda and Dan look to the floor.

What about Marsha? Amanda asks.

Come on.

Hey, Urs, Daddo says. If we're making them uncomfortable . . .

No, Mommy says. This is bullshit, guys.

She's shaking again.

Hey, language, Dan says.

What's bullshit, Ursula? Amanda says. You come over here with an absolutely insane story of an intruder in your house, you talk like it's a demon, and you're up all night all over the house! How do you expect us to react? You want me to make some cookies?

Mommy looks even madder.

What's a demon, Daddo? I ask.

Yeah, Mommy says to Amanda. Cookies would be nice. You think we want to be here?

Yeah, well, Dan says. Sounds like we're in agreement then.

Mommy and Daddo look at each other.

Sure thing, Daddo says. I mean, yeah, we're not going to outstay our welcome.

You guys just freaked us out is all, Dan says. I was seeing things up there. And the baby . . .

All right, Daddo says. But just, please, understand . . . whatever this is, being here in the middle of the night, hardly sleeping, we didn't ask for this or plan this out or anything. Something's happened and we're just trying to make sense of it.

We know, Dan says.

Mommy calls someone. In front of us.

We know, Dan says again.

Yes, hi, Mommy says into the phone. We need to come over. Yes. Now.

Amanda and Dan look to the floor again.

Thanks, yes, Mommy says. Right now.

She hangs up.

We're going to my mother's house.

Ursula, Dan says.

But that's it. He doesn't say more. Amanda doesn't either.

Come on, Bela, Mommy says.

She takes my hand and walks me out of the house and out toward the car. Daddo follows.

Fuckin' dicks, Mommy says.

We're at the car. She unlocks it and we get in.
We don't have any of our stuff. We didn't bring any here.

Please drive safe, Amanda says from the front door.

She's in her pajamas in the porch light and it's really dark in the sky above their house.

I'll drive, Daddo says to Mommy.

Mommy looks at me.

We're going to Grandma's house. We'll figure this out there.
We'll figure this out, Daddo says too.

Daddo turns the car on and turns on the lights and Amanda and Dan are already inside again and their door is closed and Daddo pulls out of their driveway and drives up the street.

What a bunch of *crap*, Mommy says.
Yeah, Daddo says. Gotta agree. That wasn't great of them.
I mean, how could they? Mommy asks. We would never do this to them.
We wouldn't, Daddo says.

He turns onto another street.

But I do also get it, he says.
Don't even start, Mommy says.
I mean . . .

You mean nothing, Mommy says. We had a very scary thing happen and we needed them to be our friends for one night and they couldn't even break their prissy pattern for *one* night to do that. We shoulda known.

We shoulda, Daddo says.

He turns up another street and a deer is staring back at us in the headlights and Daddo slams on the brakes and we all cry out and the deer slowly walks away and we're just sitting there parked in the middle of the street, breathing hard.

Well, holy shit, Daddo says.

He looks back at me and smiles. Then Mommy looks back at me too.

And then they look at each other and they laugh.

And I laugh.

And we're all laughing, parked in the middle of the street, breathing really hard.

To Grandmother's house we go, Daddo says.

And then he starts driving again and then stops right away because another deer crosses the street.

We're not laughing anymore.

Mommy and Daddo both breathe heavy and Daddo starts driving again.

Up the street.

Through the dark.

To Grandmother's house we go.

20

Grandma Ruth has a little old dog named Milky. I think it's because he's white.

But he's never all white. He's always a little dirty. He plays out in
the Loblolly Pines behind her house. Sometimes Mommy washes
Milky in Grandma's sink. Grandma's house is small, but so is
she. When all four of us sit around the kitchen table we're all
really close. Her living room is small too. Daddo said the ceilings
are low. There's a light-green carpet and a white couch in the
living room. Milky likes both. Down the hall is Grandma's bedroom. Upstairs there are two rooms mostly empty, except one
has a futon.

That's where we'll sleep tonight, I think.

But we're still in the kitchen now.

And it's late. The latest I've ever stayed up I think.

Mommy and Daddo told Grandma it's because the power went
out in our house. They told me not to say this isn't true. In the
car they told me to pretend the lights being out is real.

So I pretend. Pretending is not the same as lying.

It's lovely to see you, Bela, Grandma Ruth says. Even if it's
because the power is out.

Grandma is not much bigger than me. Even when she stands.

We can't thank you enough, Daddo says. It's a pain in the butt, to be sure.

Mommy and Daddo took some time in the car to "not look so crazy." That's what Mommy said they needed to do. But I don't know if it worked.
In the car Mommy said to me: *She wouldn't understand what's happening. And it might scare her.*

You're free to use all of the upstairs, Grandma says. I haven't been up there in six months, but I'm sure there are still two bedrooms and a bathroom.

Grandma likes to make jokes. She's funny.
Daddo smiles but Mommy doesn't. Daddo and Grandma are good friends.

We'll figure it out, Mommy says. Thanks, Mom.
Of course. What are old ladies for if not housing youth in trouble?

She looks at me and smiles, and Milky peers around her ankles and I think he smiles too.

Come on, Bela, Mommy says.
Do you need anything to eat? Grandma asks. Anything to drink?
You know what, Daddo says, some water and maybe a sandwich would be nice. I can make it myself.
Don't be silly. I'll do it.

Mommy looks bothered. Like she's tired and doesn't want to stay up anymore.

Head to bed, Grandma tells her. I'll make sure he eats.

I like being in this kitchen. It always smells good. Like Grandma always just made chicken fingers or baked a pie.

What are you hungry for? Grandma asks Daddo.
Whatever you've got.

She opens the refrigerator.

Perfect, Daddo says. You've got cheese and bread. All I need.
Come on, now, Grandma says. I've got avocado and mustard and onions too. It takes two minutes more for a sandwich to get good.
That sounds incredible, Daddo says.

Grandma looks to Mommy and me.
Like she knows something is happening.
Milky is at my feet, waiting for me to pet him.

How did you discover the power was out? Grandma asks.

She's making Daddo's sandwich at the counter.

Nothing was on, Mommy says.
But at this hour? Did you get up to use the bathroom?

Grandma looks at me like I'm gonna tell her the real story.

Yes, Mommy says.

But at the same time, Daddo says:

No.

Mmm-hmm, Grandma says.

My alarm clock goes off when the power goes out, Daddo says.

Alarm?

You know. On the nightstand.

On the nightstand.

And the fan was off, Mommy says.

Ah, yes. I know how you need white noise to sleep.

Mommy and Daddo look at each other behind Grandma's back.

And how are you, Bela? Grandma asks. Excited for school to begin?

I don't know how to answer, because it feels like school will never begin again.

Go on, Bela, Mommy says. Answer your grandmother.

She's capable of doing that on her own, Grandma says.

I know that, Mom. Bela?

Yes, I say.

Sandwich made, Grandma says.

Thanks, Ruth, Daddo says.

Of course. Eat as much as you like.

Grandma smiles. She sits down at the table again.

This close, it feels like it's harder to pretend. Maybe pretending is a lie?

I pet Milky on the top of his head.

It's dark outside the kitchen window.

Is it the whole neighborhood? Grandma asks.

What? Mommy and Daddo ask at the same time.

Grandma nods.

The power, she says.

How would we know? Mommy says.

I think so, yes, Daddo says. I don't think we saw any other porch lights on or anything.

Grandma gets up from the table and goes to the kitchen window. She looks between the yellow drapes, up at the dark sky.

No storm, she says.

It's not always a storm, Mommy says.

But you two pay your bills.

We do, Daddo says. But you know how it goes. Glitches.

He eats his sandwich. Mommy looks like she wants him to hurry.

I pet Milky on his head.

I do know, Grandma says. There was one time when Bruce and I went two weeks without power. This was before you, Ursula. Chaps Edison came out but they couldn't find anything wrong. Your father was so angry. But I found that, after a while, I almost liked it.

She smiles at me.

We lit candles, she says. We read books to each other.

Maybe we should've lit some candles, Mommy says.

Grandma doesn't smile at Mommy.

Daddo eats his sandwich.

I pet Milky on his head.

Boy, it's late, Grandma says. Sun will be up in a couple hours.

Yeah, Daddo says. We almost made it.

He smiles and some of his sandwich falls from his mouth onto his plate.

    You must be very tired, Grandma says.
    We are, Mommy says.
    Well, go on upstairs. Russ is a big boy.
    I'd rather wait.

Grandma steps to the table and puts both her hands on it.
She says,

    Are any of the three of you going to tell me what's really going on here?

Daddo takes a bite.
I look to the table.

    Mom, Mommy says.

But she doesn't lie again.

    Most people don't know if their power goes out while they're dead asleep, Grandma says. And neither of you made any mention of whether or not Bela here would like something to eat. All unlike you, I know. So? What's wrong?

Daddo and Mommy both look to me.
Then Grandma Ruth does too.

    Young ears, she says. I see. Bela, why don't you go into the living room for a moment.
    No, Mommy and Daddo say at the same time.

Grandma looks worried.

Is there real trouble? she asks.

Mommy breathes deep.

It's nothing, Mom. Just . . . we had . . . we had a . . .
It's nothing, Daddo says. Just a . . .
The power went out, Mommy says.
Fine, Grandma says.

I can tell she's worried about us. I've never seen her look like this
before.
Daddo finishes his sandwich.
He stands up.

Thanks again, Ruth, he says. That hit the spot.
Of course.

Daddo brings his plate to the sink and Mommy gets up.

Ready? she asks me.
Go on ahead, Grandma tells us.

But Daddo is looking at Mommy like he needs to talk to her.
Mommy walks over by the front door and Daddo follows her.
Grandma sits beside me at the table.

Whatever it is, she says to me, it can be worked out. That's
one of the things you discover when you get to be my age. All
these little worries don't last forever.
It's not little, I whisper.

Grandma Ruth leans toward me.

O? Is it big then?

Yeah.
How big is it?

I look to the darkness outside the kitchen window.

As big as Daddo.
Is someone bothering you?
Yeah.
Someone mean?
Yeah.

Grandma nods.
Mommy and Daddo come back into the kitchen.

We'd like to sleep down here, Mommy says. On the same
floor as you. We had a scare at home. Nothing major. But we're
all a bit rattled.
Yeah, Daddo says. We're all a bit shook. We'd just as soon
keep the whole family together down here. You included.

Grandma looks at them for a while.

Is this a . . . stalker? she asks.
No, Mommy and Daddo say at the same time.
I'm sorry to frighten you, Mom, Mommy says.
Yeah, we don't mean to freak you out, Daddo says. Just
trust us when we say everything is totally fine. We just got a lit-
tle . . . rattled. Like Ursula said.

Grandma stands up.

Well, who am I to tell you where to sleep? she says. You
wanna sleep in the living room? On the living room floor? Be my
guest. Milky may wake you. Or the sun might. Or the paperboy.
But please, do as you feel like doing.

Mommy steps to her and hugs her.

Thanks, Mom.
Bela too? Grandma asks.
Yes, Mommy and Daddo say at the same time.

We all go into the living room. Daddo turns on a lamp. Mommy arranges some cushions on the floor. Daddo puts some blankets there too.
Grandma asks if we have everything we need and then she goes to her bedroom and Mommy takes off her jacket but lies down with her pants still on and Daddo lies beside her and he tells me to come lie down too. Daddo whispers and tells me they didn't want to leave Grandma down here alone.

Whatever this is, it'll all make more sense in the morning, Daddo tells me and Mommy. When the sun is up and it's daytime, all of this will make more sense.

But Mommy is sleeping already.
And I'm thinking: Why would it be any better in the day? The park was during the day. And why is the light any more true than the dark?

O! I say.

Because Milky is licking my face. He's beside me on the cushions and I pet his little face with both my hands as Mommy snores. I look to Daddo but he's already asleep too.

Milky, I say. It doesn't matter if it's night or day.

He licks my face again and both Mommy and Daddo are asleep and then even little Milky is sleeping against me and I'm the only one in the whole house who is awake I think.

Good night, I say.

Because I like to say it. Because it sounds like a good thing to say.

Good night.

But it wasn't a good night. It was a mean one.
And now I'm falling asleep at the end of it. Because I need to
too. And because we're all so tired.
And I worry that tomorrow will be even meaner.

Milky, I say.

Because he's still licking me.
And his little face is so close to mine . . . it's hard to think the
world is mean with his little face so close to mine.

Milky, I say.

But then I'm asleep. I think.
A dream.
Yeah.
Milky licking my face.
Crouched down beside my bed in my bedroom.
Milky as tall as the ceiling, needing to crouch.
Licking my face.
And I can feel his fur. The little hairs on his arms.
And I laugh and tell him to go to sleep.

Good night, I say.

And he giggles. A little dog laugh.
As I'm falling deeper asleep.
Good night.

21

The sun is out now and the living room is bright.
Mommy and Daddo think I'm still sleeping because I'm still on
the cushions on the floor in Grandma's living room.
They're in the kitchen, talking.
Milky is panting. I snuggle him close.

> I'm a mess, Mommy says.
> Yeah, me too.
> We can't go back. We actually cannot go back to our house.
> We're gonna have to eventually.
> You're not listening. We *cannot* go back to the house.
> Ursula . . .
> If you'd seen it.
> I believe you.
> Do you?
> Yes. Honest to God. On Bela's life.
> Jesus, don't say that.

I hear a chair creak and I close my eyes.
Is Daddo leaning back in the chair to look into the living room
to make sure I'm sleeping?

Do you think it wants to hurt her? Daddo asks.

I mean . . . how can I have any idea what it wants? Mommy says. What does a tiger want? What does a snake want?

Then we'll move out right now and sell the house, Daddo says.

Mommy makes a sound like she's frustrated.

It'll suck, Daddo says. But what else can we do?

We should burn it down.

What?

If you'd seen it.

Really? Burn it down?

Nobody can go back into that house.

Urs.

I need you to understand something. Okay?

Yes. Of course.

I need you to understand that reality, for us, for the three of us, is changed now by what I saw sitting on Bela's bed.

They don't talk for a while.

Milky pants.

I put a finger to my lips to tell him to keep quiet.

This is terrible, Daddo says.

Now you're getting it.

I got it from the start.

We'll need to buy a house without any money from selling ours. Jesus, what the fuck are we going to do?

Road trip, Daddo says.

Russ.

Why not? Reality, like you said. All gone now. Why fight it? Let's get a camper. Hit the road. Leave it all. This is an opportunity.

They don't talk for a while again.

I look to the couch.

Grandma Ruth is standing beside the couch.

I didn't know she was there.

She's listening too.

How long can we stay here? Daddo asks.

I don't know, Mommy says.

Your mother will understand, Daddo says.

You're not listening. I don't want to tell anyone about what I saw. I don't want to ever think about it again.

Okay, but, it's *all* we're thinking about. And while I couldn't be more sorry that you saw this . . . we have to think of Bela. I mean, shit, Ursula, school starts soon.

You think I don't know that?

I gotta talk to work, Daddo says.

What are you gonna say?

I don't know.

Did you grab your computer?

I didn't.

Fuck, Russ.

Yeah. I imagine there are a lot of things we're gonna want to go back for.

No. Do you hear me? *No.*

I'll go alone. Without Bela. During the day. I can ask Mark to go with me.

They go quiet again.

How about this, Daddo says. How about we give it a couple days. Whatever is going on, it *just* happened. And we're acting like we're supposed to have all the answers at once.

You need an exorcist, Grandma says.

Mommy and Daddo make the sounds people do when they realize someone was listening.

Now, don't interrupt me, Grandma says. And I don't give a
shit who hears me say it. What the two of you are talking
about . . . you need to get it out of the house and out of your
lives.

Ruth, Daddo says.

I said do *not* interrupt me, and I am not done. There's a
little girl pretending to sleep on the living-room floor. You think
you're scared, Ursula? Imagine all you're feeling and tag on an
unhealthy dose of realizing your parents can't protect you like
you thought they could.

Bela? Daddo calls.

I don't answer.

You sound insane, Mommy says.

You know that's not true, Grandma says. Either what you're
talking about is real or it isn't. If it's not, you've gone mad. And
if it is? Then you need an exorcist. You need someone who understands what to do about the problem you have at home.

Mommy and Daddo don't answer.
Grandma says,

Bela. Get up and come sit on the couch, please. Grandma
would like to speak to you a minute.

I push my sleeping blanket aside and get up and me and Grandma
put the cushions back on the couch. Mommy and Daddo come
to the living-room entrance.

Mom, Mommy says, there's nothing to talk to Bela about.

Nothing? Grandma says. We'll just see about that.

We sit together on the couch.

Bela, she says. I'm going to need real answers from you, okay? I've been listening to your parents talk for some time about what was going on in your house, but I need to hear from you now. Okay?

Okay.

It's all right to be nervous. You'll learn soon enough in life that everybody's nervous about something and it's the ones who do the things they need to do anyway who end up getting the most out of it. Okay?

Okay.

Very good. Now—

Mom, Mommy says.

Now, Grandma Ruth says. How many times did you see the thing your mommy saw in your bedroom? How many?

I don't know.

Okay. I didn't think you would have a solid answer. But . . . more than once?

Yeah.

A hundred?

I don't know.

But maybe a hundred?

Yeah.

Mommy gasps.

Are you serious? Daddo says. Bela?

There's no right or wrong answer, Grandma says.

That's enough, Mommy says.

Grandma Ruth slams her hand on the couch and I've never seen her do that before.

This is your daughter, Grandma says. And if you can't talk about whatever this is with her, then you've got bigger problems than whatever you saw in her bedroom. Now, Bela . . .
Yeah.
Has this thing ever talked to you?
Yeah.
And what did it say?

Mommy and Daddo look at me. Their eyes are really big.

She talks sometimes.
She? Grandma asks.
Yeah. Other Mommy.

Grandma looks surprised at this.

Really, Grandma says. Okay. It's best that everything is out in the open. And that means everything. Why do you call her Other Mommy, Bela?
Because that's what she told me to call her.
Jesus, Daddo says.

Mommy just stares at me. Wide-eyed.

What else did she say to you? Grandma asks.
She asks me something.
What? Daddo says. What does she ask you?

I don't wanna say it out loud.

What is it, dear? Grandma says. It will help if you tell us. Perhaps quite a bit.
She asks if she can go into my heart.

Mommy puts a hand over her own heart.

You phoned the police? Grandma asks.
Of course, Daddo says.
And you're certain it wasn't an intruder?
Yes, Daddo says.

Mommy puts her other hand over her mouth.

An intruder in a costume, perhaps? Grandma asks.
I mean, Daddo says. I mean, anything's possible.
Even likely, Grandma says. Even that.

She looks to Mommy, but Mommy isn't looking back.
Grandma talks to her anyway:

This is why you need to call in an expert. Because if this is not a person . . . then no police can help you.

22

Behind Grandma Ruth's house there are a bunch of Loblolly Pines.
It's easy to remember what they're called because Grandma and
me used to sing their name. They're really tall and their bark is
like the shingles on the roof of a house.
We're out in the Loblolly Pines. Daddo and me.
Mommy is in the front yard. On her phone.
It's afternoon and it's bright outside.
Daddo says Mommy's talking to friends. He says Mommy "isn't
doing well with what happened" and he "gets that she needs
some time to process."

But you and me, he says, we're tough in a similar way.
Tough?

Nobody's ever called me that before.

Absolutely, Daddo says. It's amazing how brave you've been
through all this.

Grandma is looking out her bedroom window. I see her in her
red flannel shirt. I wave but she doesn't wave back.

Daddo and me walk through the Loblolly Pines.

> Can I ask you something? Daddo says.
> Yeah.
> When this thing . . . when this Other Mommy . . . when she asks you about . . . getting in . . . what do you say?
> Nothing, I say.
> For real? Daddo asks. You say nothing?
> Yeah.
> Okay. That's good. I think.

We walk. I look back. Grandma's house is hidden a little now, but I can still see her at her bedroom window. She's watching us.

> Well, listen, Bela, Daddo says. Because if this *is* a person, and they're asking stuff like that. Ah, Jesus.

He looks frustrated.

> This is all almost impossible to talk about, he says. And I wish your mommy was up for it because I don't know how to say anything I want to say. But . . . you said nothing, right? Nobody . . . got into your heart?
> I said nothing, I say.
> And she never touched you?
> No, I say. Not like that.
> What do you mean?
> We held hands before.

Daddo looks real upset. He turns to face the front yard like he's gonna call out to Mommy. To tell her I held hands with Other Mommy.

> Literally just hands? Daddo asks.

I try to remember.

One time she was floating above my bed and her face touched mine a little.
O, God.
We were friends back then.

Our feet crunch leaves and cones. The cones are so big. The Loblollies so tall.

What do you mean by that? Daddo asks.
I don't know.
Bela.
She didn't talk in the beginning.
Okay.
She just made faces at me from the closet.
Jesus.
And they made me laugh.
O, man.
And so I thought we were friends.
Then what?

We're far into the trees now.

I don't know.
Then what though?
Then she started coming out of the closet. Sitting with me.
Listen, Bela, what I'm trying to say is, intruder or not, nobody is allowed to touch you. You got that? I know you already know that. But this is some confusing, scary stuff. And I don't want you forgetting how important you are, how tough you are, in the middle of all this. Do you understand what I'm saying?

I hear the leaves creak like how the ceiling in the house creaks. I look up.

I mean, Grandma Ruth is talking about intruders in costumes, Daddo says. Mommy is talking about . . . monsters. And you're talking about . . . Jesus. In our house . . .

Daddo puts his hand on my shoulder. We stop walking. He kneels in front of me.

It's a lot, Daddo says. A lot. And so . . . I just feel like I gotta remind you, as your father and as your friend . . . If anybody, anybody or anything in the entire world asks if they can go into your heart, or touch you at all, you say no. And you mean it. And you feel no guilt or fear when you say no. Okay?

Grandma Ruth calls out from behind me. I turn to see her between the Loblolly Pines, coming toward us.

The hell is going on? Daddo says. What is it, Ruth?

Grandma points to the front of the house.

Come on, Daddo says.

He takes my hand and then looks at it. Like it's different now. Now that he knows Other Mommy held it too.

Ursula, Grandma says.
What about her? Daddo asks.
She left.
She what?
She took the car and left, Grandma says. She said she needed to see a friend.

Daddo looks to the street and Grandma looks at me and she
says,

     Come inside, dear. Come on. We're going to get through
this together. Okay? You and me and your daddo.
We walk toward the house.

     We're just beginning to talk about this, Daddo says to me.

Or maybe he says it to himself.

     And you gotta know you can tell me anything, he says.

I stop walking.

     I'm worried she's out here, I say.
     What?
     I'm worried she followed us here.
     Why do you say that? Grandma asks.

I look up to the trees.

     She really wants me to answer, I say. She's getting closer.
     Closer? Daddo says.

He looks up like she could be right above us.

     I mean she's around all the time now, I say.
     Okay, Grandma says. Let's get her into the house. Russ?
Get Bela into the house.
     Did you see her? Daddo asks.
     No, I say.
     Did you smell her? he asks.
     No.
     Then why do you think—

Because she really wants me to answer. She won't leave me alone until I answer her about my heart.

Get her into the house now, Grandma says. Now, Russ.

Daddo still holds my hand and we walk up the side-door steps. But he stops and faces me before we go in.

But if you answer, he says, you *know* how to answer, right?

Grandma is walking toward the Loblolly Pines in her red flannel shirt.

Yes, I say.

But I realize then that I don't. Even with Daddo telling me what to answer.

I don't know if I know what the answer is.

Mommy's gone, Daddo says. So stick close to me in the house.

Okay.

Don't leave my side.

Okay.

Then we're heading inside.

And I know Daddo's trying to help. And I know he's probably right.

But still . . . we were friends. I held hands with her too.

And I don't know the answer.

No matter what Daddo says.

I don't.

23

Daddo stands at the bedroom window, looking out at Grandma Ruth.

Why didn't you tell me you felt she was near? Daddo asks.

He's really upset. He tried calling Mommy but Mommy didn't answer.

What is Ruth doing out there? he says.

Through the window I can see Grandma facing the Loblolly Pines.

Where was she? Daddo asks. Like, where did you feel she was?
Behind a tree.
Bela, seriously?
I don't know.
Jesus.

Daddo calls the police.

I see Grandma outside, looking up into the trees.
Milky is at my feet.

Yes, Daddo says into the phone. A possible intruder. In
the woods behind the house. No. I can't give a good description.

He looks at me.

Bela?
Dark hair on the backs of her arms, I say.
Hang on, Daddo says into the phone.

He looks at me like he wants me to change what I said, but it's
the truth.

Okay, Daddo says into the phone. So . . .

He walks out of Grandma's bedroom and into the hall.
I watch Grandma facing the trees.
She looks small out there. Too small! I wonder if I'm that small,
standing on the carpet in my bedroom, small as Grandma among
the Loblolly Pines.
Her closet opens behind me.

Go *away!* I yell.

But it's just Milky. Sniffing something on the floor in there.
Daddo hurries into the bedroom.

What's going on? he says.

He's already taking me out of the bedroom. Hurrying me up the
hall.
Grandma comes in through the side door.

She screamed, Daddo says.
Bela? Grandma says.
It was just Milky! I say.

Daddo stops. Looks back toward Grandma's bedroom.
Milky barks in there.

Don't go in there, Ruth, Daddo says.

Because he knows she will.

It was just Milky, I say.
Maybe, Daddo says.

Milky barks again.

Nobody's taking over my house, Grandma says.

And she goes to her bedroom.

Jesus, Daddo says. Bela, wait here.

Then,

Dammit. I can't leave you alone right now. Ruth!

But Grandma doesn't respond. And Milky doesn't bark.
So we wait.
And Daddo paces. And he makes the sounds people make when
they're talking but they're not really talking.
Grandma comes out of her bedroom. She's holding Milky.

Nothing, she says.
Did it smell bad? Daddo asks.

Grandma looks at him like this, of all things, is the scariest thing he's asked her yet.

No.
Okay, Daddo says. The police said—

But Grandma cuts him off.

Call someone who knows more about these matters than the police do, Russ. Even if it's crazy to follow this path. Even if it's pointless. Because I'm an old woman, and all my life I can't think of a better case for better-safe-than-sorry.

24

We're at a Big Boy restaurant near Grandma Ruth's house. It's night now.

There's a lot of people eating at the other tables. We've been here a long time and people get up and new people sit down.

Daddo was outside with the police for a while a while ago. He said they looked around Grandma's house. They went through the Loblolly Pines.

They didn't find her. No "intruders" Daddo said.

Grandma stayed with me while Daddo was talking to them. She doesn't pretend everything is okay.

Daddo checks his phone.

> She's almost here, Daddo says.
> Here? Grandma asks.
> Yes.

A new waiter comes by and asks if we're okay. We've been here long enough to eat twice.

I've eaten twice.

Daddo tells him we're okay.

But we're not.

I'm going nuts, Ruth, Daddo says.
It's a lot, Ruth says.

They both look at me. They keep doing that.

Do you have to use the bathroom again? Grandma asks me.
No.
She's here, Daddo says.

He gets up and me and Grandma look out the window.
A green car parks.
Daddo goes to the front door.
Lois Anthony gets out of the car and meets him there.
They talk a little and then come to the table together.

Hello, Bela, Lois says.

She sits down.
Her eyes look extra big behind her glasses. Her green sweater
looks fuzzy and warm.

You must be Ruth, Lois says. I'm Lois Anthony.
Can you help? Grandma asks.

Lois looks at me.
Her eyes are so big you can tell how she feels.
She's nervous.

Well, I can't say yet, Lois says.

Grandma doesn't like this answer.

We have a group, Lois says.
A group? Grandma says. We?
A group of us get together. We . . . talk about . . . these things.

Grandma looks to Daddo.

At this point, you know a lot more than we do, he says to Lois.

Lois wants to smile, I think. But she doesn't do it.

Can I ask you something, Bela? she says.
Yeah.
Does this thing ever try to make . . . deals with you?

I look to Daddo. He says,

Bela said she asked to . . . well . . . get into her heart.
O? Lois says. Then to me: In exchange for anything?

I don't wanna talk about this here right now.

She said she wants to reincarnation with me. Then I would go to where she comes from.
The closet? Lois asks.
No, I say. She said she doesn't come from the closet.

All three of them are quiet a second with that.

So, Lois says. A deal, after all. You give her . . . your heart. You trade places with her.

I nod slowly because she's right, even if I didn't think of it that way before.

Possession, she says. It's trying to get in.
O, come on, Daddo says.

He sounds really upset. Scared.

Lois, he says. Don't say that.

Yes, Grandma says. Trying to angle its way in.

Exactly that, Lois says. I think it's been sizing Bela up for some time. I think this is why I didn't sense any sensitivity in Bela. This is no ghost.

Guys, Daddo says.

I feel too hot. Like I might forget how to breathe.

Bela, Lois says. Don't be scared. It's just that, it's important you never say yes. Never, never, never.

I start crying.

The waiter comes over and asks if everything's okay.

Daddo starts to tell him we're fine but then stops.

It's obvious we're not okay.

What's the plan then, Grandma asks. Because there has to be a plan.

Lois sits up straighter when she says,

We're going to try to meet this Other Mommy. And we're going to tell her to stay the hell away.

O, man, Daddo says. I don't know if—

No, no, Grandma says to Daddo.

She's smiling a real smile for the first time since she greeted us last night at her house.

I like this one, she says, pointing at Lois Anthony. I like this plan *a lot*.

25

We're on the second floor of a motel because Daddo says we can't stay at Grandma's right now. Can't stay at our house or hers.

Grandma and Lois Anthony are here too.

Daddo called Mommy again but she's not answering.

I'm trying to be okay about that. I keep telling myself Mommy is scared too. She saw Other Mommy.

But no matter how hard I try, I keep getting mad instead.

Tomorrow, Lois says. Everybody says they can be at my place tomorrow. We'll convene special for this.

Okay, Daddo says. Thank you. And please thank them.

He sounds out of breath. He keeps looking to me, then to the door, then to his phone.

Lois sits on one of the two queen beds. The bedspreads are yellow and tucked tight under the mattresses. Her green sweater looks like tree leaves next to the yellow sun.

Lois makes me feel hope. But then, every time I feel that way, the feeling goes away.

These wood-paneled motels remind me of when Bruce and I got married, Grandma says.

Grandpa Bruce, I say.

Grandma is sitting at the small table by the window. The hotel sign flashes outside and makes her face blue and pink.

You remember him, she says. That's nice. He's hard to forget. Kinda wedged himself into the heads of every person he ever shook hands with. We stayed in a room just like this on our honeymoon. Up in the UP. My God, were we young.

Beautiful world up there, Lois says.

It is, Grandma says. I've always not so secretly wished we'd raised Ursula up there. Might've grounded her a little more.

Chaps isn't Hollywood, Daddo says.

He winks at me sadly and I smile. It's the first thing like a joke he's made in a long time.

What time? Daddo asks Lois.

They said afternoon.

Daddo looks at his phone.

I tried for earlier, Lois says.

No, no, Daddo says. Anything is good.

Grandma stands up.

Can we talk a moment alone? she asks Lois. You and me?

Lois looks surprised but like she wants to talk too.

Of course, she says.

Grandma and Lois go out onto the balcony.
Daddo gets up and crouches in front of the TV. Then he stands
up again without turning it on. He walks around the room with
his hands on his hips.
He checks his phone.

    Daddo? I ask.
    Yeah.
    Are there things people can't figure out? Problems that can't
be solved?

He doesn't ask me what I mean.

    I think most things are worked out, he says. But, yes. Over
the course of human history, there are mysteries.
    Okay.
    I don't want you to worry, Bela. Seriously. Because I'm wor-
ried, and if you're worried too then we're just going to go in
circles. Look at it this way . . .

He sits in the chair Grandma was just sitting in. The lights outside make him blue and pink.

    We're fine right now, aren't we?
    Are we fine?
    Well, we can do anything we like, can't we?
    We can't go home, I say.
    Well, I mean . . .

But he doesn't finish and I feel bad for saying what I said.
The door opens and Grandma comes in alone.

    She means well, she says. And that's something, I sup-
pose.

Did she leave? Daddo asks.

Yes. She went home. Said she'll get the house ready for us for tomorrow.

Grandma doesn't sit down when she asks me,

Do you know if Other Mommy has hurt anybody before?

I don't like this question. I think of Other Mommy opening her mouth. I think of the sound of her voice.

Bela? she asks again.

No, I don't know.

Okay. Has she threatened to hurt anybody? You? Your parents?

Ruth, Daddo says. You're scaring the hell—

All questions that need to be asked, Grandma says.

She's waiting for me to answer.

No, I say.

She's never said something like, if you don't let her in, she's going to hurt someone?

I think of Other Mommy sliding on her belly across my bedroom floor. I think of her eyes on the side of her face under my bed.

I think of her floating out of the closet.

No, I say. I don't know.

You don't know? Is it possible?

Ruth, Daddo says. Why are you asking this?

Because if we're trying to invite her into someone else's home, I'd like to know what kind of guest she is.

Is Lois scared? I ask.

No, Grandma says.

But she said it so fast. I know she's pretending.

No, she says again. Lois is a very brave person.

She goes to the TV but doesn't turn it on just like Daddo didn't turn it on. They both look like they don't know what to do.

Daddo checks his phone.

I'm going to have some words with your wife, Grandma says to Daddo.

Yeah, well . . .

Yeah, well nothing, Grandma says.

She saw Other Mommy, I remind them.

Then they both go quiet. Like what I said is making them think.

Then Grandma says,

She saw her one time and she can barely keep the twine around her sanity. And here Bela said she may have seen her a hundred times.

Grandma looks at me. Like she wants me to understand how serious this is, and like she wants me to know she understands what I've gone through too.

But have I gone through something?

Am I going through it now?

I know, I say.

She smiles. Sadly. Just like when Daddo winked.

Big day tomorrow, Grandma says. You two sleep. I'll take first watch.

Jesus, Daddo says. Listen to us.

We sound like exactly what we are, Grandma says. Which is very good. I think that's the first step toward solving this.

But I think of what Daddo said earlier. That some things aren't solved. Some things are always mysteries.

I'm not tired, I say.

Daddo lies down on one of the beds.
Grandma looks like she might tell me to lie down anyway. But she doesn't.

Then come stand watch, she says. Let's face this thing with some balls. Think of it as a dress rehearsal.

The flashing sign outside makes her blue and pink.

We're practicing tonight facing this thing tomorrow.

26

Lois Anthony's friends dress just like she does.
They wear sweaters and brown pants and boots and some have glasses and their hair is long.
We all sit on foldout chairs on a rug in a circle in Lois's living room. They all have objects by their feet or objects in their laps.
The fireplace is wider than ours and I think about the first time I met Lois, at the party at our house.
But there is no fire. And the fireplace is dark.
There's a plate of lit candles in the center of the circle instead.

How are you feeling, Bela? Lois asks. It's a lot of people to meet at once.
No it's not, I say. It's okay.

They laugh at what I said. But it's true. There's just six of them. My classes at school are a lot bigger than this.

Good, Lois says. So long as you're comfortable.

She breathes deep. Then she laughs.

I'm sorry, she says. Just a little nervous. We've never done something exactly like this before.

Not even close, Lois's friend Kyle says.

Kyle has blond hair and blue glasses and his shirt has swirling colors on it. There's an old telephone on the floor next to his shoes.

If we can help, Lois says, we will.

The room is quiet for a moment. Then Lois says,

We're going to ask this thing to leave you alone, Bela.

A woman named Mary stands up.

Okay, she says. I don't mean to be negative from the start but . . . what exactly does that mean? This is heavy.

It doesn't have to be, Lois says.

We normally exchange crystals here, Lois. This is just . . . *wow*. We all brought phones and stuff.

Anybody can step outside at any time if they feel uncomfortable in the circle, Lois says.

Mary looks at the candles on the plate. She sits down again. Lois says,

Bela?

Yeah.

When you've addressed this . . . Other Mommy . . . have you called her that before? Does she know this name?

The room feels dark past the circle. Even with the sun coming through cracks in the drapes.

Yeah.

Good.

Are we really ready to try this? Kyle asks. Really ready?

We're going to talk to her, Lois says. No harm in that.

Really? Kyle says. Because there's actually a lot of harm in talking. Like, over the course of history a lot of harm in talking.

Lois breathes out long and slow.

Then they all start talking at once. Daddo looks worried. Grandma looks impatient.

A woman named Adina starts crying.

It's just so . . . powerful, she says. What we're trying to do. For her. So big.

We're trying to help, Lois says.

Yes. But it's . . . so big.

It might be, Lois says. The candles on the dish actually have meaning and each one means something different. The red one is to weaken the veil. It thins the space between this world and any other. The cream-colored one is a peace offering, an olive branch, intended to let any other know we're the ones thinning the veil, and that we do so in peace. The purple one is for protection, though I don't anticipate we'll need that. And the black one is for—

But a friend of hers interrupts.

The black one means we're serious, the man named Duane says. It's intended to remind all things that all of existence is bigger than we are, no matter what side of the veil we exist on. In any plane, we know our place.

A woman who told me her name is Ashley of the Moon says,

Do you know what a plane is, Bela?

I shake my head no.

A plane is like . . . a place of being, Ashley of the Moon says. We believe there are other worlds than our own. Do you know what I mean?

Different realities, a woman named Maxine says. Do you know what realities are?

I look to Daddo.
He puts his hand on my knee.

It's okay, he says.
Given Bela's age, Lois says, I think we can rightly assume there will be some terms she hasn't heard before. And while I would like for her to understand everything that happens here, it's more important we talk to the thing that's been talking to her.

Tell it to leave, Grandma says.

It feels like everything starts now that Grandma said that.
Lois sits up straight in her chair and takes a really deep breath.

First, Lois says, we need to make contact.

She lifts what looks like a big piece of ice from her lap.

The objects we've each brought are the closest things we have to spiritual telephones, she says.

Her friends pick up the things at their feet or in their laps.

Crystals, Daddo whispers to me.
I've brought crystals, yes, Lois says. But, as you can see, we have a touch-tone telephone here, a microphone, and even pen and paper. All were asked to bring what they consider to be the

best form of spiritual communication. For them. And everybody here has attempted to speak to the dead before.

Dead? I say.

The friends are all looking at me again.

Do you not think she's dead? Mary asks.

She looks to Lois.

What's going on, Lois? Exactly what are we trying to make contact with here?

The friends are all talking at once again.
Two of them get up from their chairs.
I've seen teachers look like Lois looks now. When the classroom is out of control.

Listen, Kyle says. I am *not* thinning the veil just so something we know nothing about can come through.

What did you think we were doing? Ashley of the Moon says. What exactly was the help you thought we were giving this kid?

We can't reach out to something nefarious, Duane says. That's madness.

They get louder and some walk around the room and Lois is trying to calm everyone down.
Daddo checks his phone.
Where's Mommy?
Where is she?
And I don't know if I want these people talking to Other Mommy. These people don't know her. They weren't there when she was my friend. When she was the only person with me in my

bedroom. When she was the only one I talked to, the only person I told about how Mommy and Daddo feel different than they used to.

Because they do!

They don't laugh at movies like they used to.

They don't hold hands like they used to.

They're always sending me ahead and fighting behind me.

They're always having secret talks while I'm supposed to talk to nobody!

But I had Other Mommy to talk to!

Now I yell, to Lois and her friends, I yell:

> *I don't know what she is!*

And the room goes quiet. And one by one the friends sit down again.

We're sorry, Bela, Kyle says. It's just . . . energy is a big deal. And when you work as hard as we do to make sure yours is okay, well, you don't wanna mess it up. But . . . we're gonna try to help.

Because we said we would, Ashley of the Moon says.

Yes, Kyle says. Because of that.

He sits down but I can tell he's still not sure.

Bela, Lois says. This part might be a little uncomfortable for you.

Then maybe she should leave the room, Grandma says.

I think it's important she's here for this, Lois says.

Why? Grandma says. Can't you talk to this thing without her?

If someone, if this other . . . well . . . this other has taken a shine to her.

A shine? Daddo says.

He looks up from his phone.

All I'm saying, Lois says, is that if this thing is interested in her, then it may not want to speak with anybody else.

Lois picks up another crystal and hands it to Grandma.

Pass this along to Bela, please.

Grandma gives it to Daddo and Daddo gives it to me.
Lois picks up another one.

This is for Russ. And this . . .

She hands Grandma a third.

. . . is for you.

It's heavier than I thought it would be. I hold it with both hands. Daddo has to set his phone in his lap so he can do the same.
Lois raises her crystal higher, so it's near her face.

Let's all close our eyes, she says. Everyone in the room. Let's speak to Other Mommy, silently first, but together.

They all close their eyes. Daddo and Grandma too.
Lois says,

I want you to imagine your voice, your true voice, traveling through you, out every pore of your body, and into your mode of communication. It can be your ideal voice. Your inner voice. I won't tell you exactly what to say, but I think we should remain civil. Tell it to leave like you would tell an acquaintance to leave your home who has given you reason to do so. No need to get combative. Not yet. Tell Other Mommy she needs to leave Bela alone. She needs to find someplace other than Bela's home and Bela's bedroom. Speak as definitively as you can, using your best inner voice, and send the words *into* your spiritual telephone, where Other Mommy may hear you, and will know, from our energy and from our communal voices, that we mean what we say. We are serious about what we do. We are the first line of defense for Bela, who does not want Other Mommy visiting anymore, who is not left feeling good, in any way, after these encounters. Bela doesn't want to see you again, Other Mommy. Bela wants to be left alone. So that Bela might grow into the beautiful human being Bela is destined to become. Everybody, together now . . . tell Other Mommy to leave . . . tell Other Mommy to go . . .

I haven't closed my eyes.

That's it, Lois says. Tell Other Mommy it is time to go.

Everyone's mouths are moving but they're talking without talking. They hold their objects tight.
I don't tell them that sometimes I *did* feel good when I saw Other Mommy.

Do you feel it? Lois asks. Yes, everyone. That's it.

Mary brings her microphone to her lips like she's whispering into it.
Ashley of the Moon lowers her face so that her hair touches the paper in her hands.
Duane slowly moves his head side to side.

Other Mommy, Lois says. Other Mommy, leave Bela alone.

Kyle stands up. His eyes are still closed.
I look to the dark, open fireplace behind his chair.

Other Mommy, everyone says now. Other Mommy, leave
Bela alone.

Grandma's lips don't move but her eyes are closed.

Other Mommy, leave Bela alone.

Kyle gasps. Eyes still closed.

She answered, he says.

Did anyone hear him but me?

Keep going, Lois says. Everybody, keep telling Other
Mommy to leave Bela alone.

I look into the dark, open fireplace behind Kyle's chair.

Other Mommy, leave Bela alone.

Kyle moves his head like someone's tickling him.
He brings the old phone he holds to his ear.

Inner and outer voices together, Lois says. Tell her . . .
everybody . . . tell her to leave Bela alone . . .

Kyle shakes his head like Milky is licking his face.
He opens his eyes.
He hangs up the phone.
He's looking at me.

Other Mommy, the others say. Leave Bela alone.

Daddo, I say.

But all the voices together are loud and Daddo doesn't hear me.

Everybody breathe, Lois says. In for two, out for three. In for two, out for three. We need to become unified, we need to be in tune. Breathe. In for two . . . out for three . . . tell Other Mommy to leave.
Daddo, I say.
In for two . . . out for three . . .
In tune, Duane says.
Leave Bela alone, they say. Other Mommy, leave Bela alone.

Kyle crosses the rug. He walks toward me.

One voice, Lois says. One strong voice . . . inner and outer . . .

He bends toward me and whispers in my ear,

She wants you to know she gave you a present.
What are you doing? Grandma asks.

Her eyes are open. She's looking at Kyle.
But Kyle is already crouching by the candles in the middle of the rug.

One voice, Lois says. One voice now! Communicate! We're right there! We are doing it.
Other Mommy, leave Bela alone . . .

Kyle blows out the candles.
Lois opens her eyes.

Kyle?

The doorbell rings. Louder than any phone. Some of them cry out startled. They all open their eyes.

Ursula, Daddo says.

He gets up fast and leaves the circle.

He was talking to Bela, Grandma says about Kyle. What was he doing?
Who? Lois asks. Kyle?

Grandma grabs my hand and we get up.
We walk out of the room and all Lois's friends are arguing with Kyle and Lois looks at me like she feels really bad about how things are suddenly going.
I hear Mommy talking to Daddo at the front door.
Mommy's here.
She says to Daddo,

He's dead.

Mommy is crying.
And Daddo says,

Who, Ursula? What are you talking about? Who's dead?

Lois is behind us now, saying she "apologizes" and she thought "they could at least try" and maybe they're all "just a bunch of old hippies" and she's so sorry and "Kyle is a troubled man" and she shouldn't have invited him and then Mommy repeats to Daddo,

He's *dead*.

Daddo says,

Who?
Frank Doherty, Mommy says.

And Daddo says,

What? How would you know if Frank Doherty is dead? Ursula . . . what's going on?

And Grandma says,

Bela, this is not something for us to hear. Let's head outside.

And I look back to see Kyle is sitting in one of the chairs in front of the open fireplace, alone.
Grandma takes me by the hand and walks me through the kitchen, and Lois Anthony says,

Ruth, Bela, please, a moment.

And we stop to face her and she says,

I'm embarrassed. I believe I can do better. I can help. I can look into this.
I think it's best we find a specialist, Grandma says.

Lois nods.

I understand.

Beyond her, at the front door, I hear Daddo say:

Ursula. Are you serious?

And then I say to Lois,

Why did that man blow out the candles?

I don't know, she says. He didn't think we were doing it the right way, I guess. I don't care. Whatever it was, he was wrong to do it.

Grandma says,

> You did what you could. Thank you for that.
> He said she talked to him, I say.
> Wait, Lois says. Kyle said that?

But Grandma is pulling me out the side door and we're in Lois Anthony's driveway and I can hear Mommy and Daddo talking on the front porch still and Mommy is still crying and she says,

> He was in the closet. Like he'd slept there.
> Follow me to the back of the house, Grandma says to me.

Some friends are leaving through the side door. Mary and Duane. Getting in their cars.
I can still hear Mommy and Daddo because they're talking loud, mad, scared.

> Really, Ursula? Daddo says. Frank Doherty?
> It doesn't matter anymore, she says. None of it matters anymore.

Then Grandma is walking me to the back of the house. There are paintings on easels and rugs on the grass.
But I can still hear Mommy.

> The closet, she says. Like he was asleep in there.

And I think of the man Kyle sitting alone in front of the fireplace. I think of him saying,

She gave you a present.

By the time we reach the paintings, I don't care that they're paintings of the sun. I don't care that they're paintings of each other, Lois's friends. I keep thinking of Grandma asking if Other Mommy ever hurt anyone or said she would and I keep thinking maybe.

The answer used to be no but now it's maybe.

Maybe Other Mommy hurt someone else.

Maybe she did.

So I say it,

Maybe . . .

And when Grandma asks me what I mean, I start crying, and she holds me, and I keep saying *maybe, maybe, maybe* between my tears.

Even when Mommy and Daddo come around to the back of the house I can't stop crying. And shaking.

She gave you a present.

And Mommy's eyes are puffy and she's watching me. Daddo is on his knees trying to make me feel better but Mommy is watching me.

Like she's thinking *maybe* too.

Like she's thinking maybe Other Mommy hurt someone too.

27

We're in the car. Daddo is driving.
Mommy isn't crying right now but she'll probably start again.
She keeps starting and stopping.
Me and Grandma are in the backseat and the sun is going down.

> We gotta stay somewhere, Daddo says.
> A hotel, Grandma says.

Our house isn't safe. Grandma's isn't safe. Amanda and Dan's isn't safe.

> Where is safe? Daddo asks.

He turns on the blinker and changes lanes.
The road feels so big and empty.

> We'll find something, Grandma says. We haven't made it this far in life without making good decisions.

I look a goose in the eye on the side of the road as we pass.
Mommy is crying again. Quietly.

She said her friend died. She saw him dead in the closet.
I'm trying not to think about presents.

Man, Daddo says. So . . . I don't think I've ever felt this way
before. We're going to figure this out. But right now? We just
haven't yet. And that's all right. And that's important for us to
keep in mind. Just because you haven't figured it out yet, doesn't
mean you won't. Right?

He sounds so nervous. He sounds like he's no older than me.

We can go wherever we want, Grandma says. We can't live
in—
Mom, Mommy says. Please just be quiet for a little bit.

So we all don't say anything for a little while.
Grandma squeezes my hand.
Daddo changes lanes again.

Lois said it's rare for two people to describe an entity the
same way, Daddo says. "Entity" was her word.
It's following us, Grandma says.
Mom, Mommy says. Please.
Well, dammit, Ursula, Grandma says. This isn't any time to
be lying to ourselves.

Mommy turns slowly to look Grandma in the face.
Daddo says,

The problem with a hotel is that one hotel becomes two. I
didn't work today and I don't see how I'm gonna work tomorrow, and Ruth is right. Man, she's right. We need to find someone who knows how to handle this.
Nobody knows anything about what I saw in Bela's room,
Mommy says.

Daddo looks at her and the car goes a little into the next lane. He straightens the wheel.

A hotel, Daddo says. And then how many of them? How many places before we can't go anywhere?

We need to face this, Grandma says.

Nobody knows anything about what I saw in Bela's room.

Outside, the sides of the road are dark. Like when the closet doors aren't quite touching.

I think of the first time I heard Other Mommy's voice from the dark in there.

Hello, there. Who are you?

That day, I thought she was hanging upside down in there. I didn't answer her. I sat in my bed and didn't answer her.

Do you mind that I'm in your closet? Do you mind if I come out?

I didn't tell her if I minded or not but she came out either way. I sat up in bed and watched her curl out of the closet. She told me we were friends. She said all kids have a friend in their closet. She said a lot of people lie about who you're supposed to be friends with because a lot of people are sad and they want you to be sad too.

The first time she talked, she asked if she could go into my heart. I didn't answer and I pulled the covers up over my head.

But she kept talking, like her mouth was touching the other side of the blanket. She talked about carnation, *rein*-carnation, and she said,

If you let me in, I can walk and talk just like you do.

But where would I go if she was inside me?

You would go where I come from.
The closet?
No, Bela. I don't come from the closet.

Other Mommy told me that people sometimes get sad when their friends don't help them out and then they start saying things they wouldn't normally say. She said she was warning me she might say something she wouldn't normally say.
Was this what Grandma meant when she asked if she'd said she would hurt someone?

Think of me like Pester, she said.

I didn't know how she knew we'd had a cat named Pester.

Think of me like Milky, she said.

I didn't know how she knew about Milky.

And think of Pester outside your bedroom door and how badly she wanted to get in. And the longer you left her out there, the more sad she would get. Until one day the sound of her meowing could drive you crazy. Until one day she could get mean.

Is this what Grandma meant?

Frank's house, Mommy says.
My God, come on, Daddo says.
I have a key.
Are you serious right now?

She cries quietly as she tells us an ambulance came and took Frank's body away.
Then Daddo slows down and pulls the car to the side of the road.

We all sit quiet in the dark as Daddo looks out the windshield.
He breathes in and out.
The road feels so big and empty. The night looks the same color
as the closet when the doors aren't quite touching.
Mommy says,

It's a house, Russ, she says.
You would know, Daddo says.

Then he turns the car around and we drive back the way we
came.

28

We're outside Frank's house.

I think he's the man who was holding Mommy's hand at the party at our house.

Daddo doesn't talk.

Grandma says things to me like "Things will be ordinary again sooner than we know." She's trying to make me feel better.

I don't feel better. I think maybe she's saying it to herself.

I'm looking to the upstairs windows of Frank's house.

Mommy opens the front door with the key.

We deserve some sleep, Grandma tells me. That's all that matters right now. Nobody ever did anything intelligent with no sleep.

The house is dark inside.

Mommy steps in and turns on a light.

There's a staircase on the left side. White steps. Ahead, I can see a small table with two chairs. It smells like another person in this house. Not like us.

Come on, Mommy says.

Let's get Bela to bed, Grandma says.

We all follow Mommy deeper inside. She walks like she knows the place.

There's a bedroom down here, Mommy says. The master bedroom.

Mommy wipes tears with her jacket sleeve.

You're acting like you were in love, Daddo says.
Let's get Bela to bed, Grandma says. And turn on more lights. Turn them all on.

We all go from room to room turning on the lights. The whole first floor.
I look up the stairs when we pass them. It's closet-dark up there.

What if someone sees all the lights on and investigates? Daddo says.
What do you mean? Grandma asks.
If someone stops by, Daddo says. We need to have a plan. What are we gonna say? Surely someone from his family could stop by.
Nobody's going to stop by, Mommy says.

We're all in the kitchen now. There are dishes in the sink.
A man died in this house today.

Bela, Daddo says. Is . . . is she here?

I wish he didn't say that. I wish he didn't ask me that.

Russ, Mommy says. What are you doing?

Daddo holds up a hand for her to be quiet.

I don't care about us right now, he says. I'm only thinking of Bela. Bela?

I don't know.

Is it something you can tell? Grandma asks. Think about it a second if you haven't ever thought about it before.

I don't wanna think about it. But I do.

Can I tell when Other Mommy is close by? I felt something in the Loblolly Pines.

Do I feel it now?

I think of the first time I saw her.

I had no idea she was in the closet.

But maybe . . . maybe other times I did.

Maybe, I say.

What do you mean? Mommy asks.

I can tell she didn't want to hear me say this.

I think about the nights when Mommy would tuck me in bed and I would watch the closet doors.

Do you sense anything? Grandma asks. Do you smell something? Does the air around you change? Is there anything that would suggest she's here?

I smelled her once, Daddo says. Am I right, Bela? In your bathroom. Right? That was her?

Yeah, I say. That was Other Mommy.

Daddo presses his lips tight.

Sometimes I hear creaks, I tell them. Sometimes I can smell her. Sometimes I just know she's there.

It's the first time I really understand this.

Okay, Grandma says. Is she here now?

We all go quiet and I listen for creaking. I think about her smell. That first night she talked to me from the closet I could smell her. She smelled like the time Pester found a mouse covered in bugs in the garage.

Bela, Mommy says. Come on. We're losing our minds here. Is she here or is she not? I can't handle this.

I listen. I think how a car passed that first night she spoke to me. How the headlights shined into my bedroom. How I saw she wasn't hanging upside down in the closet. That's just how her face is sometimes.

I don't think so, I say.
Show us that first-floor bedroom, Grandma says to Mommy.

We follow Mommy out of the kitchen and past a bathroom. The bedroom is small. The bed is not made and there's clothes on the floor and the closet door is open.
I don't ask if that's the closet where the man died.

All right, Grandma says. We can all sleep in here.
I'm staying up, Daddo says.
You need to sleep, too, Russ, Grandma says.
I'm glad you think so, Ruth.

Daddo and Grandma never fight. They're good friends. One time Mommy told Daddo she thinks Grandma likes Daddo better than she likes her. But they look like they might fight now.

Nobody ever did anything—Grandma starts to say.

I know that, Ruth, Daddo says.

You need to sleep.

Not tonight.

Then I'll stay up, Grandma says. You need to be clear-headed for—

Clear-headed? Daddo says. Are you kidding me right now?

The house is quiet around us. It's like I can hear the quiet.

We'll take turns, Grandma says.

That's fine, Daddo says. But I'm staying up first. Do what you want.

He leaves the bedroom.

Mommy sits on the bed. She's looking at the floor of the open closet.

Well, this is a real moment, Grandma says.

She walks over to Mommy and holds Mommy's head while Mommy cries.

I look out the bedroom door and can see Daddo sitting on the couch in the living room up the hall.

I walk out to him.

Hi, I say.

You wanna sleep out here with me? I'll be up.

Okay.

We'll leave the lights on.

Okay.

I go to the couch and sit beside him.

Grandma's face peeks out of the bedroom up the hall.

She should sleep in here with us, she says.

She's fine with me, Daddo says.

I think Daddo was crying too. His eyes are red.

Grandma vanishes into the bedroom again.

Daddo yawns. Even though he wants to stay awake, he's tired.
We stare ahead across the room. We can hear Mommy and
Grandma talking in the bedroom and sometimes Mommy's
voice gets louder and Grandma Ruth tells her to "keep calm."

For Bela, she says.

I listen for creaks upstairs. Creaks anywhere.

You're an unbelievable person, Daddo tells me.

Really? I ask.

Yeah. You got all this stuff going on . . . even if this scary
stuff wasn't happening . . . there's all this . . .

He flaps his hand toward the hall that leads to the bedroom
Mommy and Grandma are talking in.

. . . all this real stuff, he says.

Are you and Mommy mad at each other?

Daddo laughs but it's not the funny kind.

Don't worry about us right now. Just worry about you. I
mean . . . don't worry about anything, okay?

I know a kid at school whose parents got divorced. I remember
thinking the word sounds like what it means.

Maybe we should leave, Daddo says. I don't think I can stay
here.

Daddo, I think she might have hurt the man who lives here.

Daddo looks surprised.

> Your mommy wouldn't—
> I mean Other Mommy.

The ceiling creaks when I say her name. I look up. But it wasn't the ceiling, it was Grandma stepping out of the room up the hall.

> We need sleep, she says.
> Working on it, Daddo says.

Grandma looks at him like she understands why he's upset. But like she also wishes he wasn't. Then she goes back into the bedroom.

> What do you mean? Daddo says.

He's sitting up now. Not leaning back into the couch.

> I think she hurt the man . . .

I don't say: *for me*. But I think it.

> That's a big leap, Daddo says. Right? I mean . . . right?

I don't want Mommy and Daddo to get divorced. Was Other Mommy helping me with that? Was she being my friend? Daddo stands up. He paces.

> The guy at Lois's house said she spoke to him, I say.
> Okay, Bela, Daddo says. Just say whatever you're trying to say. Things are really piqued right now, okay?
> He said she told him she gave me a present.

Daddo's hands are covering his face the way people do when they have a lot of worry.
He lowers them slowly, staring at me.

Did he say that? he asks. Exactly that?
Yeah.

He heads up the hall and gets to the bedroom door before I get off the couch. I don't want to be in any room alone.
I follow him. I hear him and Mommy arguing. Grandma says we need to sleep. Daddo hardly ever yells. But he's yelling now.

How can you expect me to stay here? Are you insane, Urs? Or are you just mean?
Russ, Grandma says. Think of Bela. We all need rest.
Yeah? Well *you* try to sleep in the place where your wife just—
Russ, Grandma says.
O, Ruth, can it. I'm allowed to be upset! And I'm not staying here.

I hear creaking upstairs.
Mommy is crying. Daddo is talking so fast. Grandma is upset.

No person should have to sleep here under these conditions, Daddo says. I'm an open-minded person. But this? This is a step too far.
We have nowhere else to go, Mommy says.
Not according to your mom! We can go anywhere we want.
It'd be wise for us to stay here, Grandma says.
Not for me, Daddo says.

I look up. Because it sounds like the ceiling is bending down toward me.

I wanna leave too, I say.

But they don't hear me.

And Bela, Daddo says. Bela thinks her ghost had something to do with what happened here in the closet.
What? Mommy says.

She sounds really scared.

Yeah, Daddo says. Still wanna stay?
I think she's here, I say.

I don't want my parents to get divorced. I love them the way they are. I love us the way we are.
Did Other Mommy help me?
Is this what friends do?
And am I supposed to help her back?
Am I supposed to say yes?

I think she's here! I say, louder.

But they still don't hear me.

Russ, Mommy says. You knew this was going on. Stop pretending you didn't. You even said you liked the idea one night.
Wait, Daddo says. *Hold* the hell on, Ursula.
We're tired, Grandma says. All of us.
I'm leaving, Daddo says.
No, Grandma says.

I step past Daddo, into the room where Mommy is crying on the messy bed.

I think she's in the house! I yell.

They all look at me, startled.

    Jesus, Daddo says.
    Okay, Grandma says. Up.

She's helping Mommy up.

    Come on, Grandma says. Out. Now. All of us.
    Why? Mommy says. Why is this happening?

But we're heading for the door.
When we pass the stairs I don't look up.

    Out, Grandma says. Fast.
    Was she here before? Mommy asks. Was she here earlier
today?

She sounds so upset. Mr. Jeffrey once used a word that scared
me.
Hysterical.
Like when someone is so upset they can't control their own
mind.
Mommy sounds hysterical.
But we're outside now, hurrying through the dark to the car.
Grandma takes my hand.
I don't look back.
I'm scared I'll see her. I'm scared I'll hear her.
I'm scared she's gonna ask to go into my heart.

    All in, Grandma says, opening the car door.

I get in. Then Grandma gets in.
Mommy.

Then Daddo.
I don't look back when he starts the car. When he drives away.
I don't look back.
I'm scared she's gonna ask to go into my heart.
And I'm scared I know how to stop this. How to make Mommy and Daddo less afraid. How to make sure she doesn't give me any more presents.

Seatbelts, Grandma says. Even now, especially now, we must be smart. We're smart, aren't we, Bela?

But I don't answer. I just stare into the darkness outside.
I'm scared.
I don't look back.
I'm scared my parents are going to get divorced. I'm scared Mommy is being hysterical. I'm scared we're losing our minds.
Why did Other Mommy come to me? If she doesn't come from the closet . . . where did she come from when she came to me?
I'm scared she came to me because I don't have many other friends. I'm scared Mommy and Daddo are my only friends. I'm scared Other Mommy is my friend because I didn't have any other friends.
And I'm scared she's going to give me another present if I don't say yes.
That's it.
That's what I'm really scared of.
I'm scared I'm gonna say *yes*.

29

We're sleeping in the car. In the parking lot of a gas station between Chaps and East Kent. Daddo says we've been to this gas station a bunch but it all looks different to me if we have.

Everybody else in the car is asleep.

Daddo is in the driver's seat with his hands hanging over the wheel. Grandma Ruth is in the passenger seat with her arms crossed. Mommy is in the backseat with me.

It's bright here because the gas station has a lot of lights and there's some people walking around and a lot of them look at us in the car.

Do they know something bad is happening to us?

It feels like they do. It feels like people don't want to come near us. Like how Amanda and Dan were glad we left their house. I bet that man Frank wishes he didn't come near us.

Grandma was breathing hard on the drive here and I asked if she was okay and she said she is a sixty-one-year-old woman who has never experienced anything like this in her life and she's trying to "process." She also told me I am brave if I sat and talked with "that thing" in my bedroom before.

Mommy said I was wrong when I called her a woman. Said it'd also be wrong to call her a man.

But . . .

I still see her as Other Mommy. The woman whose eyes were a little less dark than the rest of the inside of the closet, the first time she ever spoke to me.

Hello there, and who are you?

She'd come like that, most nights. I'd sit in bed after Mommy and Daddo tucked me in and I'd look to the closet doors and they would open, just a little bit. I'd see her eyes in there like she was smiling. Sometimes I thought I saw her teeth, too, but when car headlights came through the window, I'd see she wasn't smiling. Sometimes it felt like she was checking to see if I was there. Like she was looking to see if I was asleep or not. One night I sat on the edge of the foot of my bed and waited for the doors to open but then I got too scared and I crawled back to my pillow and I heard the closet creak open behind me. I hurried up and got under the blankets, all of me, and pulled the blankets over my head. I heard her walking in my bedroom that night. The floor creaked and then it didn't and then it did again and then I smelled her next to my bed. That night she said,

Peekaboo.

Like Mommy used to say. Back when I was littler. Back when Mommy was happier I think and her and Daddo made jokes that made each other laugh all the time.

Peekaboo, you.

I didn't come out from under the blankets when she was beside the bed. Then she must've walked back to the closet because she said,

Do you like me better in here?

Then I did look and I saw she was in the closet again, between my hanging clothes, and the closet doors were open a little wider.
I nodded yes. I wanted her to know I liked her better in there.
Did she smile then? Did she ever?

Mommy? I said.

I think I said it because she'd said "peekaboo."

Other Mommy, she said from the closet.

Then she sunk back into the darkness between two of my sweat-shirts and the closet doors closed on their own.

Other Mommy, I say now, quietly, to myself.

Daddo was the one who picked the gas station. He kept saying we're gonna figure this out tomorrow. He kept saying it's important to be an "optimist at a time like this." Mommy said we should go home because it doesn't matter where we are. The car got quiet after she said that.
Grandma didn't talk much since we left that house. She did mention a priest, but Daddo wasn't raised like that and I didn't even know what a priest was until tonight. Not really.
But still, if one can help . . .
I don't know.
Daddo said other people might help too. He used the word "oc-cultist" but he said it slowly, like a word he didn't know. I do that all the time. Daddo, Mommy, and Grandma Ruth don't know what to do. They always know what to do. But they don't know now.

Other Mommy, I say again, even quieter this time.

I look over and see Mommy is asleep with her head against the window. Her eyes are puffy. Her lips are shaped like a frown.

If I turn and press my chest and my ear to the backseat, I can hear my heart.

Could someone get in there? Really?

I think someone could. I worry.

And it worries me that I liked Other Mommy.

I thought of her as my friend.

Do I still?

There were times I sat up in bed waiting for her to come out of the closet. Times I was just as excited as I was scared.

Because sometimes I feel angry, and upset, and like I want to scream and I think Other Mommy is like that too. She's different from my friends at school. Different from Deb. Different from Daddo and Mommy and Grandma Ruth.

She's mad too.

Are you angry, Other Mommy? Other Mommy are you there?

I wanna sleep, but I think maybe I already did a little because I closed my eyes and when I opened them I saw a worker from the gas station close to the window and he made a sign with his hands like he was sorry, he didn't mean to bother me, he was just making sure we were okay. Then he walked away and I pressed my chest and my ear to the seat to hear what my heart sounds like and if there's room in there for two.

I don't know . . .

Where does Other Mommy come from?

I try to stay calm like Daddo said I should. I've seen Other Mommy so many times. It used to be only at night. It used to be only in my bedroom. It even used to be only peeking out from my closet doors. But then one night when I sat up waiting for her to show up I smelled her and I looked to the side of my bed and saw her on her hands and knees there, looking back at me.

Other Mommy, I whisper. *I thought we were friends.*

Are we?

I don't think Mommy and Daddo would like me talking like this.

But I can't help it.

Outside by a pump, a man is washing his front window.

I like when Mommy or Daddo do that with our car. I like watching the soap get wiped away. I wish we could do that with my bedroom. Clean it up like Grandma said a priest could do.

The man is big and his shirt is too small and he keeps pulling up his pants to meet it.

He makes the window wet and then he dries the squeegee with a towel and then he makes a dry line along the glass.

I see a face in the water sliding down the glass.

I look away.

But I look back.

Yeah. There could be a face dripping down his window and he's at the garbage can and his car door is open and he's taking garbage from his car and putting it in the can and I think the face could be looking at me from across the gas station lot.

It's upside down.

And it's getting longer, drooping, until it touches where the wipers are.

The man comes back to the window and uses the squeegee to wipe the face away.

I can't tell if he got all the way down to the eyes.

I just can't tell.

Even when he drives away, as Daddo snores and Mommy sleeps against the window, even as Grandma sleeps with her arms crossed and I look out at the car pulling away, even then I can't tell if he got the whole face, if he got the eyes, or if she's still looking at me.

I close my eyes and I still can't tell if she's looking at me.

Even as I fall asleep.

Even then.

Are we friends? I don't think so. I don't think friends are this
scared of each other.

But still . . . I wonder. Mommy and Daddo sometimes seem
scared of each other.

I used to be just as excited as I was scared.

But now I just sleep.

I had a friend who wanted to yell as badly as I sometimes do. I
had a friend who wanted to scream.

Doesn't everyone want to scream sometimes?

Doesn't everybody want to scream?

30

It's hard for me to explain this to you, Daddo says.

We're sitting on a bench outside a big church.
Mommy and Grandma are inside talking to someone who maybe can help.

Because no matter how smart you are, you're still a kid. And so you've only lived so long, and so you don't have a whole life of *not* experiencing what we're going through. And so when I say someone doesn't actually know how they're going to react to something like this until they actually have to, that no amount of stories could possibly prepare a person for how they'd really feel if they *actually* saw what your mom saw the other night, I'm talking about people who have already lived a pretty long time *without* seeing something like that. See what I mean? When you're my age, a certain . . . reality takes root. I don't mean that I'm set in my ways. I pride myself on not being set. But no matter how freewheeling you are, something like what she saw, well . . .

Daddo's been talking like this since Mommy and Grandma went inside.

Are they getting help? Is it working?
Daddo turns to look at the big brown church door.

What can anyone do? he says. What can a priest do about
this thing?

He takes my chin in his hand.

I think it's time you stop calling it what you call it, he says.
Your mom doesn't like it.

He lets go and he stands up.
He walks up the sidewalk a few steps, then back a few steps.
Pacing. He keeps looking to the church door, wanting it
to open, wanting Mommy and Grandma to come out with
help.

What will the priest do? I ask.
Bela . . . I'm not sure.

He sits down with me on the bench again.

I'm so sorry this is happening, he says.
Me too, Daddo.

Then I start crying.

No, no, he says. One day this will all be something we got
through. One day, the problems you have now will be like a leg-
end in your life. I don't know a single person who got stuck in
the same problem for the rest of their life. Do you know what I
mean, Bela?
Yeah, I say.
Okay, good. I love you.
I love you too.

The church door opens and Mommy and Grandma come down
the stone steps toward us.
They don't look happy.

> They won't do it, Mommy says.
> Won't even come to the house?
> They don't believe any of it, Grandma says.
> And even if they did, Mommy says, they say they'd need
> proof. And a lot of it too. I said, Hey, how about the word of
> three adult witnesses and they started asking us questions as if
> to check our sanity. Do we use drugs. How religious are we. Is
> there anything we're zealous about.
> O, come *on*, Daddo says.
> They weren't very nice, Grandma says.
> They told us to go to the police, Mommy says.
> And you told them we already did?
> I did. Russ . . .
> What?
> We have to kill it.

Daddo shakes his head like Mommy is crazy but then looks at
her like she's not.

> How? he asks.
> I don't know. But if we want to get on with our lives, we
> have to kill it ourselves.
> But . . . how?
> It doesn't matter where we go, Mommy says like she didn't
> hear Daddo's question. For crying out loud, she saw it in the
> park, Russ.

They go quiet then.

> But how? I ask.

I think of the face Other Mommy makes when I don't answer her question.

What would it look like if I tried to hurt her?

    With a gun? I ask.

    Don't say that, Daddo says. Jesus, Bela.

    Well, Grandma says, what else are we talking about here?

    We haven't even tried shoving it, Mommy says.

She looks out across the street like she's thinking about doing that.

The church door opens and two men in black walk down the steps and when they get to the bottom they see me and then they look at Mommy like they're about to say something to her.

Then they look at each other and walk away and we can hear their shoes on the sidewalk, going away from us until we can't see them anymore.

Those were the priests, I know.

And that was the sound they make, walking away from us.

It sounded like the whole world walked away from us. Like the whole world just told us we have to figure this out on our own.

I try to imagine how to hurt Other Mommy.

I don't like thinking about it.

But I don't stop either.

I think.

How.

How can I help . . .

And which way is worse?

Hurting her . . .

Or helping?

31

We drove all around Goblin today. Up Northsouth and back down Christmas. We talked to a man who worked at a Northwoods gift shop, we talked to a psychic on Neptune Street. We saw what looked like a bright-green forest and Mommy said I'd actually been to this place when I was younger. It used to be a "tourist trap" called the Hedges and Mommy said I didn't remember it because I was a baby then and they carried me in a harness through the maze. Grandma said we needed to stop in every "headshop" and "lounge" we could, to ask who might know about these types of things. But in the end, nobody knew any more than we do. That's how Daddo said it. Then Mommy and Daddo got angry at each other and Grandma sat on one of the green city benches a few times, once in a place called Perish Park. Once in a cemetery, too, where they bury the people standing up. I like Goblin. A lot. I asked if we could move here but Mommy and Daddo didn't hear me and every time I looked at Grandma she still had a hurried look in her eyes.

I played video games in an arcade called Goblin Games while Mommy and Daddo talked in a booth. I didn't wanna hear them argue. I didn't want to see Grandma ask another person if there was any "renowned occultists" in the city. I wanted to forget all

about why we were there. I wanted to shove Other Mommy in a
closet and lock the door and never think of her again.

My family was falling apart. One minute Daddo was being
funny and the next he'd gone quiet and upset. Mommy was
"edgy" the whole time. She kept saying "night is coming sooner
than we think, we need to do something." Daddo said that's
what *he* was saying, we needed a plan, and why was Mommy
acting like he didn't understand that? Grandma just seemed
tired and impatient.

Night did come sooner than we thought, and the four of us
stood outside a closed bakery in the dark. It rained a little all day,
but just then it got bad. Grandma said "the sky opened up" and
I think she was right. I thought of closet doors parting when she
said it.

Daddo sat on a green bench in the rain and Mommy stood under
the bakery awning and none of us knew what to do.

It's a bad feeling. I'm not used to my vote counting as much as
theirs. I'm not used to them all being what Grandma called "desperate." Either way, it turned out she was the one who found us
a place to stay.

She has a friend who lives "out at the edge" of Goblin. Her name
is Evelyn, and Grandma called her and Evelyn said we could
come over. After she hung up, Grandma told all of us to keep
quiet about what was happening. She said she didn't know how
Evelyn would act if she heard the truth.

Then Grandma put her hand on my shoulder and said,

We're living a storm of a story, Bela.

We're at Evelyn's house now. We just entered. We're all wet and
we're standing in what Grandma said is the foyer. It's late and
the house is really big and there are three floors and even a room
just for reading. Evelyn has pictures of her family on the walls
and on tables, too, but she says none of them live nearby anymore. She said it's too rainy here for some people and Daddo

said he liked the rain and I think Evelyn liked it when he said that.

I made up three rooms after Ruth called, Evelyn says. I can show you them now if you like. I'm not saying you should call it a night yet. Feel free to stay up as late as you normally do. When people come into my home, I prefer they play house.

I know Grandma doesn't wanna tell Evelyn we wanna share one room, because then she might ask why.

This is all above and beyond, Grandma says. I cannot tell you how much this means to us.

Is there trouble? Evelyn asks.

No, Grandma says. Just weary travelers. The city can do that.

I don't think I've ever seen you so pale, Evelyn says.

You know how it can be with kids, Daddo says.

Then he pretend smiles.

But Evelyn really laughs.

I do know, she says. And you're right; children have a tendency to make it so we never look our best. Come on, let me show you your rooms.

Evelyn and Grandma leave the foyer and Mommy says to Daddo,

We'll just thank her and sleep in the same room.

Right.

We don't need to tell her what we plan to do.

Right.

The house is *really* big. Bigger than Grandma said it would be. We follow her out of the foyer and into a big open space with wood walls and paintings, and there are two staircases on either side of the big room. Both sets of stairs look as wide as my bed-room.

Second floor, Evelyn says. My January and July used to sleep on this floor. There was always noise and action and running around. It used to drive me crazy but I miss it now.

There are so many rooms. And each looks like a different world. Evelyn shows us one with all sorts of white blankets and chairs.

January's room, she says. A bit smaller but also gets the best sun. That is, when it's not raining. Which is hardly ever.

I see the bed is made up nice. There's a little table next to the bed and a fan above it.
The closet door is closed.

You can pick whatever rooms you like, Evelyn says, but I imagine this one is good for the child.

She smiles at me.

Come on, she says.

We follow her to the next room over.

Much bigger, Evelyn says. But also a little stuffy. July never seemed to mind. He never complained about anything until he grew up and then it was all he did.

There's a big brown dresser that Evelyn calls a "wardrobe." The walls are blue and there's a nice old blue rug to match.
The closet door is closed.

This might be nice for a couple, Evelyn says.

We follow her to a third room that's all yellow and green and it's got two small beds.

Ruth? Evelyn says. I saw you sleeping in this room. It's always been a guest bedroom. Once was, it was never empty. Friends of January and July, friends of my own and yours too. The great Wayne Sherman once slept in this room after a gathering downstairs to celebrate the city's birthday. But even he's dead now.

Thank you, Grandma says. As I've said before, nicer than any hotel in town.

Speaking of service, Evelyn says, would you four like something to eat?

Yes, Mommy and Daddo say at the same time.

They all laugh. Because it's funny. And I see Mommy and Daddo look at each other like maybe they like each other again.
Did Other Mommy make that happen?
We all follow Evelyn back downstairs and I look back to the bedrooms and I wonder which one we'll use. I can still see into the yellow room and I see the closet door is a little bit open.

Bela, Mommy says, watch your step.

She takes my hand and helps make sure I don't fall down the big steps.
It's the biggest house I've ever been in.

For as much as I'd like to present a fancy dinner, Evelyn says, all I have tonight is frozen pizza.

My God, Daddo says. That sounds *perfect*.

Evelyn likes this.

A man of high taste, she says.
I'm practically refined, Daddo says.

I think I prefer "practically," Evelyn says. It's the distance between instinct and manners where the fun lies. Come.

We follow her past many rooms on our way to the kitchen and I say,

It's so big in here!
A place like this needs people, Evelyn says. You are doing this house a favor.

We pass something she calls a "butler's pantry," but Daddo says it's a bar. There are a lot of bottles and glasses and a shiny metal ice bucket. I see us all reflected in the ice bucket and Evelyn says,

You're not in the car anymore. You don't have to all stand together in one space. You can spread out a little here.

But we don't spread out a little here.

The road, Grandma says, can make a tribe out of anyone.
You live less than an hour away, Evelyn says.

She eyes us for a second and then Grandma says,

Show us that pizza, eh?

Evelyn smiles.

I can hardly wait.

We follow her past the butler's pantry and then past a bathroom and then down a hall with more family photos and then—

Holy cow, I say. This is the biggest kitchen in the *world*!

Evelyn goes to the biggest refrigerator I've ever seen and pulls open the freezer and takes out two boxes. Grandma goes to help.

Please, Evelyn says. Let me host. It's been a minute.

But Grandma keeps helping anyway.
Evelyn turns the oven on, then looks to Mommy and Daddo and says,

Who wants a drink?
I'd love one, Mommy says.
Me too, Daddo says.
And you? Evelyn asks me. Grape juice?
Sure, I say. Thank you.

She starts to get me that, but Grandma's already doing it. Grandma even knows where the glasses are. She pours me some juice and hands it to me and she smiles and it's the first smile I've seen on her face since long before we hurried out of the house where the man died.

Follow me back to the pantry, Evelyn says to Mommy and Daddo.

Mommy takes my hand on the way.

Bourbon? Evelyn asks Daddo.
Sounds incredible, he says.
I'll have the same, Mommy says. Thank you.
You both like bourbon, Evelyn says. That's a good thing. The couple that drinks together . . . usually splits up. But the couple that drinks the same drink, usually does not.

Evelyn fills four glasses with ice from the bucket.

I know what Ruth's having, she said. And I'll have the same.

She makes four drinks and gives Mommy and Daddo theirs.
They both drink.

O, wow, Mommy says.
The first sip, Evelyn says, is always the sweetest.

Daddo lifts his glass, and he and Mommy look into each other's
eyes the way they do when they forget I'm in the room, and then
Mommy raises her glass too and they touch their glasses together.
Grandma comes up the hall.

Pizzas are in the oven, she says.
For you, Evelyn says.

She hands Grandma her drink.

And now follow me, everyone, she says. That oven takes
forever no matter what the timer says.

We follow her past the kitchen and then we're in a big room with
huge windows and a high ceiling and two brown couches and a
record player and plants and—

I've always loved this room, Grandma says.

Evelyn turns on the record player.

The Hollies, Evelyn says. Cheers, all. Now, tell me about
your adventures.

But Mommy and Daddo and Grandma don't talk right away.

I played video games, I say.

O, nice, Evelyn says. I haven't been downtown in a couple weeks now. Did you win your games?

Win? I ask.

Mommy laughs, and it's the first time I've heard her laugh in a while.

Rain strikes the big windows. The house creaks.

We drove all over the city, Daddo says. We saw the Hedges are overgrown now.

Someone needs to buy that place, Evelyn says. Start it over again. Were you looking for anything in particular?

Particular? Daddo asks.

You said you drove all over the city . . .

She looks to Grandma like she knows. Grandma looks back like she knows she knows.

Let's us go check the oven, Evelyn says.

Fine, Grandma says.

Visit the pantry as often as you like, Evelyn tells Mommy and Daddo.

Now it's just Mommy, Daddo, and me.

Mommy looks through the other records.

You like this house? Daddo asks me.

Yeah.

Want a house like this?

I don't know what we'd do with it.

Well, let me know once you do.

Mommy laughs at that. Daddo winks.

Come here, Daddo says to Mommy.

They stare at each other for a second. Then Mommy goes to him and they hold each other and sip their drinks.
I look to the high ceiling.

You could fit two families in this house, I say.

Mommy and Daddo smile again. They say you could fit ten and they drink more of their drinks and then Daddo calls out to Evelyn if it's okay to make more of them and she calls back that she already told him to drink her "out of house and home."

One day you'll like this stuff, Daddo says to me. Because it makes big scary houses less scary.
Russ, Mommy says.

She watches him go to the butler's pantry.

Come here a sec, Bela.

It's just the two of us now. She's leaning against the back of one of the couches and so I do that too.

We'll sleep in the room with the two beds, she says. You and Daddo in one, me and Grandma in the other.
Okay.
And if you have to go to the bathroom, or go anywhere at all, you get me.
Okay.
I love you, Bela, she says. And I'm sorry I've been so far away lately.
You're right here, I say.
Right now, yes, she says. And I really am sorry.

I look up to her face and see tears in her eyes.
Daddo comes back with two drinks.

You hear that? he asks.

Mommy stands up straight really fast.

What did you hear?
I heard a party going on in my hands.
Russ . . .

But she's not mad.
Daddo carries the drinks to her and I'm happy they're happy.
Rain strikes the huge windows. Above us, the house creaks.

When I think back to when I was your age, Bela, Daddo
says, it's all wood-panel walls and weird plants and yellows
and browns and my parents entering and exiting rooms. I was
a little person amongst thousands of legs. I remember a lot of
legs.
Yes. Mommy laughs. Legs and pants.
Right? Daddo says. A forest of pants. How did we even
know who our real parents were?

They sit next to each other on the couch. They look more like
Mommy and Daddo than they have in a long time.
Daddo kisses her neck. Mommy pretends she didn't like it.

Vacations were a nightmare, Daddo says. Grocery stores
too. I'd be walking with Mom and Dad, up and down the aisles,
and I'd be talking to them, telling them what I wanted to eat,
what I wanted to do when we got home, and I'd reach up and
hold their hands and some other woman would be looking down
at me, out-of-her-mind confused.

I look out the entrance to the huge room, down the hall where the butler's pantry is.
Someone is standing at the far end of the hall.

Dad got mad about it one time, Daddo says. Because back in those days there was all this stuff in the news about kidnappings and just . . . crazy stuff. Doesn't it seem like that kind of thing isn't as around as it used to be? I don't know. Anyway, Dad got mad and actually slapped me once and told me not to talk to strangers. But the point is . . .

The point, Russ, Mommy says.

The *point,* Daddo says, is that when I think back on those days . . .

It's a woman. I think. The lights are dim. She's walking up the hall. Toward me.

. . . it's all a hazy mystery to me, Daddo says. It's not like a film, but there *is* a film over it. Like the fog in a gothic painting. Purples and blues . . .

I can't see her face.

. . . and it's hard to know my exact location in it all. Know what I mean? Do I make sense?

Definitely, Mommy says. Childhood was an actual nightmare.

They're leaning back into the couch. Talking over the music.
The rain is hitting the windows hard.
The woman is halfway up the hall.

Know what I think? Daddo asks.

I almost say something, I almost yell about the woman in the hall.

But Evelyn steps into the light.
It was just Evelyn.

O my, she says. Is it ever nice to hear voices.

Daddo raises his drink to her.

The pizza is about ready, she says.

She eyes me like she knows I'm haunted.
The song on the radio ends and we all stand there for a second
before Evelyn says,

Come on. Unless you don't want to eat anymore. If you're
anything like me, you worry the food will eat back. Eat right
into that buzz you're getting.
I'll chance it, Daddo says.
Food's up! Grandma calls from the kitchen.

She sounds so far away.
In this big house.

Order up!

We all go to the kitchen and Mommy takes my hand and I'm
afraid to look up. Afraid to see some other woman's face looking back down at me.

Too bad the drinking age is twenty-one, Mommy says. It's
doing wonders for me right now.
It smells funny, I say.
Yeah? she says, smiling. Well, it used to smell funny to me
too. Then I found out one day that's because there's fun in it.

Grandma has the pizzas on the kitchen table.

Time to eat, she says. Because no matter what's going on in your head, your heart, your life, it's always wise to remember to *eat*.

Mommy and Daddo sit down at the big table.
Then Evelyn eyes Grandma when she says,

Yes. No matter what. And if I fix enough of these drinks, maybe we can forgo wisdom altogether. I've been alone here so long I've forgotten what living dangerously is like.

32

Mommy and Daddo had so many glasses they made the bottle empty and then asked Evelyn for another one.

She got them one.

Grandma kept saying "They need it" and Evelyn kept saying "I can see that."

We all danced in the living room. Evelyn clapped for me and was excited that I like to dance. I helped her put on different records. She taught me how to use the record player and I even put one on without her asking me to. But they quickly changed it because they said Joni Mitchell is really good but not the right music for a party.

We had a party.

Daddo turned the music up so loud you could barely hear the rain against the windows.

He looked funny, dancing around the big room with his face unshaven like it is. And Mommy was sweating and she looked happy. Grandma's face got red and she said that always happens when she drinks. I could tell Evelyn was glad to have us. Her and Grandma sat on the couch while Mommy and Daddo and me kept dancing. Mommy and Daddo started dancing like me and then we were all dancing the same and Evelyn and Grandma were talking while the three of us acted funny.

Daddo was really drunk. I know that word of course. He taught it to me. I was happy to see him that way. I wanted that time in the big room to last forever. I wanted to dance with Mommy and Daddo forever.

I wasn't thinking about home or closets or hearts.

Then Daddo got too drunk, I think.

> *You know who you move like?* Daddo asked Mommy.
> *Ginger Rogers?* Mommy said.
> *Tonight you move like Other Mommy.*

Mommy's eyes got wide like she might get mad but then she laughed really hard and then Daddo went to her and held her hand and he laughed and she laughed and they laughed so hard they had their heads on each other's shoulders. Grandma said they were going to "pay for it" tomorrow, but Evelyn said it's the kind of money we're supposed to spend while we're still alive.

> *I'd offer her a drink right now,* Daddo said to Mommy.
> *Who?* Mommy asked.

But she knew what he was going to say.

> *Other Mommy. Other Mother!*
> *Russ!*
> *No, I mean it! If she came into the room right now, I'd say, Hey, sit down, relax. Stop haunting our kid.*

They really laughed at this one. It sounded almost like crying.

> *What kind of drink would you make her?* Mommy asked.
> *All right, you two,* Grandma said.

She was looking at me.

That's easy, Daddo said. *I'd get her a glass of Other Bourbon. And we'd all get Other Drunk.*

Then they laughed so hard, Mommy fell on her side on the couch.
Then Daddo said:

Hey, I'm Other Daddo!

And Mommy looked over to me like maybe they should stop.
But the music kept playing.
And Daddo said:

My God, it feels good to be brave again.

Grandma and Evelyn left the living room and I watched them vanish up the hall.

Ursula, Daddo said. *Ursula, who am I?*

Daddo bent backwards over the couch so his head was upside down.
I turned away.
I looked out the window at the rain.

More music, Bela, Mommy said.

I put on a new record. Then Mommy got up and turned the volume up really loud.
They danced and I sat on the couch and watched them.

It's a good life, Daddo said. *Of course it is.*

I watched them hugging. They started dancing slow.

I wanted them to stay that way forever.

I wanted the song to last forever and for a second it felt like it was going to.

But it didn't. And the record came to an end. And the big room got quiet again except for Mommy and Daddo breathing hard for all their dancing.

And now, now they're asleep on the beds in the yellow bedroom.

The music is off. There's no more music.

Grandma went to sleep in Evelyn's room.

Before we all came upstairs, I heard Grandma and Evelyn talking in the kitchen because Mommy and Daddo were at the butler pantry trying to open a bottle of something else.

I believe you, Ruth, Evelyn said. *But just because you're open to something doesn't mean you immediately accept it in full. The mind doesn't work that way.*

I didn't want to tell you, Grandma said. *Because I didn't want you to think we'd bring trouble here.*

You need to let them handle this, Evelyn said. *Whatever this is . . . this is theirs.*

This isn't marital trouble, Grandma said.

But isn't there some of that? Isn't there some of that too?

I think they knew I was listening because they stopped talking regular and then whispered and I went back to where Mommy and Daddo were by the pantry but they weren't there anymore.

I went to the living room but they weren't there either.

I ran back to the kitchen and ran into Daddo when he turned the corner and he said,

Bela, come on. You're supposed to stay with us.

Mommy and Daddo looked at each other like they do when they worry about me, but then Daddo said,

Tonight is a good night, dammit.

I think he was saying it to himself.

Might be time for bed, Grandma said.
No to that! Daddo said.

But we did go to bed.
Evelyn turned the record player off and Mommy and Daddo had a hard time getting up the steps and they were talking funny and the steps creaked as we went. Mommy nearly fell into one of the beds.

Bela, she said. *Come lie down with me.*

Her eyes were closed already and Daddo went face first onto the other bed on top of the blankets and started snoring right away.

Come on, Mommy said. *Bela . . . come . . . on . . .*

She was asleep fast and then I got into bed next to her with my clothes on too.
Grandma and Evelyn came to the door soon after and they said they'd be up the hall if I needed anything, but also to wake Mommy or Daddo if it was really important.
Grandma watched me a second before leaving. Like she wasn't sure if she should leave us alone.
This house is so big.
And it feels even bigger right now.
Because I have to pee.
Really bad.

I'm in bed next to Mommy. They're both asleep.
I try to wake Mommy, but she's not answering me. She's just breathing heavy and sleeping really deep. I think she's dreaming.
I get off the bed and shake Daddo's head and he mumbles something but he doesn't wake up.
I'm standing between the two beds. I'm looking at the door to this room and I'm thinking I'm going to have to go out into the hall on my own.

Maybe there's something in this room I can pee in, I say.

I look around the room for a can or something like how Daddo's friend Mark says he pees in a bucket when he goes camping or how like Kelvin told me he once had to go so bad he peed in a shoe.
I wish Kelvin were here. He would walk me to the bathroom. He would wait outside the bathroom and talk to me while I was peeing. Even if he was looking at his phone he would still tell me I was okay and the hall was clear and no one was out there.

The closet, I say.

I try to imitate Kelvin's voice when I talk. Like he's here, taking care of me while Mommy and Daddo drink at a party.
I go to the closet and I peek inside but it's really dark in there.

It's okay, I say like Kelvin would. Open it. Check for something to pee in, Bela.

I think of the time Daddo said, *What's more alive than being afraid?*
I open the closet door and then the inside is all lit up because the lamps are on by the beds.
There's no bucket or bowl.

There's nothing at all.
I think about peeing on the closet floor.
Would Evelyn get mad?

Go use the bathroom, I say in Kelvin's voice.

Be brave, I think.
I cross the room.
I'm standing between the two beds again.
I'm looking to the door again.

Go on, I say like Kelvin.

Then I go to the door and I step out into the dark hall and I say,

Grandma Ruth?

But my voice doesn't sound like Kelvin's to me anymore.
It sounds like me.

I have to pee, Grandma, I say.

Which room is she in?
I open our door a little more so more light comes out into the hall, but I still can't see the other doors very well.

I have to pee, guys, I say again.

I walk out and I can see a little better now. I see one door, two doors, then three doors, then four.
The fourth one is smaller than the other ones and I think it's the bathroom.
I think of Kelvin and Mommy and Daddo and Grandma Ruth. I think that Evelyn lives in this house all the time.

I run up the hall and the floor creaks under my feet and I open the door and I think, It's a closet!
I hurry up and find the light switch on the wall and I turn it on and it's not a closet.
It's the bathroom.
I think of Kelvin telling me I did a good job.
I step in and close the door.

Evelyn? I ask.

I think that's her behind the shower curtain. It looks like Evelyn is sitting in the bathtub behind the shower curtain.

Evelyn? I say again. I'm sorry. I had to pee.

She's not moving. She's just sitting there.
I'm far from the yellow room now.

Evelyn?

I go to the shower curtain and I look through the plastic and I see her looking back at me and I pull the curtain aside.
There's nobody in the bathtub.
The wall is painted black where I thought I saw Evelyn sitting.
There's no water.
No Evelyn.
I have to pee so bad.
I lift the seat and I pull down my pants and I have to try hard to get up onto the seat because it's higher than the one at home, higher than the potty in my bedroom bathroom at home.
But I do it.
And Kelvin would tell me good job.
And Daddo would tell me good job.
And Mommy would tell me I sat on someone else's lap.

O, I'm sorry, I say.

Because it feels like I sat on someone else's lap.
But I'm already peeing.
And I look down and I see other legs beneath my legs.
But I'm already peeing.
And there's dark hair on the legs.

No . . .

I move too fast and I fall to the bathroom floor and I turn back
and see Other Mommy sitting against the bathroom wall and
Other Mommy has no face.
Her face is in her hands.

Bela?

A voice from the hall.
Other Mommy stands up slowly and she looks so big and the
bathroom door opens.

Bela?

It's Evelyn at the bathroom door and I see her face change as she
starts to yell.
I hear her scream.

O my God! Evelyn yells. *O MY GOD!*

Other Mommy brings the face in her hands closer to me and
then other hands are grabbing me and I know it's Grandma and
I'm being pulled from the bathroom and Grandma and Evelyn
are yelling and Evelyn is so scared, she doesn't look like the same
person who welcomed us into her home.

LEAVE MY HOUSE ALL OF YOU RIGHT NOW!

Grandma pulls me into the hall and I won't look back to the bathroom because I hear Other Mommy stepping out into the hall and I think of her legs beneath mine and how she felt wet like a fish and I think of the dead fish at the grocery store behind glass and how they make rows like rows of long legs.

Bela, Grandma says.

She sounds so scared.

Bela, don't look.

She pulls me and it hurts and I can't stop feeling other legs beneath my own.
Evelyn screams again and I know Other Mommy is in the hall with her now and Grandma kicks open the door to the yellow room wider and she wakes Mommy up by yelling and Mommy and Daddo wake up and they look confused and their eyes are red and then Mommy looks to the bedroom door and her eyes get so big and I know Other Mommy has followed us to the room.

Ursula! Daddo yells. *Ursula look out!*

I see Other Mommy duck to enter the room and she spreads her arms wide and all of her rises up to the ceiling and bunches there like a flat balloon, all of her, none of it not her. Daddo and Mommy are moving so fast and Evelyn is screaming at us to leave and to *"take it with you! TAKE IT WITH YOU!"* and Grandma is pulling me again and then we're running under Other Mommy and out the bedroom door and into the dark hall and to the stairs and I almost fall and Daddo picks me up and carries me down and everybody's breathing so hard and Evelyn's mind is different now I think and the house is so dark and I look up to see Evelyn coming down the stairs too, her eyes so wide, she's so mad and so scared, and Daddo carries me to the foyer and I see the sun is up a little bit outside and I realize I woke up and had to pee and that I slept a little and I think that's good, I think Kelvin would say that's good.

Come on! Daddo yells back to Mommy and Grandma.

Other Mommy growls from the top of the steps and then we're running out the door, we're running outside and everybody is yelling and everybody is scared and Evelyn's mind is different now, I know it is, I know it is, I know.

Come on! Daddo yells.

He carries me down the front steps and I realize my pants are still down and I peed on myself and Grandma is telling Evelyn to come with us and Mommy is shaking and opening the car door and she's getting behind the wheel and Evelyn is saying she's not leaving her house, she's not leaving her own house. This is MY house, she yells, *this is my house you brought this to!*

Bela! Mommy yells. Bela, are you okay?

Daddo lowers me into the backseat and he gets in too and he shuts the door and Grandma is still telling Evelyn to come but Evelyn is only screaming on the front steps of her big house, her huge house that creaks all at once, she's only screaming.

Mom! Mommy yells, rolling down the window. *Get in the car now!*

Daddo is talking so fast like he doesn't know how to talk anymore.
Grandma gets in the front next to Mommy.

Home, Mommy says. We're going *home.*

Daddo is breathing so hard and he's holding me in his arms in the backseat.
Mommy pulls the car out of the driveway fast and we're all thrown to the side and I see Evelyn still on her porch, still yelling, still screaming at us to leave.
I didn't even notice it was raining. And I peed myself. And I still feel other legs beneath my own.
Mommy drives so fast and I think about the pee on my legs and Daddo is breathing so hard and Grandma is talking about Evelyn. She's worried about her friend, her friend whose mind is different now.

We can't leave her with that thing! Grandma says. *We can't leave her with that thing in her house!*

But Mommy isn't going to turn around.
And whenever anyone talks, they yell.

We're not leaving it with her, Mom, Mommy says. *For fuck's sake!* Don't you get it? It's going wherever we go. *It's going wherever we go!*
Home, Daddo says. Ursula, you're right. Home. We tried. We *tried.*

It's still mostly dark and it's raining and Mommy is driving too fast.

Slow down, Grandma says. *Ursula, slow down!*

But Mommy doesn't slow down.

Ursula, Grandma says. We still have a child with us. *Slow down!*

Daddo is mumbling to himself. Mommy looks at me in the rear-view mirror.
She slows down too fast. But at least she slowed down.

It was in its hands, Grandma says.

I worry that Grandma Ruth's mind is different now too.
Daddo and Grandma saw Other Mommy tonight.

It was in its God-forsaken *hands* . . .

The road ends and we have to stop at a light, but Mommy just goes through it because there's no other cars and because we need to get home because there's nowhere else for us to go.
We tried.

Holding its face like a towel, Grandma says.

Daddo holds me tight and mumbles.
Mommy drives.
We tried.
Our house is haunted and we tried to leave it.
We tried.
But it's us.
It's me.
We tried.
We tried to leave the haunted house.
But we're haunted.
It's us.
We tried.

33

Home.
We're back home.
Daddo says he's worried about the money for all the alarms being put in but he said he's more worried about not spending the same money. Mommy and Daddo are worried about work. Mommy called her work today and she sounded upset with them. I overheard Daddo lying to his. But when he came out of the den he said it didn't matter and that it couldn't matter. We need alarms, he said. We need *something*.
We all slept together on a mattress in the living room last night. They took turns staying awake. Nothing bad happened, but Mommy and Daddo look tired.
And so like Daddo said, We need something.
And there's a lot of alarms. And a lot of people putting them in.
In every room of the house.
There are cameras and beepers and so much stuff I don't know what all of it's called except someone told me there are "motion detectors" now.
And Mommy says "the dogs" are on their way.
Dogs.

Mommy told me twice these dogs "are not puppies" and they aren't really "pets," but I don't care.
Dogs!
She said they're "Cane Corso" dogs and they're "kid-friendly" but I can tell she's worried about that. Daddo said a trainer is coming with them and she'll tell us all we need to know about the dogs. Mommy said she didn't know the dogs' names but that they will have names and no I cannot name them.
Dogs!
In our house.

Bela, Daddo says, make sure you stick by Mommy or me at all times. *All times.*

Mommy isn't the only one who's seen Other Mommy now.

Is Grandma Ruth coming over soon? I ask Daddo.
I don't know, Daddo says. She needed a break. Love you, but don't ask again.

A black van pulls into our driveway. I watch it through the den window.
It says:

CHAPS SECURITY: KEEP CHAPS SECURE

I run to the front door. Daddo yells behind me,

Bela, what did I just say?

More alarm people get out of the van. No dogs. Neighbors are watching our house. They're in their windows and at their doors. Some older kids don't kick the ball that's on the grass between them.
Daddo comes up next to me. He still hasn't shaved.

We're the talk of the town, he says.

The alarm people from the van carry more stuff to the front door and set it on the front porch. They're putting alarms outside the house too.
Outside and inside.
Alarms.
And dogs.
Mommy comes up the hall.

Okay, she says. I was just making sure Bela was with you.

The people look at Mommy and Daddo funny when they say things like this.

I haven't let her out of my sight, Daddo says.

I feel like Mommy and Daddo have put alarms all over themselves too. Like they have alarms and dogs inside them.
I don't want my parents to get divorced.
Should I be happy they're making the house safer? Does that mean they're trying to protect what they already have?
I think of Other Mommy on her knees in my bedroom, back before Mommy ever saw her. She was talking about reincarnation like she always does and I asked her how long did she need my heart for?

O, I wouldn't stay long, she said. A life.

I asked her what did she mean? I thought she just wanted my heart?
Then she said,

I'll keep asking until you answer like a friend, Bela. And you must be a friend. Because if you're not, then why play nice?

Then she went back into the closet and the closet doors closed.
Now all the closets have alarms and motion sensors.
What will happen the next time she comes out?
And what face will she make when she realizes the entire house
is saying no?

34

The dogs are huge!
They're black and have white patches on their chests and the trainers who brought them are women and they say the dogs' names are Kami and Kamael. The dogs are both boys and are trained to guard our house.
One of the trainers says,

We provide bedding. They'll bring that in shortly. We also provide food for the first three days, but if you want their services longer than that, then it's on you. We've already trained them to accept the three of you.

Accept? Daddo says.

Yep. When we brought them in. It's the first thing we did. All done with scent. Your wife gave us an article of your clothing. Your daughter's too. So there is absolutely no way either of them will attack any of you. At the same time . . . if anybody else comes over, even a close friend of yours, you need to be aware that Kami and Kamael have no reason to trust them. And this is exactly what you want out of them. We'll show you how to scent-train them in case you do have someone coming by.

Where will they stay? Daddo asks. Are we supposed to play with them?

No play. Not like that. But like we talked about on the phone: you have a fenced-in backyard; let them out a few times a day. Make sure to let them out before you go to bed for the night so they can prowl the first floor alone.

We want them to guard the entire house, Mommy says.

The trainers look surprised.

Their job is to guard any way in, one of them says. There wouldn't be a reason to think anyone had gotten in with these two around.

And what about ghosts? Mommy asks.

I expect Daddo to say something when she says this, but he only waits for their answer like Mommy does.

What do you mean? One of the trainers asks.

What about something already in the house, is what I mean, Mommy says.

Nothing will get past them.

Kami or Kamael looks at me and I wave, and he looks back at the women who brought him.
No play.

The dogs aren't trained to go upstairs in the homes we bring them to, one of the trainers says.

However, the other trainer says, if they hear a struggle, anywhere in the house, anywhere at all, they'll come. Kami and Kamael are without question two of the best dogs we have.

All right, Daddo says. Well, I'm glad they're here.

I am too, I say.

The trainers look at me like they're wondering if something else is going on. Something they aren't used to.

That's good, Bela, Daddo says. But give them their space. Let them do what they're trained to do.

No treats, one of the trainers says. And absolutely no human food. Kami and Kamael are working. They know this. Okay?

Okay, I say.

Mommy breathes deep and looks to the cameras in the ceiling above us.

I hope we've done all we can, she says.

I'm sure you have, one of the trainers says. In fact, I don't think we've ever seen a house as fortified as what you've done to yours.

If I were you, the other says, I wouldn't fear a thing.

35

Mommy is on the phone with Grandma. She's telling her all about the alarms and the dogs. Daddo is at his desk, but he's moved the desk into the living room so that we're all together and never apart.

We're home.

Kind of. It's our house, yeah, but it feels different now.

Kami and Kamael sit by the front door. Last time I walked by, they were staring at the door like it could open any second. I think of the trainers saying the dogs are at work.

I get what they mean now.

And everything's fine over there? Mommy asks Grandma. If anything remotely unsettling happens, come here immediately. But remember we have these guard dogs for at least the next few days. We were taught how to get them to accept you. Yes. Accept.

Daddo is on his computer. He still hasn't shaved and he looks funny. Not exactly like Daddo.

And Mom, Mommy says, thanks for all you've done here.

Mommy ends the call.

> You hungry, Bela? she asks.
> Yeah.

We go into the kitchen while Daddo types. The TV is off. Mommy and Daddo don't turn the TV on. No music either. They say they don't want to confuse the dogs, but I don't think that would confuse the dogs. I think Mommy and Daddo just want to be able to hear the whole house.

> Mac and cheese? Mommy asks.
> Yeah.

I sit at the table. If I lean back in my chair, I can see Kami and Kamael down the hall, up at the front door. They're both sitting with their faces toward the door.
I wonder what they think about when they work.

> Can we keep them? I ask.
> No, Mommy says. Remember what they said: these aren't pets.
> How about we get one just like them? I say. Then we can feel safer forever.
> That's something to think about, Mommy says.

She puts the pot on the stove.

> Maybe if we got two they could be friends like Kami and Kamael are friends.
> Bela?
> What?
> Did you mean what you said about . . . her giving you a present?

One of the dogs growls by the front door.
Daddo stands up.
Mommy steps to the hall so she can see them too.

Ursula? Daddo says.

But Mommy is already walking toward the dogs.
Me and Daddo follow
Neither of the dogs turn to look at us.

Probably just a neighbor, Daddo says.
Maybe, Mommy says.

All three of us jump a little at the sound of water sizzling and
Mommy goes back to the kitchen because the pot is overflowing.
No one is at the door. We see a neighbor walk by on the sidewalk
through the window.
He looks at our house the whole time he passes.

Good dogs, Daddo says.

He doesn't pat their heads. He just watches them watching the
door. Until Mommy says the mac and cheese is ready and Daddo
says he'll have some, too, and then all three of us are eating at
Daddo's desk in the living room, surrounded by cameras and
alarms and bells and those two amazing dogs that growled at a
regular old person outside our house.
I don't say what I'm thinking. But maybe I should.
I'm thinking it's my fault Mommy and Daddo are so worried.
It's my fault the house has so many alarms now. It's my fault the
dogs can't be played with. It's my fault Grandma saw Other
Mommy at Evelyn's house.
If I'd just said yes, none of this would be happening.
I think.
But then . . . who would be me right now?

Would she?

And where would I go? Is where she comes from a worse place than this?

Mommy and Daddo look different now. I bet I do too.

I put my hand on my neck and feel my pulse. Does my heart beat louder than it used to?

Me and Other Mommy used to laugh. I heard her laugh once anyway. When Mommy and Daddo were out with Mark and Kelvin was watching me at home. I was in my bathroom and Kelvin was talking on the phone in my bedroom and then he started talking about reincarnation and how the best thing a person can do is to help their friend live. He said *come to life*. He said a good friend helps a friend *come to life*.

When I came out of the bathroom he wasn't in my bedroom. But Other Mommy was.

She was standing by the window with her back to me. I heard Kelvin outside, down in the yard, on his phone for real. Other Mommy laughed then, like Kelvin laughs. Then I realized she wasn't facing the window, she was facing me.

She said to me,

> *Do you hear that, Bela? I can sound just like everyone you know.*

And she laughed then in her real voice.

I don't wanna think about her real voice.

> You okay, Bela? Daddo asks.
>
> Why are you asking her that? Mommy asks. What is it, Bela?
>
> She's just staring off into space, Daddo says.
>
> Bela? Mommy says.

I'm worried it's my fault Mommy and Daddo have alarms on themselves now too. They have a framed picture in their bedroom upstairs of a woman dancing. One time Mommy told me the woman is "free." When Other Mommy was pretending to be Mommy, she said a lot of things about how I get in the way of her being free. Other Mommy has been right about a lot of things, hasn't she? She knew about the man who died. And she knows what things make me happy and sad. She knows how to make me feel safe and to make me feel scared.

Does Mommy really think I make her not free?

Bela? Mommy says.

She puts her hand to my head like she's checking for a fever.

I was just thinking, I say.
About what? Daddo asks.

I can hear every room, I think. Maybe it's because there are dog ears in the house now.

Kelvin, I say.
What about him? Mommy asks.
I miss him, I say.
Well, I'm sorry to report, Daddo says, you won't be seeing Kelvin for a while. We won't be seeing anybody.
Do you understand why that is? Mommy asks.

I do. Nobody can come near us because I keep saying no. And the more I say no, the more Other Mommy will meow like Pester outside my bedroom door, until she gets mean.

Yeah, I say.
But do you? Mommy says. For real? Tell me for real.
Yeah.

They go quiet for a minute. Then Daddo says,

Let's at least put a movie on silent. I can't sit here like this, just staring at the rest of the house.

He turns the TV on and turns the volume all the way down. After a minute he looks at his phone. I see it's the screen that shows him what the cameras see.
And so, even with the movie on, Daddo still stares at the rest of the house.

I'm sorry, I say.

But neither of them say anything back. Daddo is still looking at his phone and Mommy is staring at the screen and they both seem like they're in other places and while I don't want to be alone in the house I feel like I am.
I feel like I have the answer for all this. I feel like I can make it all go away.
But where would I go?

How long do you think we'd have to go without an incident for us to feel back to normal? Daddo asks.

Then he looks like he didn't really wanna say that out loud.
And Mommy doesn't answer him.
And it feels like we're stuck here. Just like this. Without knowing the answer to that.
Forever.

36

I gotta use the bathroom, I tell Daddo.

Mommy is asleep on the mattress they brought into the living room. I was, too, but then I woke up and saw Daddo sitting up on the couch, staring up the hall.

> What are you looking at? I ask him.
> Nothing, he says.
> I gotta use the bathroom, I say again.
> Okay, Daddo says.
> Will you take me?
> Yeah. Of course. Just . . . give me one second.

But he doesn't move. He just looks down the hall to where the dogs are sitting.
The dogs are looking up to the ceiling.

> Daddo? I ask.
> I don't know, Daddo says. It's pretty windy outside. Maybe the wind woke you.
> No, I have to pee.

Well, okay. But the house has been creaking.

I don't want him to say this. I don't want to go to the bathroom anymore. I want to pee right where I am.

No, no, Daddo says. In a totally normal way. I mean it. And these dogs . . . they're incredible. That's all. I promise.

He watches them a little more and then says,

Are you ready? I'll take you.

We both get up and Daddo turns on another lamp and he looks back to make sure it didn't wake Mommy. He watches her a little and I don't think he wants to leave her alone.

Okay, he says. Let's hurry.

We go up the hall and into the bathroom and Daddo turns on the light and he lifts the top potty cover and he tells me he'll wait outside.

No, I tell him. Just wait here.
Okay.

I sit and it's just a potty and Daddo faces the open door and he sticks his head out and looks both ways. Up and down the hall, up and down the hall.
My pee sounds like a whisper.
It sounds like someone is whispering below me.
I slide to the side and look down and make sure and I'm done and I clean up and get up and Daddo is still looking up and down the hall.

You good? he asks, without facing me.

I look in the mirror.
I look more like a big girl now. I really think I do.

Yeah.
Okay. Wash your hands. Hurry.

I wash my hands and the water sounds like a whisper, like someone is talking to me or about me in a whisper.
Then Daddo takes my hand and we go back down the hall to the
living room.
Mommy is sitting up on the mattress.

Was that you guys? she asks.
What did you hear? Daddo asks.

Mommy thinks about it.

I heard you two laughing in the kitchen.

We look to the kitchen.
There's the stove and the sink and the refrigerator and the rack
where we put the dishes to dry.

We need to remember that houses make sounds, Daddo
says. In a normal world, houses make sounds.
We gotta take shifts, Mommy says. I'll go first.
Okay, Daddo says. But if you have to use the bathroom,
wake me.
Okay.
Wanna put a movie on?
No.
No?
I don't wanna stare at one place. When you stare at one
place you create corners of the eyes.

I'm not sure what Mommy means, but Daddo nods like he does.

Let's sleep, Bela, Daddo says. So that Mommy can go to sleep after us.
Okay.

We get back on the mattress, back under the sheet and blanket.
One of the dogs is standing at the entrance to the living room.
I think it's Kamael.

Jesus, Mommy says. The dog scared the shit out of me.

Kamael looks to the kitchen for a second. Then he looks at us again.

Hi, I say.

But Kamael doesn't wag his tail or smile.
He just turns around and goes back up the hall to the front door.
We hear him sit down again.
After a while, Daddo says,

Maybe we'll both stay up a minute.
Okay, Mommy says.
But you try to sleep, Daddo says to me.
Okay.
Good night, Bela, Daddo says.
Good night.

37

There has to be someone who can help us, Daddo says. Not friends, family, police, priests . . . I don't mean any of them. We just can't . . . be stuck. It's literally impossible. Nobody is ever just stuck. You hurt yourself, you go to a doctor. You need money, a car, you get a loan. I don't know. We can't be stuck.

Everything is so piqued, Mommy says. We gotta talk about something else.

But Daddo's been talking like this for a long time.
He's at his desk in the living room. He's looking up people he thinks could help us. And he keeps looking at the cameras on his phone. I don't like looking at them. I don't like how small my bedroom looks on the camera. And how empty.
Mommy's on her phone, texting with Grandma. Grandma said she's gonna come over soon. But she said that a while ago. I worry she was changed at Evelyn's house. I'm so worried Grandma was changed.

Like, how about this couple, Daddo says. From Samhattan. They say they specialize in . . .

He looks over at me like he doesn't wanna say what he was going to say.

. . . in this kind of thing, he says.
I don't believe them, Mommy says.
What? Just by the pic?
I don't believe them.
Well, we gotta believe *someone*.

Daddo saw Other Mommy too.
They're all changed, I think.

Are you tired, Bela? Mommy asks. Russ, maybe we should go for a walk.

Daddo looks up like he could see the sky through the ceiling.

In fact, he says, there's another couple from Samhattan that says they specialize in the same thing. And in their description . . . they say that first couple is bogus.

He looks upset.
I am tired. I'm curled up on a blanket on the couch while Daddo searches for help online. I think of Grandma at her house sleeping all alone, the closet in her bedroom opening.

All I can find are people who investigate, Daddo says. But does that mean they also exterminate?

The word sits in the room, it feels like.
Like Daddo tossed a black ball in the air.
All the lights are on. Most will be on all night.

My God, he says. Each one is worse than the last.

That's fine, Mommy says. Then I don't want them in our house.

All right, but someone's gotta come, Daddo says. We need—

I know what we need, thank you, Mommy says.

I'm touching my neck. I can feel my pulse. My heart.

What would it feel like if I say yes?

One time I told Other Mommy I was scared of what would happen and she didn't smile or make a mean face, she just stared at me for a long time like she was hungry.

I mean, this guy from downstate is *insane,* Daddo says. Look at him, Urs. Come here.

Russ, I don't wanna think about this right now.

Okay, but—

Please. Stop.

Okay, but . . . just look. Looks like a Satanist. Looks serious.

Bela, Mommy says. Sleep if you need to. Rest is more important right now than ever.

I close my eyes. But I don't sleep. Not yet.

I don't even know if I'm searching for the right thing, Daddo says. Are there differences?

I need you to stop talking about it, Mommy says. I need to think clearly and everything you're saying is making me feel crazier.

Is she still awake? Daddo asks.

I am.

I don't know. Mommy says. I think so.

I am.

It's not even the money, Daddo says. But that's outrageous too. I just think, if we had a bunch of people here, like when Chaps Security was installing the alarms . . .

It showed itself at the party, Mommy says.

But at least we weren't alone with it when it did.

I have dreams, Russ, Mommy says. I feel trapped. I have an entire life to live and instead I'm stuck in this house. This house of all houses only because it doesn't matter where we go, this house follows us there. It's insane and I want it to be over.

I'm working on it. What are you doing?

Are you seriously implying there's a *right* way to react to this?

There's gotta be a wrong way.

Russ.

Leave if you wanna. Go for a walk. A drive.

I can't leave Bela. And that means I can't leave whatever the fuck this is. It's like I didn't read the fine print on the motherhood manual where it said, *You might have to stay home for a haunting.* I feel tethered, Russ.

Yeah, well, that's not the nicest thing to say to the person you're tethered to.

And even if I did go out tonight, Mommy says. Let's say I *could* go out tonight: What the hell would I do? What would I say? When someone asks me how I'm doing, how we're doing, what the hell would I say? O, Marsha! We're fine. Things are really great. Bela starts school soon and Russ is working his tail off and I'm getting closer and closer to all my dreams.

Maybe if you said all that, it would come true. I don't know.

There is a life I want to live, Mommy says. There *is* a life I want to be living instead of being stuck in the living room of our own house. For hell's sake, Russ, I was at my wits' end *before* all this. And now?

That one guy is starting to look good now, Daddo says.

What? Mommy says. Who?

The man in all-black camo or whatever, Daddo says. He's starting to look good compared to some of these other people.

The house creaks. But I'm falling asleep to the sound of Mommy and Daddo. Their voices are like a movie. They go back and forth, back and forth, and the creaking sounds like the lid of a box, closing over me, tucking me into the dark.
I sleep.
And I wake.
In my bedroom.
In my bed.
In the dark.

Mommy?

I sit up and look for her.
We're not sleeping upstairs anymore. That's the rule.
Where are they?

Daddo? Mommy?

Do I hear them downstairs, still talking? I listen close. But it's hard to tell.

Daddo? Mommy?
Hey, Bela.

I almost scream at the voice. The closet is so dark, I can't tell if it's open or closed.

Kelvin? I say.

Because it was his voice.

Yeah, hey, Bela. How you doing?

I hear him but I don't see him.

Where are you?
Right here.

I see his eyes. If white-blue were a color, his eyes would be white-blue.

Your mom and dad said you needed a friend, Kelvin says.
They did?

But I know they did. They've been talking about that.

Yeah, Kelvin says. They're having a party downstairs. Can you hear the party, Bela?

I think I can. Yes. Voices. Yes. And music too. But I've never heard Mommy or Daddo play music like this before.

They called me up, Kelvin says. Told me to come watch you. They really want you to have a friend.
How did I get up here? We're not supposed to be up here.
I carried you, Kelvin says. And it's your bedroom. Of course you're allowed to be in your bedroom. If you're not allowed, no one is.

It sounds like a party downstairs. But far away. Like it's two downstairs.
Kelvin's eyes are white-blue in the dark by the closet.

Mind if I sit with you? he asks.
No, I say.

I'm sitting up in bed. There's no blanket on me. I look to the hall
and there's no light. No nightlight. Only the moon coming
through my bedroom window.

Thanks, Kelvin says.

His eyes get bigger for a second, like he's coming toward me
really fast. Then I see him, Kelvin, coming out of the dark. He
sits on the side of my bed.

You guys have been out on the road for a while, he says.
Yeah.
But you came back home.
Yeah.
That's nice. That's where you should be. Do you think your
mom and dad are doing well, Bela?

It sounds like a wave goes over the voices and the music downstairs.

I don't know.
But you do, Kelvin says.

Daddo was talking about how other people in the house would
make him feel better. Like the Chaps Security people did. Is that
why they're having a party?
Kelvin reaches out like he's going to put his hand on mine but he
just touches the bed.

It's okay to admit they're not doing too hot, he says.
No, they're not doing too hot.
No. But I think I know how to help with that.
You do?
Mm-hm.

Another wave, like all their voices and the music slows down and then goes fast again.

I'm the person your parents call to help with things, Kelvin says. And so listen to me closely when I tell you how.
Okay.
Okay.

He gets up and steps into the darkness where my dresser is.

If I were you, he says, I would be able to fix this.
What do you mean?
Well, I mean I know more about these things than you do, Bela.
Yeah.
Yeah. And so if I were you, even for a day, if we switched places, I could say all sorts of things that would make your mom and dad love each other again.
They do love each other.

The voices downstairs get louder. Whose voices are those?

No, they don't. Not right now. But they *could*. If you said and did the right things to make it that way.
What should I say?

His eyes blink white-blue by the dresser.

It's too much to teach you, he says. But I could do it for you.
Will you?
Yes. But you're going to have to let me be you. Just for one day.

I hear a woman crying downstairs. Is that Mommy's cry?

Who would I be? I ask.

His eyes get bright and the shape of them looks upset.

You would be you, Bela, Kelvin says. And I would be you,
just for one day. Should we try it?
I think I should go downstairs.
They told me to make sure you didn't do that.
Why?
They want you to rest. And they think you need time with
a friend.
Okay.

I'm thinking of the dogs. How Mommy and Daddo would've
had to get the dogs to "accept" all those voices downstairs.

Are the dogs outside?
Look for yourself.

I swing my legs over the side of the bed and the carpet is cold. I
walk to the window but it shows me mostly the side of the house.
I can barely see the fence for our backyard.

They're right there, Kelvin says.

I back up at the sound of his voice because he's right next to me,
his chin close to my shoulder. He points to the glass and his finger is dark with hair.

You see them?

I lean forward until my head is touching the window and I'm
suddenly scared of falling through the glass.
When I turn to look at him, I see his face move in the moonlight
so that it looks like Kelvin again.

Yeah, I say.
Did you really see them?
I think so.
So what do you think, Bela?

He's standing close to me. My back is to the window.

About the party?
No. About letting me be you. Will you let me in?

I hear a growl and at first I think it's Kelvin. I think he's going to jump at me.
But it's the dogs. I know it is. Down at the foot of the stairs by the front door.

I wanna go down to the party first, I say.

Kelvin just stares at me. He's not moving. I can't tell what part of me he's looking at. It's like he's looking at all of me.
I step to the side to get around him and he's still just staring where I was. Like I'm still there.

I'll be right back up, I say.
Bela, he says.

His voice is lower now.

Bela, I can keep your parents together.
Thanks, I say.

I'm backing away from him. He's still standing by the window.
I think his clothes only cover the front of him. I think the back of him is crouching in the dark.
He turns my way.
He steps toward me.

And I hurry out of my bedroom and into the hall. From the top
of the stairs I see the dogs down at the bottom. The voices and
the music get so loud, then get quieter again.
Kelvin comes out of my bedroom. I hear him behind me.
I hurry down the steps. I hold on to the railing as I go.
Kami and Kamael are growling, looking at the top of the stairs.
I pass them, get to the bottom, and hurry down the hall.
There is no music.
No voices.
And no light either.

Mommy, I say. *Daddo*.

I pass the dark bathroom and I run into the living room.
The dogs bark behind me.
Someone moves in the dark living room.

What's going on? Daddo says.

Then his face lights up from his phone.
He turns on the flashlight and shines it on me.

Bela? What's happening.
Let's hurry, I say. Let's get outside.

The stairs creak.
The dogs bark.

Russ?

Mommy's awake now too.

What's happening? Mommy says.

She's up and she turns on the light.

Daddo is looking at his phone and his eyes get wider.

> Kelvin was upstairs, I say. He carried me up there.
> What? Daddo says.
> O my God, Mommy says.

She grabs my wrist. Leads me toward the back door.

> Russ, she says. *Russ,* now.

The dogs bark.
The three of us hurry to the back deck door.
Daddo is still looking at his phone.

> The footage, he says.

But he doesn't say any more.

> Why did you turn off the lights? Mommy asks him.
> I didn't. Why did you fall asleep?

She doesn't answer. She pulls me outside and then all three of us
are out there and Daddo closes the door and we're backing up to
the grass.
Daddo has his phone to his ear.

> Hey, Kelvin, he says.

Daddo called Kelvin.

> Hey, yeah, Daddo says into his phone. Well, I don't know
actually. Are you in our house right now?

Mommy puts me behind her legs. Puts herself between me and
the house.

We're all looking at every window at once.

It's a weird question, Daddo says. I understand. And I didn't think you were. Thanks, Kelvin.

He ends the call.

What are you doing? Mommy asks him.
I don't know. I think I was hoping.
Russ, Mommy says. You're right. I'm sorry. You have to get someone here. Now. Anyone. It doesn't matter.
I know, Daddo says. I know.

He looks through his phone.

Front yard, Mommy says. Come on.

She leads me to the backyard fence and we exit together. Daddo follows, still searching his phone.
We walk along the side of the house and I look up to my bedroom window.
I don't see Kelvin. But I think I see where my head was touching the glass.
He was so close to me.
Now Daddo's calling someone.

We're getting someone, Mommy says to me. Someone will come.

We're in the front yard now.
I think of Kelvin saying he could help Mommy and Daddo.

Hello? Daddo says.

He sounds surprised.

I'm sorry I'm calling so late, he says. O, are you? A night owl? Yes, I guess we've been keeping odd hours ourselves lately. Listen, yes. No, we're not religious. But we're not sure what we believe in right now and anyway that doesn't matter. The only thing we care about is getting rid of it. Yes. Absolute proof. I'll tell you everything. Can you help? Really? You're up for that talk right now? Well . . .

Daddo looks to Mommy and me.

Go ahead, Mommy says. Why waste one minute more?

We back up all the way into the empty street. Mommy still keeps me behind her legs. Putting herself between me and the house.

All right, Daddo says into the phone. All right. Here's what's happened so far . . .

38

His name is Brian and he's big. Bigger than Daddo.

He has no hair on top and he wears all black and even a pair of black gloves. Mommy said he looks "very serious." She said that to him. He didn't say anything back. He just looked down the hall and up the stairs and he said,

I'm gonna need a tour.

And so we gave him one. All of us together, because we can't be alone right now. Not even when the sun is up and outside on the lawn. We showed him my bedroom and the closet and the bathroom. We showed him Mommy and Daddo's room. He eyed the photo of the dancing woman on their wall for a while. We even showed him the linen closets, places I used to think would be too small for her to hide.

Kami and Kamael have "accepted" him because Mommy and Daddo did what the trainers said to do. I think they used his gloves. Now we're in the backyard. The sun is out. It makes Brian's black clothes look ever blacker.

He's staring at the house while he talks.

I asked if you're religious because I won't work with people who are. You spend half the event disagreeing with the client and trying to convince them of something the world hasn't convinced them of and so there's no point in trying.

The event, Mommy says.

That's what it'll be, Brian says.

He has a flashlight on his belt. A camera. Other things too.

What do you think it is? Daddo asks.

I don't care what it is, Brian says. It's just got to go. I won't call it a ghost or a demon. I don't give them names. It's a pest, is what it is. A very big pest.

He looks down at me and he's so big it's like he's a building in our backyard.

What's your plan? Mommy asks.

Don't know yet, he says.

We need it gone now, Mommy says.

Doesn't work that way. I was told its story last night. I'm seeing your house for the first time right now. I'm just meeting you people as we speak. So . . . I don't know yet.

Mommy looks to Daddo like she's upset and Daddo says,

Well, the sooner the better. We're . . . we're losing our minds here.

Brian takes his flashlight from his belt and says,

Mind if I take a look around the house alone?

Is that something you need to do? Daddo asks.

It's something I'd like to do.

Well, all right then.

And the dogs? Brian asks. Can you bring the dogs outside?

Why? Mommy asks.

I want to go through the house, like I said, alone.

Mommy starts to say something, and Daddo says,

Sure. I'll get the dogs.

Daddo goes to the back deck door and Brian says,

The camera footage means nothing to me.

Are you suggesting we're lying to you? Mommy says.

Did I say that? I'll know in person and in person only if this is the real thing.

It's the real thing. The fact you're debating that worries me greatly.

Ma'am, like I said, I just got here.

Mommy stares at him, quiet. Then she takes my hand as Daddo brings the dogs outside.

Brian doesn't say anything else. He just goes into the house alone.

He's going to steal something, Mommy says.

Maybe, Daddo says.

We're literally letting a stranger go through our home alone.

Yeah, he might steal something, Daddo says.

Then they both go quiet and Daddo reaches down and pats me on my head.

We watch the house.

We can see Brian's light going through the rooms where the lights are off.

>   It feels so hopeless, Mommy says.
>   Don't say that, Daddo says. Please.

But he sounds tired.

>   What can he possibly do? Mommy says.
>   This is us trying, Daddo says. We're trying.

Mommy steps closer to the fence and looks out toward the street the way people do when they're thinking heavy.
Daddo goes to follow her.
I watch the light moving around the house.
He's in my bedroom now.
The light stops moving. Like he's only looking at one thing now.
I think of Kelvin up there, last night.
I think of him saying he could make Mommy and Daddo happy.

>   This is us trying, Daddo says again to himself.

He tries to hug Mommy, but she steps away from him.
The light starts moving again in my bedroom.
Then it's out in the hall I think.
The dogs sit together on the grass, watching the house. They're still working.
Brian comes out the deck door.

>   All right, Brian says to Mommy and Daddo. And you definitely saw it?
>   Jesus, Mommy says.

Yeah, Daddo says. And not just us. Ursula's mom, friends.
A number of people have seen it now.

All right, Brian says. I think I know what to do.

What? I ask.

Brian faces our house and puts his hands on his belt and says,

I'm going to trick it.

39

Brian is in the dining room. He has a bunch of "gear" on the table in there. That's what Daddo calls it.

Mommy's worried he has a gun. She's worried he's a "scam."

Daddo asked him if he wanted to see what the cameras see, but Brian told him he doesn't "trust video of anything." Mommy said he should want to see it because he should want to have "every tool at his disposal." She doesn't like him. But Daddo hopes he can do something.

They whisper-argue about it in the living room. But sometimes they raise their voices.

I think of Kelvin upstairs, saying he can fix it.

He's just sitting there eating, Mommy whispers. *He's not* doing *anything.*

We don't know that, Daddo says. *Give him a chance.*

It's a waste of time.

Well, we called someone, didn't we?

Call someone else.

Hey, Ursula. At this point in time, he's literally the only other human being who is helping us in any way.

But this isn't true. Mommy's phone dings. It's a text from Grandma.

She's here, she says.

We all get up and head up the hall to the front door. As we pass the dining room, I see Brian sitting at the table. He's eating a bag of chips.
We head outside. The dogs look past us, to see who's here.
Always working.
Grandma Ruth gets out of her car. She's wearing her red flannel shirt and she looks better than the last time I saw her. Still, she looks up at the house like it's haunted.

You trust this man? she asks Daddo.
No, Daddo says.
Not at all, Mommy says.
But what can we say, Ruth? Daddo says. We're desperate.

Grandma takes my hand. She saw Other Mommy at Evelyn's too.

And you? she asks. How are you doing, Bela?
I hope Brian knows what to do, I say.
Yes, Grandma says. That's what we all want.

Then she says to Mommy and Daddo,

Can we talk alone for a minute?
About what? Daddo asks.
About what, Mom? Mommy asks.
Alone? Grandma Ruth says.
We're not leaving Bela alone, Mommy says.
I just mean up the sidewalk, Grandma says.

They walk with her up the sidewalk and I stay on the front lawn.

I step to the side of the house and I can see Brian through the window. He's still just eating like Mommy said.

Then he pauses and looks up to the ceiling.

Mommy is arguing with Daddo, and Grandma is trying to calm them down.

Kami and Kamael are at the front door.

Brian still looks up.

I look up too. To my bedroom window.

Brian gets up and he takes his flashlight from his belt and he leaves the dining room.

I climb the porch steps and through the brick windows I see him go upstairs.

I cup my eyes against the glass. I can see up the stairs. I can see down the hall. I can see Daddo's desk in the living room.

I look up the street.

Grandma is doing most of the talking now. She's got a hand on each of their shoulders.

I cup my eyes against the window again and Brian's face is looking back at me.

I almost shout, he scared me so bad.

But he's not looking at me. He's just standing by the dogs, looking down the hall, looking up the stairs.

He has something in his hand. I think it's a tape recorder.

He puts it close to his ear and he puts one foot on the first step and he looks up the stairs like he might go up again.

But he goes into the dining room instead and sits at the table again instead.

Mommy grabs me hard by the arm.

Ow!

What did we say? Mommy says. Do *not* go close to this house without us. Don't go anywhere without us!

A neighbor lady sees this from the sidewalk. She looks worried about us.

Grandma comes to the porch.

You won't get any sympathy from me, she says. Your mom's right.

Did you bring the clothing I told you to bring? Daddo asks Grandma.

Yep.

She takes off her flannel shirt. She's wearing a yellow T-shirt underneath that says:

WORLD'S TOUGHEST GRANDMOTHER

She hands Daddo the flannel.

I'll introduce you to the dogs with this first. Then you'll meet the guy. You can tell me how dumb I was for calling him.

Daddo lets the dogs smell Grandma's flannel, and he keeps saying, *friend*. I think of Kelvin upstairs and I think how friends would do anything for friends.

Once we're all inside, Daddo starts to introduce Grandma to Brian, but Brian raises a hand to say not right now.

He has the tape recorder up to his ear and he's nodding along to what he hears.

Did you get something on tape? Daddo says.

What would it matter? Mommy says. The last thing we need is proof.

I think normally she'd walk away after saying that. I think normally she'd head up the hall into the kitchen, angry.

But she stays next to us. Because, except for Brian, none of us want to be alone in this house.

40

Mommy is on Daddo's computer. I think she's looking for other help.

Grandma went home when the sun went down.

It's dark out now.

But the lights are on in the house.

Brian wanted to turn them off, but Mommy and him had an argument about it. Brian kept saying he had to be allowed to "do his job" or else they would have "an excuse" not to pay him and Mommy said she'd give him all the money in the world if he did his job but she said "no way in hell" about turning off the lights.

He's sleeping at the dining-room table. I know because Daddo and I went to the front door when we heard the dogs growling at something outside. A neighbor couple was walking by and I peeked into the dining room and saw Brian asleep.

Now I'm quiet on the couch because Daddo is asleep too.

Bela, Mommy says. Come sit with me.

I do.

We'll wake your daddo when we get tired, she says.

She already told me we can't all be asleep with this man in our house. She said she was "worried enough already."

It's not his fault, Mommy says. It's not your daddo's fault he's making poor decisions. We're tired. We're scared. Nobody should have to go through something like this. I'm proud of you, Bela.

Me?

O, man. Yes. Do you have any idea how strong you are? Ninety-nine out of a hundred kids your age would've fallen to pieces by now. But you . . . you're still with us. You're keeping it together as much as we are. And maybe that's not saying much. I don't know.

Did you find someone else to come help? I ask.

She looks at the computer.

No.

Up the hall, the dogs sit facing the door.

Your daddo's always snored, Mommy says. Even when we first met. The first time I ever slept over at his dorm he was so loud and I was like, Nope, I'm not dating a guy this loud when he's unconscious.

I smile. I like when Mommy talks about when she and Daddo first met.

I tried to stop him, Mommy says. I plugged his nose. But he just woke up and looked at me like I was crazy. I tried putting a pillow like a wall between us. I even tried putting the pillow over my ears. But . . . there was no escaping it.

I look at the computer and see the word: EXORCISM

Back in college, Mommy says, there were a lot of kids interested in ghosts and stuff. It's the kind of thing you get into in college for whatever dumb reason. There was one night your daddo and I went to a lecture at Madison Hall. It was a guy who claimed to be an expert. He talked about a lot of stuff and your daddo liked him, but I walked out of there rolling my eyes. I somehow feel vindicated about that right now. Not sure why.

Daddo snores.

Before you were born, Mommy says, we went camping. And he was so loud I heard people in another tent asking each other if there was an animal outside.

I laugh.

They were like "Go check!" Mommy says. They unzipped the tent and actually checked. I remember feeling so secure. Because this loud man was mine now. That's hard to explain, maybe. But I was glad for it then.

On the screen, beneath that other word: DEMON

He's always been like this, your daddo. He's always been optimistic. Something happens, he says okay we'll fix it. Something really bad happens he says okay we'll get through it. It started to drive me crazy. The way he'd just pop back up after we'd get knocked down. It happened all the time. From things as big as worrying about a house payment to things as small as someone stealing your parking space. Russ would say, "It'll be a nice walk if we park farther away." But thing is . . . and this is something he's never gotten to understand . . . thing is, sometimes it's nice to just *vent*. Sometimes when you complain, it's not because you want to be told how to fix it. You just wanna say it sucks. Because sometimes it just sucks.

Mommy is talking to me, yes, but it feels like she's also talking to herself.
She looks up the hall to the dogs. Then down to Daddo. Daddo has a full beard now.

I think maybe it's our biggest difference, Mommy says. That thing. Some people find strength in complaining. And I don't mean doing it all day. But you ever notice how most old people are also real nit-picky? Your grandma's not that old. I mean *really* old people. The ones who make it to a hundred and sit on their porches and point out all that's wrong with the world. A lot of them got that far on spite. Your daddo . . . he has none.

I think of Kelvin, of Other Mommy, saying she could fix them.

No edge, Mommy says. And sometimes we wanna cut ourselves on our partners. Sometimes we wanna feel that sting together. That's hard to explain. But there's a lot of people in this world who make their way to the underbelly of society not because they're failures but because there's some truth to be found down there. I'm not saying only darkness is truth. And I'm not saying all truth is darkness. But your daddo . . . he doesn't have a single light turned off in his body. There isn't one shadowy hallway inside him. Not one corner for something to hide. No closets.

She clicks out of one screen and goes to another and it's a picture of a bunch of people standing in a foggy basement, looking at the camera. Mommy goes to a different site.

'But I have closets, she says. I do. I love your daddo more than you'll ever know, but sometimes I wonder if you're supposed to marry someone with a similar floor plan.

She's talking the way she does when she thinks I'm asleep. But I'm sitting right next to her.
I think we're all changed by Other Mommy.

Maybe I'm not saying it right, Mommy says. Then again, what are you going to remember about this in a year, in five, in thirty?

She takes my hand.

Your daddo is a great man.
I love Daddo.
I know you do.

On the computer screen is a list of names. I don't understand them. They're written how words were written thousands of years ago I think.

Bela, Mommy says, why are the dogs looking in the dining room?

I look up the hall.
Both dogs are looking into the dining room.
Mommy stands up. I follow her out of the living room and into the hall. She walks quiet on purpose.

Brian? she says, quiet.

But when we get to the dining-room entrance, we see he's standing up by his chair, looking somewhere we can't yet see.
He puts a finger to his lips and says,

Shhhh.

He points to where we can't see.
Mommy steps into the room, looks where he's looking.

O God, she says. Bela, don't—

But I'm already in the room too.
I see her too.
Other Mommy is on her knees in the dining room.
Brian steps toward her.

Nobody move, he says.

Other Mommy just stares at him. Her eyes are at the top of her head.
I think of the list of names on Daddo's computer.

Russ, Mommy says.

But not loud enough for Daddo to wake up in the other room.

Nobody talk, Brian says.

He gets closer to Other Mommy.
I can hear her breathing. I see her knees don't touch the ground.

Ursula, Daddo says.

He did hear her. He's with us now. In the dining room.

O my God, Brian whispers. O my *God*.

Other Mommy's mouth starts to droop toward the floor.

Brian is too close.

Get away from her! I say.
What are you doing? Daddo yells at him.

But Brian doesn't seem to hear him.
He reaches out with a hand. He wants to touch her.
Other Mommy's mouth stretches all the way down to the carpet.

Bela, Mommy says. Get back. Get back right—

Other Mommy yells.
And her voice is loud as an earthquake.
And wind fills the dining room.
And I'm thrown back to the carpet and Mommy's hair is wild and Brian floats in the wind from Other Mommy.
The wind doesn't stop.
The dogs are barking, the dogs are so loud.

Bela! Daddo yells.

He reaches for me, but the wind shoves him back.
Other Mommy's mouth is so big. Big as the doorway.
She keeps yelling.
It doesn't sound like a voice anymore.
It sounds like it's every sound at once, like her yell has always been in this house.

Bela!

Daddo is still reaching for me. But I'm flattened to the carpet just like Mommy is flattened to the wall behind me.
Brian reaches forward, still trying to touch Other Mommy.

He's smiling. He looks so happy.
He reaches.
His fingertip touches her face.

Take my hand! Daddo yells to him.

He wants to pull Brian out of the dining room.
Mommy is yelling at Daddo to stay away from Other Mommy.

Take my hand! Daddo yells again.

But Brian doesn't take it. And Daddo reaches farther . . .
Farther . . .
Farther . . .

Daddo! I yell.

Other Mommy's mouth gets even wider, wider . . .

Bela, look out! Mommy yells.

But then Brian flies forward against the wall and falls to the floor.
I can sit up. I sit up.
The wind's stopped.
Other Mommy's voice is gone.
And so is Other Mommy.

O my God, Bela, Mommy says.

She comes to me. She helps me up. She pulls me out of the dining room.
The dogs are at the foot of the stairs, looking up.

Are you okay? Daddo asks Brian.

But Brian is already gathering his stuff from the dining-room table.

> We warned you, Daddo says. Wait, what are you doing? Come on, you can't leave.

Brian is moving fast. He seems so happy.

> I've seen one, he says.
> Yeah, Daddo says. We told you—
> Where are you going? Mommy asks Brian.
> I've seen one, Brian says again.

He's heading for the front door now.

> Hey, Daddo says. Whoa. You said you had a plan.
> I've seen one! Brian says again.

At the door he turns to look at Daddo and he says,

> It's all I've ever wanted. To *see* one.
> You son of a bitch, Mommy says.

Brian opens the door and hurries outside and Mommy chases after him.
Then me and Daddo do too.
Brian is walking fast to his car.

> You *motherfucker!* Mommy yells.

Brian is still smiling.

> You don't get it, he says as he puts his stuff in his car. This is so much bigger than you. I saw it, with my own eyes. Not on video. I touched it!

What's going on? Daddo says. You can't be serious.

He *used* us, Mommy says. Then, to him: You *used* us, you piece of shit.

Is that really what happened? Daddo asks Brian. You're really leaving us?

But Brian isn't waiting. He opens the driver's door.

Hey, he says. I don't really give a shit what you think. I've been doing this for a long time, and tonight . . . I saw one.

Daddo swings a fist at him but misses and Brian swings back and hits Daddo in the face.
Mommy runs at Brian but he ducks into his car.
He slams his door closed.
Mommy kicks the door and he starts the car and Mommy kicks the door again and Brian drives away and he's smiling as he leaves us.
Daddo is holding his face, lying in the street.
Mommy is yelling at Brian's car as it leaves.

FUCK YOU!

Her hands are fists.

YOU FUCKING FUCK!

Lights go on in some homes.
Some neighbors are looking out their windows.
Brian is gone.

Why did he leave? I ask.

But Mommy goes to Daddo and touches his face and Daddo winces.

We have to do it ourselves, Daddo says.
I know, Mommy says.
We have to get rid of it ourselves, Daddo says.
I know, Mommy says.

They're both shaking. Daddo gets up and then sits down on the curb and Mommy bends enough to check how bad his face is hurt.

Why didn't he help us? I ask.
He was never going to help us, Mommy says.

She's so mad. *So* mad.
I look back to the house.
I think of Other Mommy's mouth stretching to the carpet.
I think of the cold wind.

How? I ask. How are we gonna do it ourselves?

I'm crying now.

It doesn't matter, Daddo says. That's all there is to it. We have to.

A neighbor comes out of his house and crosses the street to us.

Are you all okay? he asks.
No, Mommy says.
Do you want me to call the police?
No, Daddo says. No police. We have to do it ourselves.

The dogs are at the front door. They're looking out at us.

Are you sure? the neighbor says.
Yes, Mommy and Daddo say at the same time.

Then they bring their foreheads together so that they're touching and their eyes are close together and they nod together, like that, like they're one person out here on the curb, one person making one big decision.

And blood drips from Daddo's nose.

And tears roll down Mommy's face.

But they look like they believe they're making the right decision.

And the neighbor slowly walks away.

And Mommy and Daddo nod like that, like they're talking without talking, through their touching foreheads, making a big decision, unaware the neighbor is leaving, maybe not really aware he was ever there at all.

41

They think I'm sleeping. But I don't know if that matters to them anymore. I think they'd talk this way no matter what now.

We need to be strong, Russ. Mommy says. We need to find something inside us we haven't ever even looked for before. You remember at State when we used to sit up all night in my room? We'd talk about taking on the world like there was nothing that could stop us? We had so *much* nerve then. So much. God, Russ, if we could've bottled that. But, thing is, I think living it once, believing it once, *is* bottling it. I think we did bottle it and we've had it in us this whole time. Only, we haven't really needed to use it. The things we thought were hard before . . . they weren't. This is hard. *This.*

I know, Daddo says. I agree. I'm with you one hundred percent. And I'm ready to do it. Tonight if we have to. We can't go on like this. It's unbearable. Look, we know it can be touched.

Yes.

He touched it.

Right.

And so . . .

Daddo whispers now:

> . . . *the next time we see it, we have to go at it.*
> Yes.

They're facing each other in two chairs near the couch. I'm on the couch. I have my eyes open a little bit. Their faces are close and a movie is on with some volume. I think they don't want Other Mommy to hear.

> How do we make sure we see it again? Daddo asks.
> Are you kidding? It's the only thing we can count on right now.
> But like . . . should we . . .

They look to me at the same time and I close my eyes tight.

> No, Mommy says. That's crazy. We can't do that.
> Right, Daddo says. We can't do that.
> What about weapons? Mommy says.
> Knives, Daddo whispers. We have a lot of those. Do we need a gun?
> But it can look like other people. We have to be sure we don't hurt someone else.
> O God . . .
> Right, Mommy says.
> We gotta get close.
> We have to be fearless.
> I don't know if that's possible, Daddo says.
> Think about what you always tell Bela. You tell her she's survived everything she's ever been afraid of.
> But this . . .
> This is just what she's afraid of now.
> Okay, I like that, Daddo says. Then: When we used to stay

up all night in your dorm, we also used to joke about having a family. And now look at us.

I know.

Just saying. If that worked out, maybe this can work out too.

Their faces are close together. They don't want Other Mommy to hear.

But I worry she hears everything. No matter how quiet you say it.

I'm so scared, Mommy says.

Yeah, same.

It may have killed Frank.

I know. It's all I can think about.

But it hasn't killed us.

They go silent a second.

But if something happens to us? Mommy says.

I close my eyes as they both turn to me.

It won't, Daddo says.

It might, Mommy says. Russ, I love you. I love the way you see the world. But this is very dangerous. We need to be aware of that. In a way we've never been aware of it before. This isn't like making sure she's in sight at the mall. This isn't parenting.

This is survival, Daddo says.

Yes.

And that's why it'll work out, Daddo says.

That's why it might, Mommy says.

Their foreheads are touching now, just like outside.

We're a team, Mommy says. Whether we meant for it to be like this or not. We're a team.

Yes, Daddo says. Always.

Whether we asked for this or not.

Yes.

We can do this, Mommy says.

Yes.

Fuck, Mommy says.

What?

I can't get it out of my head. What it looks like. How it moves.

I know. Don't think about it like that. Think about it like it's a big animal. Think of the nature docs we've watched. The stronger ones don't always win.

Yes. Good. You're right.

We're a team, Ursula.

Yes.

Always.

Daddo is crying a little.

It's all right, Mommy says.

It's not, Daddo says. But maybe . . .

Their foreheads are touching and they're crying and then they think it's funny that they're both crying and they both smile and wipe away each other's tears and they laugh just a little bit.

The next time we see it? Daddo asks.

The next time we see it, Mommy says.

No matter where it is?

No matter where it is.

That could be any minute, Daddo says.

That could be right now, Mommy says.

They look up the hall.
Kami and Kamael are facing the front door.

> Knives, Daddo says.
> Knives.

They kiss. When they pull apart they look to me again and I close my eyes again.

> We know you're awake, Bela, Mommy says.

I open my eyes.
They each put a hand on my shoulders.

> We're a team, Mommy says.

And Daddo says,

> Always.

42

Daddo's shaving.
Me and Mommy are in the bathroom too.

After this, Mommy says, we'll get dressed up. Clean clothes anyway.

Daddo's face is half done now.

And we'll shower first, Mommy says. Yes.
It feels good to take care of ourselves, Daddo says.

They sound a little crazy.
He's almost done now. Me and Mommy watch his face get clean.
It's daytime. The house is bright with the sun.

It's been a minute since we cared about us, Mommy says.
Yep, Daddo says. Just that.

Then he's done and he turns on the faucet and washes his face and when he looks in the mirror he looks like Daddo again.

Are we going somewhere? I say.

They're acting like we are.

> No, Daddo says.
> Nope, Mommy says. We're caring about ourselves. That's it.
> Just that, Daddo says.

But it's like they're getting ready to go out.

> Sometimes you need to feel good about yourself, Daddo says. In order to do certain things.
> Don't you always feel good? I ask.
> No, Mommy says.
> It's more complicated than that, Daddo says.

He reaches back and takes Mommy's hand.

> Let's head upstairs, Daddo says. Shower. Get some good clothes.
> Hey, Bela, Mommy says. We're going upstairs now. Okay? Absolutely no wandering up there. Zero. *None.* We're going to shower. Daddo first, then you and me. We'll all be in the bathroom and we will not leave each other's sight. Understood?
> Yeah.

The dogs watch us pass. They watch us go upstairs.

> Nothing too constricting, Mommy says to Daddo. No dress shirts.
> Already thought of that, Daddo says.

We go into their bedroom and Mommy turns on all the lights. She goes to the closet and pulls some clothes aside and I close my eyes.

But nobody's in there.

Here, Mommy says.

She puts a shirt on the bed for Daddo.
We all go into the bathroom and Daddo turns the water on.
Mommy takes my hand and we stand near the sink and she says,

How you dress can actually change how you feel. Like when you want to wear those certain clothes for the party.

She opens the drawer and takes out small scissors and starts to cut the ends of her hair.
She looks back to Daddo in the shower to be sure he's okay.

Here, she says.

She cuts my hair a little bit too.

Listen to me, Bela, she says. No matter what happens in the coming days, or even today, you're going to have to steer clear of it.
What do you mean?
It means Mommy and Daddo may need to take action. And if we do, you don't.

I think I understand.

When?
I don't know, Mommy says.
I'm good, Daddo says.

He's out of the shower and he's drying off with a towel and Mommy cuts my hair a little more.

You look nice, Daddo says to Mommy.

She takes off her clothes and then takes off mine and we both go into the shower.
The water is warm.

I clean up well, Daddo calls to us.

He looks like Daddo again.

It's incredible, he says. Given all this . . . we're still us.

We shower as Daddo cuts his hair by the sink.
When we're done, Mommy turns off the water.
Daddo hands us towels.

All right. Let's get dressed. Bela?
Yeah.
What do you want to wear?
I wanna wear my party clothes.

Mommy and Daddo look at each other.

Those clothes are in your bedroom? Daddo says.
Yeah.
All right, Daddo says. Then we get them together.

I see knives on the bed.

I'm so close to being me again, Mommy says as she looks in the mirror. I can practically see her.

We leave the bathroom and Daddo puts on his salmon shirt and nice pants and Mommy gets dressed in a green blouse and her brown pants and then she checks her hair again in the closet-door mirror.

You look great, Daddo says.
So do you.
Ready?

We hold hands as we cross the hall and go to my bedroom.
The closet is wide open and empty. My clothes are still in piles.
Mommy finds my party clothes and hands them to me.
I get dressed.

What do we do now? I ask.

I realize Mommy and Daddo are both holding knives.

Come on, Daddo says. Bela, you walk in the middle. Between us.
Okay.

We leave my bedroom. The dogs are at the bottom of the stairs looking up at us.
Mommy goes first and then I go and then Daddo goes and Daddo is looking behind us the whole way down.
When we get to the bottom, Mommy says,

This is our house.
Yes it is, Daddo says.
This is our child.
Yes it is, Daddo says.
This is our fight.

43

It's night again.
We're all awake, sitting, dressed up and clean, on the couch.
The dogs are sitting up, facing the front door. Working.
Mommy and Daddo still have knives.

> Are you hungry? Daddo asks me.
> No, I say.

I lean back into the couch. I close my eyes. When I open them,
Mommy is at the kitchen counter and me and Daddo are at the
table.
I sit up fast.

> You fell asleep, Daddo says.
> Okay. Wow.
> You feel rested now?
> I don't know.
> You might not feel rested for twenty years, Mommy says.
That's probably what we all have to look forward to.

The TV isn't on and the house is quiet.

There's no bowl or food in front of me, so I lay my head down again. Just for a second. But when I wake up . . .

Mommy?

I'm still at the kitchen table, but Mommy and Daddo are standing in the middle of the living room, looking up at the ceiling.
They both hold knives.
I get down from my chair.

Bela, Mommy says.

She doesn't look at me.

Do not leave this room right now, she says.

I look up the hall and I see Kami and Kamael are looking up the stairs.

Is the house creaking? I ask.

Mommy and Daddo don't answer.
Either Kami or Kamael growls.
Mommy steps closer to the entrance to the living room. She waves for Daddo to do the same.
They're together, looking up the hall.

Okay, Mommy says.

She breathes deep.

It's upstairs, she says. We know it is.
I don't think there's any question about it, Daddo says, quiet. Then: What about Bela?

We sure don't leave her down here, Mommy says.

We bring her up with us . . .

Yes, Mommy says. Bela?

What?

This might be scary now. This might be a lot to take in. But we need you to come with us. Stay within sight of us. But don't get too close. Understand?

No.

I start to cry a little.

Bela, Mommy says.

Daddo is still looking down the hall. His knife is up like he's going to use it.

Mommy and Daddo can't be Mommy and Daddo right now, Mommy says. We need to be something we've never been before. Something outside our nature.

Outside our nature, Daddo repeats.

Like they're building themselves up. Like they have to.

I imagine the knives going into Other Mommy's face.

I don't want to go upstairs, I say.

Is she a friend? Wasn't she once?

That's okay, Mommy says. We're all going to do something we don't want to do now.

Daddo steps into the hall.

The dogs growl, quietly, looking up the stairs.

Now you, Mommy says to me.

I step into the hall behind Daddo, and Mommy comes in after me.
We walk slow. We pass the bathroom.
We pause at the bottom of the stairs.
Then Daddo starts climbing without talking about it. I start to
follow, but Mommy holds me back. She goes first. She holds my
hand behind her. Holds me close to her. She looks back over my
head, then ahead again.
We get to the top of the stairs like this.

The storage closet, Mommy says.

It's a closet at the end of the hall where we keep a vacuum.
Daddo once called it a "second pantry," but there's no food in
there.
A person can fit in there.
Daddo once hid there when we played hide-and-seek.

Mommy, I say.

But Mommy puts her hand over my mouth.
We keep walking.
All dressed up, all clean. They hold their knives.

Stop here, Bela, Mommy says.

The thin door is open a little, and Daddo gets to it first. He
looks to Mommy before he reaches into the darkness and tries to
find the light switch.
I hear him flip the switch, but no light comes on.
Daddo pulls his hand from the room.
He looks back to Mommy.
She steps to the door. Puts her mouth near the darkness.
Says,

Leave our child alone.

Daddo's hand is shaking. The knife is shaking.

This is your last chance to leave our child alone, Mommy says.

She pushes the door open.
The smell comes out of the second pantry.
Other Mommy is in the second pantry.
Daddo starts to make a sound I've never heard him make before.
Like he's about to do something he needs to be brave to do.

No matter what happens now, Bela, Mommy says. Do *not* run.

Daddo is yelling to be brave and Mommy starts yelling to be brave and I know they're going to run into the second pantry, I know they're going to try to kill Other Mommy.
They raise their knives.
And Other Mommy says,

Hello, and who are you?

And the dogs start barking like crazy downstairs.
Mommy is yelling to do it and Daddo is yelling to do it and the dogs are barking and Mommy starts to move toward the darkness of the second pantry.

Do you like me better in here? Other Mommy says.

I can't see her. But I smell her. And I can imagine her face when she talks.
Mommy and Daddo step closer to the second pantry.

Bela? Other Mommy says. Why would they do this to me?

And Mommy and Daddo run the rest of the way, stabbing into the dark, screaming, sweating, stabbing, and—

What's that? Mommy says.

The doorbell rang.
It rings again.

Bela? Other Mommy says. Why?

The doorbell rings again.
Mommy and Daddo pull back from the second pantry. All dressed up, shaking at the end of the hall. Their knives look so small.

Where is she? Daddo asks.
We can't lose our nerve, Mommy says.

The doorbell rings again and the dogs are barking like mad.
My bedroom door slams behind us and we all cry out at the sound.
Daddo reaches into the second pantry again and finds the light and flips the switch and—

It's not in here, he says.

He sounds crazy. They look crazy. I can't look at them.
I look up the hall.
My bedroom door is closed.
Other Mommy is in my bedroom.
The doorbell rings again.

Come on, Mommy says. We *have* to do this now. We can't lose our nerve.

But I think they did.
They're not yelling anymore. They're not stabbing anymore.

We all walk slowly to the top of the stairs, passing my bedroom door.

Who the fuck is here? Daddo says.
Was it in the bedroom the whole time? Mommy asks. Bela? Do you know?

She gets to the stairs first and her hands are shaking and she's walking down the stairs backward, I'm second, and Daddo is making sure I don't fall.

Can it just go from room to room like that? Mommy asks. *Bela?*

The doorbell rings again and we're halfway down the stairs and Mommy is yelling who is it and they're both shaking and we get to the bottom and Mommy holds her knife to the stairs and Daddo opens the door and the dogs are growling and I see her outside on the front porch.

Lois? Daddo says.

Lois Anthony is here.
Mommy goes to the door.

What's going on? Mommy says.

They look so scared. Mommy and Daddo look so scared.

O my God, Lois says. What have I interrupted?

Daddo grabs my wrist and Mommy holds back the dogs and we all get out the door and onto the front porch where Lois is standing alone in the night.

What are you doing here? Mommy asks.

Mommy looks so crazy. I can't look at her.
Lois starts to speak, but Mommy cuts her off.

I didn't mean to—
Out with it, Lois! Mommy yells. What are you *doing* here?

Lois looks to the knives. Looks to the house.

I'm sorry to come unannounced, she says. But also . . . also I'm not. I'm not sorry at all.
What's going on? Daddo asks.
Please hear me out, she says. It's all I could think about. Since you left my house. All I could think . . . that I let you down. That I didn't know what I was doing and I let you down.
Lois? Mommy says. What the fuck are you doing here?
Hear me out, Lois says. Please.

We step farther out onto the lawn. Mommy and Daddo still hold their knives.

I learned, Lois says.
Learned what? Daddo asks.
I learned how to get rid of the thing in your house.
O, fuck, Mommy says. Are you fucking *kidding* me?

Lois looks to the knives in Mommy and Daddo's hands.

You can't hurt it like that, she says. And you can't talk to it. You can't tell it to leave. What you have is so much more serious than anything me and my circle could've imagined.

The dogs still growl inside.

How? Daddo says. *How,* Lois? How do we do it then? As maybe you can see, you caught us at a *real* piqued moment.

Then, like he's realizing it right now,

Holy shit, he says. We tried to stab it. Holy *shit*.

A neighbor is out on her porch now, watching.

You need to get rid of what it wants, Lois says.
What does that mean? Mommy asks.
It won't leave till it has what it wants.
Okay, but what does that *mean*? No more hippie-speak! We're past all that!

Lois looks at me.
And it feels like the whole world is looking at me with her.

It wants Bela, she says.
Okay, Mommy says, you can leave now. *Now.*
And it won't leave until it has her.

She has tears in her eyes.
But she looks strong.

Leave, Mommy says.

But she sounds tired. Like she used all her bravery upstairs. Like Mommy and Daddo used all their bravery and now they're just people with small knives.

You have to make Bela less appealing, Lois says. Less appealing to *it*.

Mommy and Daddo lower their knives.

You have to make Bela less appetizing to whatever is inside your house.

I don't . . . Daddo starts to say.

Come with me, Lois says. Let's go somewhere and talk. Somewhere to clear our heads. Somewhere we feel more alone.

She looks to the house like it can hear us.

Mommy laughs but it's not the funny way, it's sharp.

It follows us, Lois. In case you didn't know. No matter where we go.

We're at our end, Daddo says.

But he looks like maybe he doesn't feel it's the end.

I understand, Lois says. I swear I do. But if you can't get rid of it, that means it's always present. And if it's always here, then why not give me an hour? One hour to hear me out.

She looks at me again.

I'm sorry, Bela, she says. Sorry for underestimating what you were going through in this house.

Mommy and Daddo are breathing hard.

They're sweating.

The dogs are quieter now.

Lois says,

I know you're at your wits' end. I know you feel like you're out of options. But I'm coming to you with a clear head. Clearer than I've ever had before.

Daddo looks to Mommy, and Mommy sounds like she's about to tell Lois Anthony to leave again. She breathes in the way someone does when they're about to yell.
But she doesn't do that.

All right, Mommy says. *All right,* Lois. Tell us what you learned.

Lois watches Mommy a second before taking a step back. Like she's worried what Mommy will do when she says what she has to say.

I need you to let this sink in before you respond, Lois says.
Lois, Daddo says. Come on.

Lois breathes deep, slow.

The thing in your house is attracted to Bela's innocence. We have to take that innocence away.

44

Daddo says the Big Lake is more than one hundred miles from our house, and that the trip is going to feel really long for me. He's right.

But Lois has been talking a lot in the car and that helps. She's in the backseat with me. Daddo called the trainers and they came and got the dogs and they seemed upset they had to do it so late at night, but Mommy and Daddo said an emergency happened and so that was that.

Before we left, Lois said,

We need to go somewhere where maybe it can't hear us. You haven't tried to go far away yet. I understand why. You have a house. This is all new. It's followed you wherever you've gone. But this thing, it must have a limit too. Can it travel a hundred miles to Lake Michigan? Will it? And where will it hide if we're out on the sand, if there's no house for it to haunt?

It can hide in the sand, Mommy said. It can hide in the air.

But Lois felt like hope to me.

She's right that we haven't tried anything like this, Daddo said. *Goblin isn't far.*

Lois was right to take that step back from Mommy before she said her plan. Mommy stepped toward her with a growl and Daddo grabbed her and eventually calmed her down. They talked for a long time out in front of our house. Neighbors watched. Some were on their phones while they watched. Like they were describing it all to their friends.
But Mommy and Daddo don't have any other plan. And Lois talks with hope.
I think she came at just the right moment.
What might've happened upstairs if she didn't?

You gotta give us more than just that, Daddo said, meaning about the innocence. *A lot more.*

Then Lois said something that really got Mommy and Daddo's attention. She said,

Russ, when the four of us were at the motel, Ruth asked to speak with me out on the balcony.
Yeah, I remember, Daddo said.
What did she tell you? Mommy asked.
She told me everything, Lois said. *She felt I could only help if I knew everything.*

Mommy and Daddo got quiet then.
Then Lois talked a lot about how I needed to learn the truth of the world and my life in the world and that was "revoking innocence" and Mommy was mad and Daddo was mad at Mommy and I didn't look up to the windows in our house because I didn't want to know if Other Mommy was watching from one of the rooms.

I could smell her. Even when we were outside I smelled Other Mommy in the house.
I wonder if I'll ever not feel like she's near.

It's near Glen Arbor, Lois says now in the car. I know several spots along Sleeping Bear Dunes where we can stay out on the beach.
This is insane, Mommy says.

But we're doing it.

It is, Lois says. All of it.
My God, Daddo says suddenly. We tried to stab it . . .

He's talking like he's been thinking about this the whole time in the car.
I was thinking about it too.
Other Mommy in the dark second pantry.

Distance, Lois says. That's first. And we've already got some. Hopefully.
But how do we *know* what it wants? Daddo says. We don't know it has anything to do with innocence.
Whatever this is, Lois says, it's attracted to Bela either because it wants to corrupt something, anything, or it thinks Bela's not strong enough or mature enough to know she's being tricked. It wants to trick her. It's trying to trick her. What we're seeing here is a magnifying glass, held above the entity's attempt to possess. All of this has been the entity's attempt to get in.

We're all quiet for a while, like if what Lois said was still being said.

Are there bears at the lake? I ask Lois.

No, she says. It's called that because the hills of sand look like a bear lying down. Sleeping.

Still. I think of us running from Other Mommy and running into bears instead. I'm thinking of Mommy and Daddo with their kitchen knives trying to fight.

It's going to be all right, Daddo says. It simply cannot continue.

Then Mommy looks back at me like she's thinking hard about something.

We'll have to tell her, Mommy says. If it's what we're going to do, then we have to do it.

Daddo shakes his head silently.

Tell me what? I ask.

But nobody answers. And when I look at Lois to see if she knows, she's just looking out the window, her eyes big and worried.

First, distance, she says. Then the talk.

45

Daddo and Mommy are sleeping under the umbrella Lois brought to our house. She brought things like blankets and pillows too.

She was prepared for her plan.

The sun is high up, but it's windy and Lois said the lake is like a "big air conditioner." She said it cools the whole state.

Up the beach I can see big sand cliffs.

Daddo said it's like California and Mommy said it's better than that and then Daddo said maybe Lois was right that we all needed to get far away and then they all asked me if I thought Other Mommy was close.

I told them I didn't know.

Me and Lois stand where the water touches the tips of our shoes. The lake is loud. And it's big. And everything is so pretty, it feels like the opposite of Other Mommy in the dark second pantry.

You'll hear some things tonight that will change your understanding of the world, Lois says. And while it isn't fair, or natural, it's likely necessary. Do you understand what I'm saying?

You guys want Other Mommy to go away.

Yes. That's it exactly. We want Other Mommy to go away. But not just for a little while. We want it gone forever. Okay?

Okay.

Do you think that is possible? I think it's probably helpful if you think that's possible.

I don't know.

I get it, she says. What's unfair is that people are supposed to learn the secrets of life gradually. They aren't supposed to be told a hundred truths at once. But if you think of it like a ritual, I think that will help. When your parents wake up, I'll get a fire going. You see nobody's up and down this beach, we're alone. And I think we should do what we came to do right away. I think all this will make Other Mommy less interested in you.

Okay.

You sound sad about that. Are you?

I thought Other Mommy was my friend.

I see.

The water goes a little farther and curls around the tip of my shoe.

Your parents have been through a lot, Lois says. And what they're experiencing is just as unnatural as what you are and what you will. They've been so worried about you and your house. It's a really big thing, what they're dealing with. One day you'll be an adult, too, and you'll look back on these days and you'll see what your parents did for you and how they behaved when they had to, and I imagine you'll love them deeply for it.

I look back and see Mommy and Daddo sleeping beneath the white umbrella. They're sleeping like people do who are so tired all the noise in the world won't wake them.

Can I ask some questions? Lois says.

Yeah.

Okay. When Other Mommy first came to you . . . were you scared?

No.

Did you tell Other Mommy anything personal about yourself? Things you like? How you feel about things?

Yeah.

I'd rather talk about the sand. The sand is so pretty. So cool.

And did Other Mommy tell you anything about . . . Other Mommy?

What do you mean?

I don't know exactly. Do you know as much about her as she does about you?

I don't think so.

What *do* you know about her?

That she comes from someplace other than the closet. And that her face changes. And that she wants to get into my heart.

Lois looks like what I said makes her feel sickly.

Has she ever told you what she would do if you said yes to that? Lois asks.

Yeah.

And? What was it exactly?

She said she would come back to life. Carnation.

Reincarnation?

Yeah. I keep forgetting. That's it. And one time she told me that when I say yes, it'll be as easy for her as slipping into a dress.

She said that? Those exact words?

Yeah.

And how did that make you feel, Bela?

I don't want to tell her that I liked it when Other Mommy said that.

    I don't know. I thought it sounded pretty.

    Okay, Lois says. I think, for now, let's just be happy to be far away. And when your parents wake up, we'll do some more heavy talking. All right?

    Yeah.

    All right.

We watch the water together and we both look up the beach, way far away, because we both heard a sound like a dog, and there's something on all fours way far away up the sand and it looks like it's crawling toward us, a dog, I think, and the wind comes in strong and the clouds pass in front of the sun and I think I can see the color of the dog for a second, and for a second it looks like the dog has dark fur.

Me and Lois watch the dog for a while and it keeps looking like it's crawling up the sand toward us, the big skinny dog, but it doesn't get any closer and it seems like no matter how long we watch it, it keeps crawling but doesn't get any closer.

Then Mommy wakes up.

And she calls for me.

And I go to her and Daddo beneath the umbrella and I see Lois is still looking up the beach.

    What happened? Mommy asks. Did something happen?

    Nothing happened, I say.

She looks to the water.

Well, holy shit, Mommy says. That's the first time in a long time I've *not* woken up in the middle of something horrible.

She wipes sand from her shirtsleeves.
She looks at me and I can tell she's thinking something big with a lot of feelings.

But I guess we're still in the middle of it, she says.

46

Mommy and Lois make a fire out of the wood they got in the big grass behind us.

Daddo sits in the sand and looks out at the water.

He's been doing that most of the day. I sat near him and watched the sun go down.

But it's not all the way down yet. And the sky is purple and pink and orange.

And there's the moon, white against the colors. And its reflection is in the water. So, two moons. Two moonlights.

And a fire.

Mommy and Lois didn't talk as they collected wood, and Daddo's just been staring out at the lake. So it surprises me when he says,

Hi, Bela.
Hey, Daddo.
You don't . . . sense anything?

Then he smiles, but it seems sad.

What an insane question I just asked you, he says. I'm sitting on a Lake Michigan beach and just asked you if you

sensed an entity from our house. I mean . . . is this insane or
what?

Daddo seems nervous.

    I think we're okay, I say.

But I don't know. I just don't want Daddo to be any more nervous.

    Good, Daddo says. That's really good. And it's good to
have a good thing at a time like this.

He breathes deep and the fire gets bigger and more of him is in
the orange light as the sky gets darker.
Mommy and Lois are getting more wood. Their flashlights are
bouncing around the big grass now, and I can tell they're staying
near each other because they don't want to find something scary
out there alone.

    It's such an interesting moment in time, Daddo says. Think
about it: there are enough people, so much fascination with
things like the thing we're dealing with now, think of all the stories and TV shows centered around stuff like this, and yet, there
isn't anybody to call if such a thing happens to you. Here's a
subject we're all drawn to, the occult, or whatever word you
wanna use, yet, when the rubber hits the road, nobody raises
their hand to help or even knows someone who knows how.
    Lois Anthony raised her hand to help, I say.
    You're right, Daddo says. And I should've thought of that
before I said that. She did, didn't she? She's here. She took us
here. And she didn't have to do this.

Mommy and Lois come back with more wood and put it near
the fire.
We have blankets on the sand and more blankets to sleep be-

neath because it's a little windy but it's not so cold. Lois said we might wake up to the sun being really hot on us but she also said she heard that whenever you sleep by the lake, you wake up a little wet even if you're nowhere near the water.

Maybe we should all sit closer to the fire, Lois says.

Mommy looks over to Daddo, but Daddo just looks out at the water.
I get up and sit closer to the fire and Lois sits to the right of me and the fire makes the sand look red, like we're sitting in real red sand.
Mommy is standing and staring into the fire.

Ursula? Lois says. Russ?
Lois, Mommy says, cut us a break.
I understand, Lois says. But we're here to do this. It should be done.
Yeah, well, Mommy says, some things are easier said than done and some things are harder to say. Okay?
Yes, Lois says. Okay.
When did you learn to make a fire? I ask Lois. Were you littler like me?

She smiles, but like Daddo's, it's sad.

No, she says. It wasn't until I started getting into the kind of things I'm into now. That's when I learned how to make fires and do all sorts of things on my own. Because of . . . rituals, I suppose.
Rituals, I say.

I like the word. Daddo once told me that some words sound exactly like what they mean. I think "ritual" maybe is a word like that.

That's cool, I say.

Yes, Lois says. And it's something to keep in mind. When you grow up, you ought to find an interest that serves many purposes at once. It means you're doing the right thing if the thing you do serves you in more than one way.

Mommy steps closer and says,

A kid isn't supposed to grow up all in one night.

The fire crackles.
Daddo moves so he's sitting across from me on the other side of the fire.

Maybe I should start, Lois says.

Mommy and Daddo don't tell her no.
Mommy sits down. Now the four of us make a square around the fire.

Do you know what innocence is, Bela? Lois asks.
No.
Okay, Lois says. Well, there's a purity to being innocent. Being unaware of the bad things in the world. Being unaware of the bad things people can do. Even people close to you. People you love. Animals are innocent because they aren't motivated by things other than survival. For the most part, animals want to eat, find shelter, nest, procreate, and play. This is why it's so terrible when you hear about an animal being hurt by a person. Almost any animal is innocent, like we all are, until we grow up and learn things and see things and experience things, and then we're not innocent anymore.
This is insane, Mommy says.

Daddo is staring at the fire.

I can stop talking, Lois says.

You make it sound so frightening, Mommy says.

What?

Innocence.

It *is* frightening, Lois says. Because the innocent are targeted first.

All right, Mommy says. Just. Enough. We'll do what we came here to do.

She runs her hands down her face like she's trying to wipe away all we've seen.

Russ? Mommy says. Who should go first?

Daddo takes a while before he answers.

I don't know what I think anymore, he says. I do know we're dealing with a really bad thing right now. And out here, with this fire, and this lake, it's easy to think it's behind us. That it's only back home. Back in Chaps. But I keep thinking of that thing coming into the bedroom at Evelyn's. I keep seeing its mouth stretching to the floor.

Everybody is quiet and for a quick second I see Other Mommy's face in the fire.

Upside down.

Looking back at me.

All right, Mommy says. Me, then.

She clears her throat.

Bela, she says.

Yeah?

I'm going to tell you a story now.

Okay.
And it's not a good story.

I don't like what Mommy is saying.

And it's going to make you see the world differently, and I guess that's what Lois is aiming for. Do you understand?
No, I say.
Of course you don't, Mommy says.
Ursula, Daddo says.
What, Russ?

But Daddo doesn't answer. And Mommy takes a few moments before speaking.
Then she says:

47

When I met your father, I was married to a man named Douglas Cain. I can't believe you just heard those words come out of my mouth. If you only knew how often your daddo and I have talked about when we would tell you this. Sometimes, if I drank too much, I'd argue we never should. And the fact I was married to someone before I married your daddo isn't even the worst of what you'll hear tonight. I'm sorry, Bela. But this is how it went and this is how it is. I married Douglas young. My name for a brief time was Ursula Cain. I loved the name. It almost made getting married worth it to me, at the time. That's how young I was. Young and dumb enough to think a good name was worth an eternity pact. We didn't have much between us, me and Douglas. He thought I was attractive. He was about ten years older than me. We had almost nothing in common except we both went to the same bars and we liked to close them. This means we drank as much as we could until we were asked to leave. I don't expect you to know what that means, not entirely. I'm just trying to paint a picture of what it was really like back then. I had no goals. No ambitions. No drive. And neither did Douglas, and maybe that's what we saw in each other. Maybe we saw the bottom in each other and we didn't want to be found at the bottom alone. So we met and we dated and we got married and there was a whole wedding with bridesmaids and groomsmen and a man who married us and flowers and a cake. I fooled myself into thinking Douglas was the right man for me in the same way people tell themselves they like a job they have no love for. I suppose I felt Douglas was something I had to do. There was no fire in that relationship. No electricity. There was only companionship there at the bottom. And I was too young to be content with living my life at the bottom, the underbelly, *rock bottom* as some people like to call it. It feels like rock. Believe me. And you can hear the echoes of every dumb decision you make, echoes off that rock. And so . . . I guess, given the lack of love between Douglas and me, it was only a matter of time before I started cheating on him. There was no conscious decision to do this, understand. I didn't formulate some plan or write out a list of goals, people I wanted to sleep with behind my husband's back. But that's exactly what I did. And it wasn't just a little bit, Bela. It was with friends of his. People we knew through his job and some of the stupid jobs I had back then too. There were one-night stands, and ten-night stands, and longer. And all this, Douglas knew nothing about any of it. I don't think you're old enough to understand exactly what that last statement illuminates regarding my marriage. But it sheds a lot of light. It says: Douglas and I were so far apart, naturally, that he didn't even notice the fact his wife was sleeping with his best friends. Some of them in our very house. And while I feel absolutely crazy telling you this, now, and for the reason I am telling you this now, it's also a glimpse, I suppose, of the world Lois was just referring to. The bad things people do and the bad people who do them and how even your mommy isn't the bastion of golden purity most children imagine their mommies to be. But again, this isn't the worst of it and I'm going to tell you the worst of it because that's why we're here and because we're just desperate enough to try anything to protect you from what has become obsessed with you back at our house. So here it is, the worst: I met your

daddo in the fog of this rudderless life at a bakery in downtown
Chaps, a place that isn't there anymore. Your daddo was in line
behind me and he asked me what I was going to order and I told
him and he said he was going to get the same thing because it
sounded good. And then we laughed and I realized, right there
in Mart Street Bakery, that I wasn't happy with Douglas and no
pronunciation of Ursula Cain could convince me I was. It was
the first time I'd laughed without a drink or without pretending
I'd found something funny and, more than that, it was such a
pure and, yes, innocent, laugh I was nearly startled by the sound
of it. I ordered and your daddo ordered and we got to talking
outside and I suppose you could say the innocence ended there,
as I knew immediately this would be the beginning of yet another affair. And it was. And your daddo and I saw each other on
the side for many months as I was still married to Douglas and
it even got to the point where your daddo factored me into his
plans when he got his first apartment. We lied to you when we
said we met at college. We didn't. We both went to the same
school, but we didn't meet there. And so whenever your daddo
and I have talked about hanging out in college together, what we
were *not* telling you was that these hangouts happened in an
apartment in downtown Chaps, a place I visited regularly behind my husband at the time's back. So, you see, Bela? A lot to
be learned tonight. But this, of course, isn't the worst of it because ever since I saw that thing sitting on your bed that night, I
understood I'd become part of something I wouldn't be able to
voluntarily pull myself out of. I understood immediately that
my reckoning had come, this darkness would not simply pass,
and that I would likely have to do something similar to what I'm
doing right now if I wanted us to make it to the other side. I got
pregnant, Bela, while sleeping with your father. Yes, I got pregnant while cheating on my husband, sleeping with your father in
his tiny apartment in Chaps, and I knew I was pregnant even
before I missed my period or showed any signs. I felt it immediately. I knew I was no longer one person and that I was now two,

and I suppose this is one of the perks of being someone who feels ultimately alone, the ability to sense when you are *not* alone anymore, sense it better than any social butterfly ever could. I told your daddo right away. And he went with me to the drugstore we used to frequent and we got a test and I tested positive in your daddo's apartment bathroom and I stared at that test for a long time, doing the math, adding up the numbers, trying my hardest to make sure I knew whose child it was. Because, you see, Bela, just because a person is sleeping with someone else doesn't mean they aren't sleeping with the person they made a vow to, and in fact, they're much more likely to sleep with their spouse *because* they are trying to maintain airs, to make it all look like nothing is happening on the side. And so, finally, with that test in hand, I left the bathroom and showed it to your daddo and he said he wanted to keep it and I said keep what? And he said, My child. And I said, How do you know it's yours? And so your daddo and I lost our own innocence that day, if such a word applies to anybody in this story that I can't believe I'm telling you. And I'm sorry that I'm crying now and I hope you can hear the words between the tears and I hope you're understanding even half of what I'm telling you, but I also kinda pray you don't understand the other half. Because I might've been able to hide an affair from my husband, but you can't hide a pregnancy, and so the whole world became a ticking clock for me. I could hear it in the clouds, in passing cars, in the house. It was like the house was creaking, leaning into me, telling me I had to talk to Douglas, and I couldn't just pretend this wasn't happening like I'd pretended so much before then hadn't. And just when it felt like I couldn't stand the sound of all that creaking in the house anymore, I told Douglas about the baby. And he was excited. He was *so* excited about this baby and I did all I could to hide the fact I'd taken the test in the apartment of another man and I did all I could not to break apart into a thousand pieces as he started coming up with names, as he asked no questions, as he had *no idea* there was even a possibility the baby might not be his. But I did it. I maintained this unfathomable front. I *pretended*, Bela. Just like I've pretended a lot of things with you. And I'm sorry that I'm crying. But I can't imagine I'll ever stop again. I did enough research to learn the earliest I could get a paternity test was nine weeks into being pregnant. What this means, Bela, is that I could take a test to make sure who the baby's father was. But I would need the blood of one of the men in order to do this. Your daddo offered his up one night in that tiny apartment in Chaps. He got a knife out not that different than the knife he carried just last night when we stood like maniacs outside the upstairs hall closet in our home. And he cut his palm and he bled into a little plastic cup he had in the bathroom. We didn't sleep that night because our minds were racing with all the possible futures haunting us. It was like we could see the *possible* us walking around the apartment, or walking through a future home, *other* me, *other* Daddo, and who we might become once we found out who the father of this child was. And in the morning, I went to the doctor's and they took some of my blood and I gave them your daddo's blood and I drove home to my house where I lived with Douglas as his wife and I waited for word. And I waited. And I was so scared, Bela, the most scared I believed it was possible to be before these recent incidents have shown me there's always more to be afraid of. The phone didn't ring that day, and I barely slept as Douglas slept smiling beside me, he with an idea of raising a baby, he with all these dreams and visions of his own, just like your daddo and I dreamed earlier in the day. And while Douglas slept I thought about waking him. I saw myself *telling* him the baby wasn't his. I knew the exact words I'd use and I even rehearsed them in the bathroom, and worked on my expression, the face I would make when I told him the baby *was not his*. And about exactly when I had it right, at about the exact moment when I walked back into our bedroom and saw the sun had come up and found it within myself to wake this man, this man who had no idea of his wife's affairs, the phone rang. And it was the doctor. She had the results of the paternity test. I could breathe again because this would be the moment I'd hear it was your daddo's child and I, galvanized by this information, would wake Douglas and tell him I was sorry, so sorry, but my life had taken a turn without him. But . . . Bela. That's not what the doctor said. The doctor did not tell me the child was your daddo's. The doctor told me the blood I'd brought in was not the blood of the father of the baby I carried. And so there I stood, phone in hand, as my husband slept proudly, rightly believing the baby to be his.

Mommy stops talking, and her eyes are puffy from crying and Daddo is staring hard into the fire.

Your daddo is not your father, Mommy says. Not your biological father. You father is a man named Douglas Cain. A man who, when he discovered I was indeed seeing your daddo, when he followed me one night to that tiny apartment in Chaps, when he knocked on the very door of that apartment, suddenly wanted nothing to do with me, nothing to do with the marriage we had, and nothing to do with the child within. And it was that night, after Douglas left, that your daddo said he would raise you, Bela. That he would be the father to you that Douglas no longer wanted to be. The night he chose to be your daddo.

I'm standing up and I didn't even mean to. I don't remember deciding to stand up.

And I'm so sorry I'm telling you this now, Mommy says. And I'm so glad I'm telling you this now. So that maybe the world will stop creaking and the sound of this clock can finally go away, and the only reason I'm telling you this now, when you're way too young to hear it, is because your daddo and I were told it might help get rid of a monster, by replacing it with another monster, one there's absolutely no way to get rid of, and here I am, feeling worst of all for trying to get that monster to like you less, because even now, *even right now*, I don't want anything in this world to like you less than it does Bela, not even a monster, I don't even want what we found in our home to like you less because I want everything in this world and any world to love you.

I'm walking through the sand. I don't remember deciding to walk.
Lois is telling me to stay near and she's asking if I'm okay and she's telling me it's okay to cry, it's fine that I'm crying but I don't remember deciding to cry.

Is this innocence revoked? Daddo says behind me.

He's talking to Lois.
I turn to look at him, but I can't look at him because suddenly he looks like he's in disguise to me. The fire plays with his face and it makes it look upside down and I don't understand what Mommy just told me and why did she say it at all?

Yes, Lois says. I believe it is.
Then we're done, Daddo says. No more talking. Please.

Mommy is crying and I'm crying and Lois is telling me it's okay and she's next to me now and she's got her hands on my shoulders, but I push her off and I start to run along the beach to where we saw the dog so far away and I think how Mommy said animals are innocent and I think she doesn't understand that animals are the smart ones. Animals are the ones who know everything and Mommy and Daddo don't know anything at all.

Bela! Lois shouts.

And I hear Mommy and Daddo behind me too. And they're all running for me because we can't be alone anymore because

Other Mommy can grab me and she can ask if she can go into my heart and they're trying to make her like me less but all they did was make me like everything less and so I'm running and hoping to find that dog so I can tell it that Mommy and Daddo don't know *anything,* but now there are hands on me, hands in the dark, and I say,

Other Mommy!

But it's not her. It's Mommy. And Daddo and Lois Anthony too. And they're all in the dark with me and the fire is so far away! I ran so far away. And the wind is loud and the water is loud and all of them are on their knees in the sand and they're talking to me and crying and we're all crying and I can hear either Mommy or Daddo or Lois or all of them saying,

Yes, this is innocence lost.

And I don't like it! I don't like it one bit! Why are they taking it away from me? Why are they making me feel so bad? Why won't they let me be happy?

Bela, Mommy says.
Bela, Daddo says.
Bela, Lois says.

And I say,

No! *No!* It's not true! You're all lying!

But they tell me again it *is* true. And they all hug me and try to block the wind but through them I can hear it.
I can hear the dog.
Crawling up the beach.
It's far away but I can hear it.

Yes.

I can hear the dog crawling where the lake and the beach are married and I can hear it breathing and I don't wanna tell Mommy and Daddo *anything* anymore because they'll just turn it into a lie.

> Bela, Daddo says.
> Bela, Mommy says.
> Bela, Lois says.

And I say,

> Other Mommy isn't here.

But I don't think that's true, and I just want to lie to them like they just lied to me.
Yeah.
I want to tell them lies and make them believe stuff that isn't true because all they ever did was lie to me.

> Other Mommy doesn't want me anymore, I say. Other Mommy is gone.

Lies. I can lie too!

> Other Mommy doesn't want me anymore. Other Mommy didn't follow us here. Other Mommy isn't crawling on the beach.
> Bela, Mommy says.
> Bela, Daddo says.
> Bela, Lois says.

And they're all so sad!

> It's okay, I say. We're okay!

Because I can lie too. Because I won't tell them I can see her, yeah. See her on all fours up the beach. I won't tell them I can see her between Mommy and Daddo, I can see her dark hair in the moonlight, I can hear her breathe and can smell her like she's as big as the lake.

It's okay, I tell them. We're okay! Other Mommy doesn't like me anymore.

And they cry.
And they hug.
And I lie.

Other Mommy is gone, I say. Forever. It worked. She's *gone*.

And I'll keep telling them that. I'll keep telling them.
I'll keep telling them
LIES!

48

Daddo walks behind me on the beach.
The sun is up.
I slept but I don't remember sleeping.
Lois told me someone stayed awake all night and that "nothing is out here with us" but I didn't say anything back.
I woke up and went for a walk and when I look back now I see Daddo walking along the sand too.
Mommy is way back with the umbrella and I don't think she slept all night because her face looked like she didn't.

I just wanna walk alone! I yell to Daddo.

But it's windy and the water is loud and I don't know if he can hear me.

Leave me alone! I yell.

There's a tall, sandy cliff ahead. The water is so blue and in some parts green and yesterday Daddo told me the shallow water is a different color from the deep water and I can't remember which is which. But what does he know anymore?

I look back.

Daddo is a little closer now.

It's not fair because his legs are longer.

You're not my dad! I yell.

Then I turn to the lake and the wind and I scream as loud as I can and my whole body yells and the wind takes my yell and I hope it gives it to Mommy and Daddo and Lois Anthony too.

Bela, Daddo says.

He's right behind me now. That's because I stopped to yell.

Mind if I walk with you? he asks.

I want to walk alone.

Okay, I understand, Daddo says. But I feel really bad too. And we're best friends, you and me. And I could use to talk it over with you.

He looks sad, and I don't like when Daddo looks sad.

But I don't know who these people are anymore.

I start walking and Daddo walks right behind me and he says,

You're gonna have your own secrets one day, Bela. I know that doesn't mean much to you right now, but it's true. It's one of those things you accumulate in life without even trying. Nobody sets out to keep secrets. Not me. Not you. And yet . . . here . . . your mommy and me, we had a big one. We have many. Not as crazy as what you learned by the fire last night. No. That's the biggest secret we had. And for as bad as it's making you feel, it's making me feel worse. Yet . . . at the same time . . . I'm glad you know now. Still, I'd like to explain how a secret like this comes to be. How you set out to do the right thing and end up doing the wrong one. This happens in every house in every city in every country in the world. The man Mommy told you about last night was an angry man. Mean too. And he was prepared to leave Mommy alone with you and that was too much for me to allow, because, well, because I care deeply about Mommy. You know that. You can tell. And so I said, hey, I can help. And so I did. And so I have. You think Mommy gets stressed and serious now? You should've seen her when she was pregnant with you. And I was there. For her. For you. Here she was, pregnant one minute, and the next you come out and we're both crying with happiness that you came out. And neither of us are thinking whether what we're doing is right or wrong. We're just . . . so happy to see you. But then, it struck me, right there in the hospital, seconds after you were born, it struck me how now . . . *now* Mommy and I had a secret. Because now we were no longer two, we were three. Yet, when you were a baby, we couldn't tell you the secret. Right? Because babies can't understand that kind of thing. And so the question became . . . when? When do we tell Bela this secret? When you were one year old, you were still too young. Then two. Then three. You see? When was the right time? So, this idea that started with good intentions then became a bad thing. And honestly, Bela, if you think about it, I don't think it's me or Mommy you're mad at. I think your mad at the news. The secret. Just like I'm mad at the secret. And the fact I had to carry it for these years, this most recent year especially, as you seemed to be getting closer to the age where, hey, maybe you should know the truth. Me and Mommy, we talked about this. A lot. And we argued about it. A lot. And we decided . . . not yet. Over and over we settled on not yet. But at the same time we agreed upon *someday* soon. You see? Then . . . all this started happening. And the things Mommy and I saw. And the things *you* saw. And I can't believe how insane all this is and then Lois comes along and, I don't know. I guess she gave us a nudge to tell this secret now. And maybe we shouldn't have. Maybe agreeing to coming out here was another in a line of bad decisions. But here we are. And if you noticed, there wasn't an incident last night. Not one like the ones we've been suffering.

I wanna go home, I say.

Home? Daddo says. Really? But home has been the hardest place of all.

I wanna go home.

We stop walking and Daddo is quiet.

What do I call you from now on? I ask.

He looks at me like I'm crazy and he says,

O, I don't . . . I don't know. I think you can call me whatever you want, Bela.

I don't tell him that I want to call him liar.
I walk back toward Mommy and Lois and the umbrella.

I wanna go home, I say.
I don't know if we're ready for that, Daddo says.
I am.

Up ahead, Mommy and Lois stand by the umbrella and the blankets and they're talking and the clouds go over the sun and the lake is loud and it's windy out here and Daddo is still talking about secrets behind me.
Other people come out of the big grass and they walk down to the beach. It's a couple, I think. Younger than Mommy and Daddo, I think.

I don't wanna be out here, I say.
That's fine, Daddo says. But we have to be smart. We have to—

But I don't wanna hear him anymore, so I turn to the lake again and I scream and it feels like my whole body is yelling, not just my mouth, and I open my eyes and I see the clouds look like Other Mommy is in the air, in the wind, and her face is one big mouth and she's yelling, too, back at me, or maybe she's swallowing my scream, yeah, she's swallowing my scream. Daddo touches my arm, and I shove him away and then I'm in the water, I'm running, I don't even have my suit on, I'm just going out into the waves and Mommy and Daddo and Lois are all yelling and the water and the wind is so cold and I go under and I yell under there, too, I yell until I'm all one big mouth, too, and I open my eyes and I see her legs, yeah, I see Other Mommy's hairy legs and her feet with three toes on the rocky bottom and I keep yelling and I don't wanna come up, I don't wanna be here with these people who lied to me.

I want to be home with Other Mommy.

Bela!

It's Mommy. They're all pulling me out of the water and they're holding me so I don't go under again and they're all so scared for me and yelling at each other and the water is *so* cold and when they carry me back to the sand I think I see the very top of Other Mommy's head far out in the water.

Do we need a doctor? Lois says.
No, Mommy and Daddo say at the same time.

Then Daddo says,

What we need is a family.
We have one, Mommy says. Whether or not we've done right by it, we have one.

I'm cold under the umbrella and Mommy and Daddo are drying me off with towels and Lois is standing in the sand. She's still wearing her sweater and pants and her big glasses and she looks like she's never been on a beach before.

     We love you, Bela, Mommy says. I understand why you're mad. But we're still your parents and you aren't going out to sea on us.

Lois looks like she sees something in the water.
She looks back at me.

     We love you, Bela, Daddo says. We love you so much.
     She could've drowned, Mommy says.

Lois comes over to us and says,

     Did any of you see anything out in the water?
     What? Daddo asks.
     I just . . . I thought—

Mommy stands up and slaps Lois Anthony's face and her glasses fall to the sand.

     O, no, Daddo says. Ursula.

Lois holds her face and Mommy steps back and Daddo goes and picks up the glasses and gives them to Lois.
I'm cold and wet under the umbrella.

     Thank you, Lois says like a whisper to Daddo. I think maybe it's best if I rented a car and headed home now.
     Yeah, Mommy says. That's a good idea.
     Lois, Daddo says.

But then he doesn't say anything else.
Lois puts her glasses back on.

Her face is red.

She's shaking.

They're all so scared and embarrassed and full of lies.

I hope we did some good work out here, she says. I hope you three get to lead a normal life.

Mommy turns her back on Lois, but Daddo says,

Thank you, Lois. And I'm sorry.

No, no, Lois says. Just . . . please. Be careful.

Then she picks up a towel and walks away from us.

I watch her go up the sand.

I look to the water.

I need a minute, Mommy says. Holy shit. I need a minute.

She walks away and leaves Daddo and me and I think Daddo is going to tell her to be careful.

I don't tell her I can smell Other Mommy.

Everything's a mess, Daddo says. Literally . . . everything. And it feels like only minutes ago it was all put together. It feels like someone dropped something valuable in the house. Like something we treasured just fell. Doesn't it?

I don't answer.

It's like I can hear it, Daddo says. The echo of it shattering. Something made of glass. And now I feel like I knew all along it was too close to the edge of the table.

I don't say anything.

Bela? Daddo says.

I don't say anything.

We tried to do the right thing, Daddo says. And one day you'll know that. Me and Mommy . . . we love you.

I look to the waves. One of them isn't moving, I think.
Mommy is walking way up the sand.

It's amazing, Daddo says, how one incident can lead to so many more. How one cracked possession can lead to stepping on the glass, then bleeding on the floor, then not getting the stain out, then forever needing to explain the stain to anybody who ever steps foot in your house.
I wanna go home, I say.
I know, Daddo says. And that's where we're going. Know why?

I don't answer.

Because I think a time comes when you realize the whole world and all of life is your house, Daddo says. And so you might think something bad is going on at home, but no. It's going on in you. And I think that's the innocence Lois was talking about, Bela. I really do. I think maybe you're not the only one whose eyes were opened out here.

He's quiet now and I watch Mommy coming back.
I think about her hitting Lois.

Bela? Daddo says.

I don't answer.

Do you think it worked?

I don't answer.

Do you think Lois was right? Do you think we got rid of it?

I don't answer.
I watch Mommy walk back and I think of things breaking in our house and I don't answer.

I hope so, Daddo says. Because I'm not sure we have it in us for another scare. Not one more. Not one.

49

This is all my fault, Mommy says.

She's driving. I'm in the back alone.

I don't know how I didn't see this before, Mommy says.

Ursula, Daddo says. I don't know I have the energy for this right now.

Russ, I'm realizing something. I'm *realizing* it right now. *Think*. Other Mommy. Other Daddy. Don't you see? I made this happen somehow. It's like . . . it's like there's an invisible pocket or something and everything you do goes into it and then it forces other stuff back out.

What are you talking about?

I'm talking about comeuppance, Russ. I'm talking about just dues.

You don't deserve this any more than we do, Daddo says. This isn't your fault. Are you crazy?

Yeah, I might be, Mommy says. I just might be.

We've been on the highway for a long time. There aren't many other cars.

The sun is almost down. It's almost dark out.

But I'm serious, Mommy says. Forever I've treated relationships like they're meaningless. I don't need to tell you
this.

Daddo looks back at me like he doesn't want me to hear this.
But things are different now I think. So he doesn't say anything
to me about covering my ears.

You know, Mommy says. You of all people know, Russ. I
mean . . . I've been so terrible. And because of that, now we have
to deal with this. All of this. From this fucking monster to this
fucking secret.

We haven't done anything wrong.

How can you say that? Sure we have. I've taken everything
for granted and you've enabled it.

Come on, Daddo says. I was the other man once, remember?

That's just it, Mommy says. That's it exactly. Both of us,
we figured out ways to keep acting terribly, by using these little
phrases like "I was the other man once, remember?" And then
we just nod and say hey, yeah, you were, and so I guess you deserve to be other-manned too.

O, come on, Daddo says.

No. *Think,* Russ. What do we have that I haven't appreciated for years? I'm serious. We've had family. We've had food.
We've had a house. And now it's all torn apart and haunted because I can't remember the last time I said thank you to anybody
for anything, for the things we had. Instead I was out . . . looking
for other stuff to have. Other people. Other homes. Other beds.
This is all my fault.

You thanked your mother for helping us.

Did I?

Yeah.

I see a woman walking along the trees far off the highway.
I see dark hair on her shoulders.

I'm a terrible mother, Mommy says. And I'm a terrible wife. Do *not* try to tell me I'm not. When's the last time I *appreciated* what we have? Right now it feels like what we *had*, Russ, and it's really scaring me. It's really, really scaring me right now.

All right, Daddo says. But you're also driving us home. So maybe let's talk about this when we get there.

Ah! Mommy says. When we get there. All will be better once we just get back to our house and home.

I think I hear something move in the trunk behind me.
I look to Mommy and Daddo, but they don't look back. They're talking loud. Loud like the lake.

People go through stuff, Daddo says. This is life. This is how it works.

I don't think so, Mommy says. I don't think what we've been experiencing is life. Nope. No way. This is just deserts, man. This is retribution. I sent some bad stuff out and some bad stuff came back.

Okay, Daddo says. But Bela? You think this is retribution for Bela?

No, Mommy says. Bela is an innocent in this. No matter what batshit plan Lois Anthony had. Bela is an innocent. And we're just dumb enough to have listened to her.

Desperate, Daddo says. We're desperate. There's a big difference.

I hear it again. A sound in the trunk behind my seat.
I lean forward because it's pushing against my back.
I see something push against the seat.

A fingertip, I think.
From the trunk.

I don't know, Mommy says. I'm not into this crap that Lois pushes but . . . I don't know, man. Maybe there's something to the energy you put out and the energy you get back.

You've been a great mother, Daddo says. Don't even say what you're saying.

Have I? Have I told you how many times I just wanted to drop her off at a friend's house and never come back? How about the time you found me drunk at Mark's place and I was supposed to be watching Bela but I asked Mark's fuckin' nephew Brad to watch her? That kid was eleven, man. Do you have any idea how many times I wished I didn't have to watch our kid, how many times I wished I was out at the bar, how many times I wanted to be doing *anything* other than parenting?

Daddo looks back at me and he sees I'm looking at the seat and so he looks at the seat but he doesn't see it because it doesn't happen while he looks.

Bela doesn't need to hear this, Daddo says.

Why not? Mommy says. Thought this was all about sullying our golden child's innocence, right? My God, what have we done?

Desperate, Daddo says again.

The sun is down and every car looks black. Like it's covered in dark hair.
Something pushes from behind my seat.

Hey, I say.
Doesn't matter, Mommy says to Daddo.

Her voice is loud like it gets when she really means what she's saying.

Totally doesn't matter. You think every family in every house would react the same exact way we have? No. There are people out there who would've known what to do. And if they didn't know, they would've figured it out. But us? O, Russ. We haven't got a clue.

We're trying. This isn't like missing a mortgage payment, for crying out loud.

It's about me, Mommy says. Why do you think there's "Other Mommy"? Think, man. It's because this Mommy is shit. It's because this Mommy took everything for granted and cared more about herself than she did her kid and her husband and you know what?

Don't say it, Daddo says.

It's true, Mommy says.

She laughs in a mean way.
Something kicks against my seat and I turn and try to pull the seat forward a little bit.
I can smell her.

And the worst part, Mommy says, is that despite everything I'm saying right now? I'm not sure I feel any different. I'm not even sure if I've learned my lesson.

I pull the seat a little farther out.

Hello? I say.
You're under duress, Daddo says. We all are. Literally nothing we're saying or doing counts right now. None of it matters and none of it is a reflection on the real us. This is traumatic, Ursula, what we're going through. And nobody, I mean nobody would keep it together with the shit we've seen.

Some would, Mommy says. Some would.

Did you say something, Bela? Daddo asks.

I don't answer.

Ah man, Mommy says. If I had to do it all over again . . . what would I do?

Not now, Daddo says. We need to get home. Just get us home safely, or I can drive and that's all we need to think about right now.

Mommy laughs meanly again.

That's so you, Mommy says. So fucking you.

O, come on, Daddo says.

Even now, even *now,* you have to see the bright side of things. Do you have any idea how much pressure that's put on me?

To do what?

To be *dark.*

Okay, now you're just talking crazy.

O, really? And meanwhile, while I was parenting our kid, you were becoming Bela's best friend.

And that's bad?

No. But also yes. Balance. You are light. So who's dark? See?

Our exit is coming up.

I'm tellin' you, Mommy says. There's something here. An answer to all this. And I'm just not seeing it.

Nobody deserves what we've been going through.

Maybe some people do, Mommy says.

I look into the little bit of space where I pulled the seat out.

So now we go home, Mommy says. Here. Our exit. Now we're close. And then what?

I bring my face closer to the open space. I can't see anything in the trunk.
Just dark. No smell.

We work and we live and we love and we carry on because that's what strong people do, Daddo says.
We're not strong, Mommy says.
We always have been.

Mommy makes a turn and we're close to our house now because I recognize the Dream Cream on the corner.

I love you both, Mommy says. And I'm sorry I haven't thanked the world for anything in a long time.

She turns again and I push the backseat back to where it's supposed to be.
We're on our street.
There's our house.
Mommy pulls into the driveway.
Grandma's car is here.

What? Mommy says, seeing Grandma's car.
I texted her, Daddo says. Thought we could use a friend when we got here.

I open the door right away and then Mommy and Daddo get out of the car and Grandma gets out of her car, too. She walks over to me.

Hi, Bela, she says.
Are you really my grandma, Grandma Ruth?

She doesn't look to Mommy and Daddo when she says,

Absolutely.

Then the four of us are in the driveway, facing the house.
Just one little family on one little street.
Facing the house.
And everything that happens inside.

50

I hear you got some heavy news out by the lake, Grandma says.

We're on the couch in the living room. Just me and her. Mommy and Daddo are upstairs.
I don't know if they think the house is safe or if they don't care or maybe it's because with four of us nobody ever has to be alone.

I don't want to talk about it, I say.
No, neither do I, she says. But that's the thing, we probably should. You'll notice, the older you get, that it's the topics people say you shouldn't talk about that get all messed up beyond repair. My whole life, people said don't bring up politics and religion and, well, look at things now. Subjects can become sick just like people can. They need care. They need medicine. They need *talk*. So, while I wish I'd asked you about the water and the sand, we really should talk about the news you got. That's the trick, Bela. The whole trick. With aging, with living, with enduring this life. It's all about *heart*. How long can you maintain an open heart and an open mind in this world, how long can you

sustain being kind to other people, no matter what they say or do. Now, keep in mind, some things are beyond the pale. Of course. There are killers and cruelties that surpass our wildest imaginings. But this . . . what your parents told you . . . this was born of heart. Your mother might not think so, right now, but even she'll come around and stop beating herself up for not telling a child a truth that even an adult couldn't rightly process. And your daddo . . . well . . . do you have a better friend? Is there anybody in this life who has been better to you than your daddo? You see, Bela . . . *heart.* I want you to think of your heart like a house. This house, if it's easier. There's only so many rooms, right? But at the same time, there's a lot of room. That's the same with your heart. Here we've got the dining room and the living room and the kitchen and the foyer and the stairs and the bedrooms and the hallways and the bathrooms. But those are just the defined spaces, you see? Those are the spaces with names. But what about the spaces *between* these rooms? What do you call it when one foot is in the dining room and one in the foyer? Where are you then? And when you're more than halfway up the steps . . . are you then upstairs . . . or down? We say the living room and the kitchen are different places but isn't there only a counter between them, and doesn't that make them one? There are so many hidden spaces in a house, Bela. And there are so many hidden spaces in your heart. Some of them in plain sight. So what we need to do then, we need to determine what we'll allow *in* to our home, what we'll allow *in* to our heart. With a home we have furniture. We have pets. We have guests. But there are also *feelings* allowed into a house, just like you have feelings in your heart. And the trick of aging, the trick of getting through this life with your sanity, is deciding to let the right feelings exist inside your house and your heart. Some people let in a lot of dark feelings and some people don't let any dark feelings in at all, but that's a lot of work and I think it's best to let in a good healthy mix of both. Still, the feelings to look out for are the ones that are immovable, the ones made of stone. Last night your parents told you something that justifiably upset you, and there are people who would take the feeling you have now and make a statue of it, so that in their house, there is always this solid, unremovable statue that remains long into old age. And the reason I tell you this now is not because I think you should get over these feelings immediately, but because I know that the longer a statue remains, the harder it is to take out of the house. So, please, just think about it. Think about your house and your heart and think about what you would allow into both.

Grandma looks at me like she's wondering if I understand everything she's saying.

How many rooms are in this house? she asks me.
I don't know, I say.
Guess for me.
I don't know.
Guess.
Like . . . ten?
Okay. There are ten rooms in this house. Now, how much *room* is in this house?

I think of the video I saw of my bedroom. I think how small my bedroom looked on the little video.

Not as much as I thought there was, I say.

Grandma looks like I surprised her.

O, but think about it, Bela. You could learn the piano in this house. And what if you did? And what if that led to you playing concerts all over the world? Then wouldn't this house become big as the world? Sometimes, when people are all grown up, they come by to visit the house they grew up in. You know why? Because their childhood took place in that house. And your childhood is taking place in this house. And childhood has a habit of playing a major role in the rest of your life. Doesn't that make this house bigger? Doesn't something so important give this house more room?

I don't answer. I don't know what to say.

It's room we're looking for, Grandma says. All our lives. Room to grow, room to love, room to prosper, room to get out of a jam, room to succeed, wiggle room to chase our dreams. And every house has a lot of room because every house has people in it and those people are infinite insomuch as they go on to do an infinite number of various things. Just because Mommy and Daddo are raising you here doesn't mean you're going to grow up to be Mommy and Daddo. You see? Am I just like Mommy?
 No, I say.
 Exactly. And you're not just like Mommy and you're not just like Daddo, though you're more like him than you are Mommy.

I hear Mommy and Daddo talking on the stairs. They're talking about where we're all going to sleep. Daddo is saying maybe Lois's plan worked and we don't have to worry about this any- more. Mommy is saying we have to worry until we know we don't.

Room, Grandma says. Room and rooms. And anything can happen in any room. And when one thing leaves your house or heart it makes room for another thing to take its place. This is why it's unwise to make solid statues inside. A statue takes up that space without moving, without flowing, without growing. You see?

Mommy is telling Daddo we need to take turns sleeping still. Daddo is saying maybe we can all just live like normal people again now. He says he went through the camera footage of when we were gone and nothing was in the house.

And some rooms have secrets, Grandma says. And some secrets have a lot of room. I think this one, what you learned last night, that has a lot of room. A lot of room to be taken in different ways, to be examined over time, to make sense to you. But that doesn't change the fact that the house, like the heart, has corners and closets and places for things to hide. That's really what I wanted to say to you right now. That you may not even know that something's hiding in your house or heart unless someone like me, a friend in your life, told you that such things can be. Do you understand what I'm telling you?

Yeah, I say.

Good. That's good.

Mommy and Daddo come down the hall, into the living room.

Someone's gotta stay up, Mommy says.

It's late now. It's dark outside. The sun went down when we drove home.

I'll stay up, Grandma says. I'm wide-awake.

But you really have to stay up, Mommy says.

I said I would, didn't I?

We don't mean to tell you what to do, Daddo says. It's just . . . we're tired.

Say no more, Grandma says. I understand.

She puts her hand over mine.

What about you? she says. Are you tired?

No, I say.

'Cause I'm not. I feel like I could never sleep again.

We can sleep in the dining room, Mommy says. So you two can watch a movie or something in here.

Grandma squeezes my hand and we get up and Mommy and Daddo bring couch cushions and beach blankets into the dining room and Grandma asks me what kind of movie I wanna watch or would I rather do the Michigan puzzle and I tell her it doesn't matter, the puzzle is fine.

We'll see you in the morning, Daddo says.

I don't answer him.

Bela, he says. I'm sorry.

I don't answer him.
But suddenly . . . I kinda wanna.
I think about what Grandma told me and I kinda wanna tell Daddo it's okay, I won't make a statue of what they told me.
I don't want it in my house.

Good night, Daddo says.
Good night, Mommy says from the other room.

Then Daddo heads up the hall and Grandma puts the puzzle on Daddo's desk in the living room and she says,

You're a good person, Bela.

Then we try to put pieces together and it's hard because so many of them look the same. When we do get two together Grandma gets excited. We have most of the fish together and the apple blossom is easier because it's got pink, but the water is really hard.

I hear a creaking from upstairs and I look up.

When I look to Grandma again, she's smiling because she just fit three whole lake pieces together.

We're gonna do it, Bela, she says. By God, we're gonna solve this.

51

Turns out I'm sleepy after all.

Me and Grandma are doing the puzzle and I close my eyes and my head gets closer to the puzzle and Grandma touches the top of my head and tells me to stay up just a little bit longer, let's get more of this done, she says, "keep each other company." I keep telling her I'm awake. Because I am. I'm just sleepy is all. I'm not asleep. So, I keep putting pieces together but it's getting harder and Grandma got a little bit of a beach done and she says,

This is where you guys stayed. Right here. This exact beach, I think.

It looks so much smaller when it's just pieces of a puzzle, but I think I can see the spot where Mommy and Daddo told me their secret and I close my eyes and open them and Grandma has more of the beach done and more of the water and even some of the big grass and I say,

I remember that.

Right you should, Grandma says.

I close my eyes and open them and Grandma has done a lot really fast, it feels like, because there's more big grass and more of the water and it looks like the water has waves in it and I'm looking at the waves and I think I see one of them that isn't moving.

I lean closer to the puzzle.

I open my eyes when Grandma touches the top of my head. I didn't even know I had closed them.

Keep me company, she says again.

I do. I put two pieces together but then her hands come over to my side and she takes the pieces apart and says no, no, that's not right, those don't go together, and I close my eyes and open them and she has even more done.

More water. More beach.

I see, yeah, one of the waves isn't a wave.

And I see tiny dots on the beach and I think of Mommy and Daddo telling me their secret.

You're my real grandma, I say.

That's right, Grandma says.

She adds more pieces and now there's a little bit of a road and Grandma says,

This is the road you took home. Right here. This one.

And it looks so small just like my bedroom looked so small and I say,

There's no room for a family on that road.

Sure there is, Grandma says. There's always more room than you think there is. And more to a room.

I close my eyes. I open them.
Daddo is snoring in the dining room. Maybe Mommy is too.
I think I hear her breathing.
I look to the kitchen because I thought I heard Mommy breathing in there.

What if they die in their sleep? I ask.

I'm worried they'll always think I hate them if they die in their sleep.

That's the best way someone can go, Grandma says. In their sleep.

I'm trying to stay awake.

This is the exact road, Grandma says. Just hours ago you were here . . .

She touches the beach.

And now you're here.

She points to the actual room we're in, the living room.

So you see? Your house is much bigger than ten rooms, Bela. It's as big as everything you ever experience.
Yeah, I say.

But I can't keep my head up and I close my eyes and when I open them Grandma has done so much of the puzzle that I can read the name CHAPS.
I look really close, and I think I see a tiny car on the road from the beach to Chaps.

It's getting easier, Grandma says. It's like the door has been unlocked.

Where's our house? I ask.

She points to a spot by the name CHAPS and I see a little hair on the back of her finger.
I look up at her and she's not sitting there.
She's standing in the kitchen.

Needed a snack, she says. You keep nodding off, but I'm wide-awake.

I close my eyes, and when I open them, Grandma is not in the kitchen. She's not in her chair.
She's standing across the living room, staring at me.

Grandma, I say. You're my real grandma.

She doesn't say anything, and I close my eyes and open them and she's not in the room anymore and I look to the couch and see she's not there and I hear Daddo snoring in the dining room and I hear Mommy breathing close and I look to the chair across the table and Grandma is sitting in the chair.
Her face seems lower on her head.

O! I say.
Every house is just one room, Bela, she says. One room filled with decisions. Put a wall here, put a door there. Make a corner here, make a closet there. Make a happy home, make an unhappy home. Make a lying home. Make a cheating home. Make a cold home. Make a colder home. All one room. All up to you.

I look to the hall. I wanna wake Mommy and Daddo.

Would you have closets in your home? Grandma asks.
Grandma Ruth? I ask.
Would you invite other people into your house? she says.

I know what she's gonna say next. I don't want her to say it.

Into your heart?

I get down from the chair.
I run.
Out of the room and up the hall and to the front door. I hear creaking from the living room behind me.
I open the closet in the foyer and I get inside and I close the door and I hear the house creaking, creaking in the hall, and Daddo snoring, and Mommy snoring, and I want to call out to them to tell them to help but I don't want Other Mommy to know where I am.

Help, I say.

I say it quiet.
But now I just listen and I hear creaking from up the hall and then creaking on the stairs but it's quiet creaking like maybe the house has always creaked and usually I just can't hear it but I hear it now and I feel around in the closet for something to help me like a broom or a stick or—
Grandma yells from upstairs.
It sounds so bad.
Mommy and Daddo come awake in the dining room. I hear Mommy ask Daddo what that was.
And I want to tell them Other Mommy is here, but I don't want Other Mommy to know where I am.
She's gotten closer.
As close as she can get.

Bela? Daddo says.
Mom? Mommy says.

Grandma yells again.
She's upstairs and she yells,

Stay away for me!
It's Mom, Mommy says. Jesus Christ, Russ, it's *Mom.*

I feel for something to help me, but all there is are jackets and coats.

Mom! Mommy yells.
Ursula, Daddo says. *Where's Bela?*

The whole house is creaking and I look up but it's dark in here and Grandma yells again and Mommy and Daddo are running for the stairs and they're so close to me now and I yell,

I'm in here! Mommy! Daddo!

But their feet are loud on the steps and Grandma is yelling and Other Mommy is growling upstairs.

Mom! Mommy yells.
Ruth! Daddo yells.
I'm in here! I call.

And they sound so far away, in the dark, so much noise, like thunder on the stairs, and Grandma is in trouble up there and I reach for something to protect myself with and I feel a hand in the closet between the jackets and coats.
I scream.
And I kick open the closet door.

And I can see, from the light from the living room, I can see Grandma Ruth is in the closet.
Her eyes are closed and her hands are folded over her chest.

Mom! Mommy yells upstairs.

Other Mommy growls.
Grandma yells.
But Grandma isn't upstairs.

O, Mommy, I say. O, Daddo.

I look up the stairs and the light is off up there and it's so dark and I hear Mommy screaming and I hear Daddo groan and I hear a heavy thud like the time Daddo asked me to help him move a table and we dropped it and a glass bowl fell and broke and he said don't go near the glass and then he said what was I doing asking a kid to help move a table and then we laughed because it was scary and because it was loud and because all we had to do was take the bowl off before moving the table.

Daddo . . .

The whole house is creaking.
Mommy is screaming and then Other Mommy's voice gets so deep, it rattles the windows and I hear another thud like the time Mommy saw me trip when I was running to her from my bedroom because I heard something move in my closet.

Mommy, I say. Daddo . . .

And the house
Goes

Quiet.

And all the room in the whole house is quiet and I look up but I can't see where the stairs end.

Mommy, I say. Daddo . . .

I take the first step and make it creak.

Mommy, I say. Daddo. It's me. It's Bela.

I take the next step and it creaks. And the third step creaks and the fourth step creaks and I hear a door close upstairs and I call,

Mommy! Daddo! It's me! It's Bela!

And the fifth step creaks and all of them are so noisy because I'm running because I'm running upstairs.

I stop at the top.

Mommy? Daddo?

I see there is a little light coming from my bedroom, my bedroom that I always thought was so big but then I saw was so small.

It's me, I say. Bela.

I look in my bedroom, and Mommy is lying down with her face in the carpet.

Mommy, I say. I'm awake. It's okay to sleep. I'm awake for us.

I go in my bedroom.

Daddo is lying with his face in the carpet.

It's okay, Daddo. I'm awake for us. I'm on guard.

I walk to my bed.

It's me, I say. It's Bela.

I climb up into bed and everything is blurry because I'm crying and my bedroom is blue like the moon makes it blue and I get under my blanket and I say,

Good night, Mommy. Good night, Daddo.

And Other Mommy steps out of the closet.
She looks at me like she looked at me the first time I saw her and I bring the blanket up to my nose because I'm crying and I need to wipe my nose with my blanket.
I need a friend.

Hello, you, Other Mommy says. It's you. It's Bela.

She walks over to my bed and crouches next to me and she says,

Can I go into your heart?

And I think of how happy Mommy and Daddo could be. I remember them laughing at jokes in movies and holding hands at the zoo.
And I say,

Yes.

Other Mommy's eyes are suddenly where they're supposed to be. They show white-blue and then . . .

. . . she disappears.

And I feel like I'm being asked to leave my own house, I feel like there's a closet going up around me, I feel like I'm in a corner that nobody knows about and that if I ever make a sound again someone will think it's me, me Bela, me who is haunting my house.

Other Mommy, I say. Where are you?

But I know where she is.

She's sitting on my bed now. Just where I was sitting a second ago.

And her face is wet with tears.

And she needs to wipe her nose.

And I think I know where I'm going.

Yeah.

Up ahead I can see where Other Mommy comes from now.

And it's not a closet.

No.

There's so much room.

And it's not a heart.

No.

But maybe I'll find a friend in there, in all that room, someone to carnation for me.

Maybe.

I feel like I'm in a corner of a space big enough to hold everything I've ever done and everything everyone's ever said.

And I don't think there was enough room in my heart for more than Mommy and Daddo and me.

This is where Other Mommy comes from.

This is where she lived.

And I hear my voice, someone says:

Hello, I'm Bela . . .

* * *

AND THERE'S ROOM.
So much room.
But it's not a house my voice speaks into.
And it's not a home.

—Michigan
Autumn 2023

Acknowledgments

In some ways, a book is like a stage production. The rough draft is usually close to a solo performance, a lone monologue under a single overtaxed stage light. It's an amazing place to be. But the finished thing is much more involved. And much better for that. "Behind the curtain" (one might say), a lot goes on. I'd love to thank the following great people for taking part:

Kristin Nelson, Wayne Alexander, Ryan Lewis, Tricia Narwani, Scott Shannon, Keith Clayton, Alex Larned, Ayesha Shibli, David Moench, Ada Maduka, Ashleigh Heaton, Tori Henson, Sabrina Shen, Diane Hobbing, Cindy Berman, Scott Biel, Ross Jeffery, Ryan Malerman, Jonathan Janz, James Henry Hall, Jim Burning, and Allison Laakko.

And thank you to Dave Simmer, ever and always, for opening the closet door.

About the Author

JOSH MALERMAN is a *New York Times* bestselling author and one of two singer-songwriters for the rock band the High Strung. His debut novel, *Bird Box,* is the inspiration for the hit Netflix film of the same name. His other novels include *Unbury Carol, Inspection, A House at the Bottom of a Lake, Pearl, Goblin, Daphne,* and *Malorie,* the sequel to *Bird Box.* Malerman lives in Michigan with his fiancée, the artist-musician Allison Laakko.

joshmalerman.com
X: @JoshMalerman
facebook.com/JoshMalerman
Instagram: @joshmalerman

About the Type

This book was set in Sabon, a typeface designed by the well-known German typographer Jan Tschichold (1902–74). Sabon's design is based upon the original letterforms of sixteenth-century French type designer Claude Garamond and was created specifically to be used for three sources: foundry type for hand composition, Linotype, and Monotype. Tschichold named his typeface for the famous Frankfurt typefounder Jacques Sabon (c. 1520–80).